PAYBACK IS A BITCH

PAYBACK IS A BITCH

THE KURTHERIAN ENDGAME™ BOOK ONE

MICHAEL ANDERLE

Payback Is A Bitch (this book) is a work of fiction.

All of the characters, organizations, and events portrayed in this novel are either products of the author's imagination or are used fictitiously. Sometimes both.

LMBPN Publishing
PMB 196, 2540 South Maryland Pkwy
Las Vegas, NV 89109

First US edition, May 2018
Version 1.02 June 2018

PAYBACK IS A BITCH TEAM

Thanks to our Beta Readers

Bree Buras
Dorothy Lloyd
Tom Dickerson
Dorene Johnson
Diane Velasquez
Nat Roberts

Thanks to the JIT Readers

Kelly O'Donnell
Sarah Weir
James Caplan
Peter Manis
Tim Bischoff
Kelly Bowerman
Kim Boyer
John Ashmore
Daniel Weigert
Thomas Ogden
Larry Omans
Sherry Foster
Micky Cocker
Michael Pendergrass

If I've missed anyone, please let me know!

Editor
Lynne Stiegler

To Family, Friends and
Those Who Love
to Read.
May We All Enjoy Grace
to Live the Life We Are
Called.

CHARACTERS AND RACES

• **ADAM** - AI, TOM's partner, Bethany Anne's advisor, resource, presently resides in organic Kurtherian computer in Bethany Anne's body (which was placed there by TOM [see below] when she was enhanced).

• **Addix** - enhanced Ixtali, Spymistress for High Tortuga, fighter for Bethany Anne.

• **Akio** - Michael's sidekick, Elite Guard, Queen's Bitch, human vampire, originally from Japan.

• **Anne** - enhanced human, saved by Bethany Anne in Las Vegas, now heads her own R&D team.

• **ArchAngel** - Ship's AI and battleship lost in the war with the Yollin upper caste Rebuilt by General Lance Reynolds and used in covert ops.

• **ArchAngel II** - **AI**, and the superdreadnought ***ArchAngel II***, Admiral Thomas' ship.

• **Az, Az Th'loo** - Leath, Head of KGB company, CEO and President.

• **Baba Yaga** - Bethany Anne's alter-ego, Witch of the Empire, Empress' Witch.

• **Bach** (Old Patch-Eye) - Shrillexian, mercenary on *Kiss my Ass.*

• **Barnabas** - Changed by Michael into a vampire, super-enhanced human, one of the seven first-born, former monk.

• **Bartholomew Thomas, Admiral** - Admiral of the Etheric Empire Fleet. Semi-retired - BA wants him back on board.

• **Bethany Anne (Nacht)** - Heroine, main character, super-enhanced human (vampire), altered by TOM on Earth. Carrying Kurtherian symbiont TOM (see below) resides physically in her body, and she also carries an organic Kurtherian computer implanted by TOM when she was enhanced. Other Titles: Empress, Queen, Queen Bitch. Approximately two hundred years old in this story. Can walk through Etheric dimension.

- **Ch'urn** - Zhyn, pirate.
- **Charles** - Security Pit worker.
- **Darryl Jackson** - Queen's Bitch (enhanced fighter/personal bodyguard for Bethany Anne after events in Florida Everglades). African-American.
- **David (Nacht)** - Human vampire. Michael's son, who tried to kill him after escorting BA to TOM's ship.
- **Drock** - Ch'urn's cousin, pirate.
- **Eric Escobar** - Queen's Bitch (enhanced fighter/personal bodyguard for Bethany Anne after events in Florida Everglades). Hispanic.
- **Eve** - EI in short human android body, Yuko's companion. Created by ADAM before they parted when ADAM went to space.
- **G'het** - Works for KGB Corp, P'rok's partner.
- **Gabrielle Escobar** - Bethany Anne's friend, Stephen's daughter, head of the Queen's Bitches, human vampire, took husband's name on marriage instead of Nacht.
- **Glorious Pain in the Ass** - Kurtherian belonging to TOM's clan. Found him while Bethany Anne and her people were setting up the BYPS satellite protection system around Earth.
- **Gorath** - Captain of Pirate ship *Kiss My Ass*, Skaine.
- **H'ick** - Zhyn, works in Engines, pirate.
- **Hirotoshi** - Elite Guard, super-enhanced human vampire, one of Tabitha's advisors.
- **Humans** - originally from Earth, but have now spread throughout several galaxies after Gating into Yollin space from the Loop (Milky Way) Galaxy.
- **Imon** - Shrillexian, KGB Senior Partner in charge of Security.
- **Ixtalis** - alien race from Pan Galaxy.

- **J'erlong** - Zhyn, works in Engines, pirate.
- **Jacqueline** - Were, Pricolici, daughter of Gerry (New York), Mark's significant other.
- **Jean (Dukes/Grimes)** - Weapons R&D Genius, creator of the famed Jean Dukes pistols, married to John Grimes, enhanced human.
- **Jennifer** - Security Pit, Communications, Analysis.
- **Jennifer** - Stephen's mate, Were.
- **Jesse Verrette** - Guardian, Watson's partner.
- **John Grimes** - Queen's Bitch (enhanced fighter/personal bodyguard for Bethany Anne after events in Florida Everglades).
- **K'rillick** - Peaceful alien race, destroyed by the T'sehmion Clan.
- **Kael-ven** - Enhanced Yollin, former and current captain of the *G'laxix Sphaea,* ex-planetary potentate.
- **Kiel** - Enhanced Yollin mercenary and Marine officer, Weapons officer *G'laxix Sphaea.*
- **Kurtherians** - Alien race, clans, seven Clans that are selfishly focused on themselves, five clans that focus on the true benefits for others. Some of the Five help prepare species for attacks from the Seven.
- **Lance Reynolds** - Bethany Anne's father, enhanced human, stayed behind to manage relations of the former Empire with the new Federation. "The General." Married to Patricia, his former secretary on Earth.
- **Lady** - EI for *The Lady Princess.*
- **Leath** - Alien race from Pan Galaxy.
- **Lerr'ek** - Zhyn businessman, works for Baba Yaga on High Tortuga to help prepare the base.
- **Mark** - Vampire youth saved in New York by Michael, Jacqueline's significant other.
- **Michael (Nacht)** - Fiancé of Bethany Anne, father of her offspring, and the original human modified well over a thousand years ago. Can change

to a form called Myst and pass through tiny spaces as well as the Etheric dimension. At the time of this book he is about 1500 years old.

• **Noel-ni** - Alien race from Pan Galaxy.

• **Patricia** – Enhanced human, Lance Reynolds' wife, Bethany Anne's stepmother. Pregnant when last seen in Book 21 of The Kurtherian Gambit.

• **P'rok** - Works for KGB Corp, G'het's partner.

• **Peter Silvers** - Queen's Bitch, super-enhanced Were, Pricolici. Bethany Anne helped save him from Michael's rules about revealing themselves to humans when he was a youth.

• **Rahj'k** - Radar operator, *Kiss my Ass.*

• **Ranger Two** - see Tabitha.

• **Reynolds** - EI & superdreadnought that has left to seek Kurtherians.

• **Ricole** - Noel-ni female youth.

• **Ryu** - Elite Guard, super-enhanced vampire, one of Tabitha's advisors.

• **Sabine** - Human with some enhanced abilities, saved by Michael and Akio, trained by Akio, picked up from Earth. Amazing shot.

• **Scott English** - Queen's Bitch (enhanced fighter/personal bodyguard for Bethany Anne after events in Florida Everglades).

• **Sean Royale (Johnny)** - Ranger, worked with Lance, Barnabas and Tabitha, Enhanced/Cyborg.

• **Shrillexians** - Alien race from Pan Galaxy.

• **Skaines** - Alien race from Pan Galaxy.

• **Stephen (Nacht)** – Human changed by Michael into a vampire, one of the seven first born and Michael's genetic sibling.

• **Tabitha** - Super-enhanced human vampire, "Ranger 2" during the Age of the Empire (the 150+ Years between leaving Earth and returning to place a protection system around the planet) Former hacker from Earth, enhanced. Major character, leader of many adventures.

- **Tar** - Communications Specialist, *Kiss My Ass*
- **Terry** - Security Pit, Communications.
- **The Queen** - See Bethany Anne.
- **TOM** - "Thales of Miletus," Resident alien entity, Kurtherian, hosted within Bethany Anne's body. Has unpronounceable name that is mathematical expression so BA calls him "TOM".
- **Torcellans** - Alien race from Pan Galaxy.
- **Uleq** - Torcellan, KGB Senior Partner, Operations.
- **Watson Stewart** - Guardian, Verrette's Partner.
- **William** - Enhanced human. Part of Team BMW (Bobcat, William, Marcus, and now Tina, Marcus's wife).
- **Witch of the Empire** – See Baba Yaga.
- **X'ern** - Zhyn, pirate with Drock.
- **Yaree** - Alien race from Pan Galaxy (aka Karillians).
- **Yollins** - Alien race from Pan Galaxy.
- **Yuko** - Enhanced human, Political Liaison in Japan while Bethany Anne was off Earth.
- **Zhyn** - Alien race from Pan Galaxy.

More information available in the Kurtherian Gambit Wiki at:
https://sites.google.com/site/kurtheriangambit/

BABA YAGA

ART BY ANDREW DOBELL

QUEEGERT

ART BY ERIC QUIGLEY

KAEL-VEN

IXTALI

ADDIX

ART BY ERIC QUIGLEY

SKAINE

ART BY ERIC QUIGLEY

SHRILLEXIAN

YAREE

ART BY ERIC QUIGLEY

NOEL-NI

ART BY ERIC QUIGLEY

LERR'EK

ART BY ERIC QUIGLEY

KRENLOCK

ART BY ERIC QUIGLEY

LEATH MILITARY

THE KURTHERIAN GAMBIT

1

Planet Devon, Code-Named "High Tortuga"

The raven-haired woman stared at the planet below through the docking bay's forcefield. The field allowed ships to pass from the bay into the vacuum of space.

Bethany Anne's alter ego Baba Yaga had begun the process of acquiring a majority interest in most of the interplanetary and interstellar companies on the planet.

Using the wealth she'd acquired as the former Empress of the Etheric Empire, Bethany Anne had spent liberally. Using her Empire's AIs she crushed the competition, making any operation that shipped to or from High Tortuga a losing proposition.

Then she bought the remaining shipping companies for a fraction of their previous worth. Some might call what she did immoral or unethical.

She called it *business*.

There was a method to her madness, but those who had

witnessed her real madness saw nothing but intelligence in her efforts to hide High Tortuga's existence.

She feared that former Etheric Empress Bethany Anne was going to become a pariah in the near future as the Federation stretched its baby legs. She needed a place to stay out of the limelight.

It had to be far enough away that no one would find her, but close enough to bring down the hammer of her warships if the future brought danger.

One danger was the collapse of the effort to create a new Federation of Peoples. Aliens and humans working together to become strong together.

The Kurtherians were still ranging the galaxies taking over other races, and there were most likely other entities willing to overpower others in their quests for domination as well. They might be races no one in the nascent Federation had yet encountered, or they might be from within the Federation itself.

She and her people would be ready when that time came.

Bethany Anne turned away from her scrutiny of the planet and headed toward Michael, her lover and the father of their child. He was waiting for her to board the ship which would take them down to the planet below.

It was time High Tortuga went through its own birthing pains to transform into the planet Bethany Anne believed it could become.

The prototype for…well, she would be calling it "Utopia" but that was way too formal. She'd just call it the Motherfucking Practical Political System instead, or MPPS, and it would be an advanced but practical form of government she would transplant (if they could accomplish the mechanics) to her home planet of Earth.

Centuries in the future.

High Tortuga, Hidden Space Fleet Base, Queen's Personal Quarters

Bethany Anne sat down at the conference table and dropped an old-fashioned notebook on it. For whatever reason, doodling notes on the paper-like substances helped her gather her thoughts.

Michael, on her left, was reviewing some documents on his tablet and Akio was next to him. On her right was Barnabas, who had come back for this, and then Stephen. While more of her people were involved in her plan, she wanted some of the oldest—the ones who had lived through the best and worst of humanity—to listen to and vet a plan she was hatching.

"ADAM?" She spoke aloud so the AI inside her would do so as well for the benefit of the others.

"Yes?"

"Please record these proceedings and discussions and provide my dad with a transcript when possible. Secured, of course."

"I will, Bethany Anne."

Michael had been modified on Earth by a Kurtherian now known as TOM sometime during the dark ages. TOM had by happenstance piloted his ship to Earth well over a thousand years ago and had crash-landed in a hidden valley.

Michael had stumbled across the spaceship and TOM

had tried to enhance him with nanocytes, but he had not known enough about human physiology to affect a completely successful change.

By the time Michael had left the ship, the nanocytes had taken control and he needed human blood to continue living. What no one except TOM had known at the time was that what he was drawing from blood was Etheric energy.

He had been the Earth's first vampire.

The vampire mythology was patently false. One example was the Kurtherian alien known as TOM (an acronym for Thales of Miletus, a name TOM took as his Kurtherian name was a mathematical expression.)

TOM had come to Earth to modify the inhabitants and prepare them to defend themselves against those of the seven Kurtherian clans who would use them for nefarious purposes.

TOM was presently living inside Bethany Anne, a situation that hadn't been part of the plan when Michael had brought her to be upgraded by the same ship that had upgraded him.

Until he'd met up with Bethany Anne again, Michael had been completely unaware that the alien was still alive.

Bethany Anne knew TOM was located inside her somewhere near her spine, but having killed a Kurtherian who had taken up residence in another alien, she didn't really want to know the details.

She sure hoped the baby or babies she was carrying didn't put her interior space at a premium.

Damn! She was going to look like a bowling ball with arms, legs, and a head no matter how small her child.

Michael was somewhere between thirteen and sixteen hundred years old—he wouldn't admit his age. Nor would his brother (and vampiric son) Stephen, who was here with her as well. Barnabas wasn't that much younger. Akio, on the other hand, was about eight hundred years old now.

Hell, she was close to one-ninety herself.

Her brows furrowed. ***TOM?***

YES?

I'm curious. How old are you? You are obviously older than Michael or you wouldn't have been out in the galaxy in your spaceship carrying so much responsibility. But are you like a little older than Michael, or a bunch older?

Ahhhhh… TOM was being evasive again, something that he had been doing more and more since they met the other Kurtherian—the one she had nicknamed "Glorious Pain in the Ass," back near Earth. **I'm older than Michael by at least two.**

Two* what? *Decades? Centuries?

Centuries is closer to reality than decades.

Huh, so that makes you the oldest person at this meeting. You ready to offer your wise insight and thoughts?

I but live to serve, TOM quipped.

"Gentleman, and Michael," she started. Michael smirked and closed his tablet, turning his attention to her.

He would wait an appropriate amount of time before returning the jab. "Yes, child? I understand you requested our august presence to provide you with wisdom from our considerable life experiences?"

Ok, so he *wouldn't* wait.

"Keep it up, old man, and I'll…" She frowned. Since she was pregnant she couldn't spar right now; certainly not energetically. Further, he had figured out how to work inside the Etheric dimension so she couldn't just toss his ass in there until she got him out. "Make you sleep on the couch…es," she finished lamely.

She sighed. "I've got to work on my threats." She turned to Stephen. "You and Barnabas are in charge of helping me figure out new and inventive ways to threaten Michael."

"Why me?" Stephen asked, neither surprised nor bothered to be tasked with the challenge.

"You're his brother; you have to know what annoys him."

"We were apart for hundreds and hundreds of those years. On *purpose,* I might add."

"You hated me," Michael supplied, smiling.

"You were a monumental *asshole,*" Stephen replied, shrugging. "If it helps, I've forgiven you."

"He hasn't completely stopped being an asshole," Bethany Anne assured them and patted Michael on the wrist. "But if it helps, honey, you have a nice ass."

Everyone there noticed when Michael stopped himself from reacting to the comment. He had started to look downward, but he closed his eyes for a moment. A small smile played on his lips as he opened his eyes. "Touché."

He could be a bit vain about his looks at times.

"Ok, everyone has their drink of choice, so let's start. I asked you here so that we can start working on what I'm calling the MPPS project." She put up a hand. "I'm not trying to implement an impossibility. What I'm trying to do is this…"

Planet Soboth (Previously Territory 7732), Undisclosed location, Open Out-ring, Non-Federation

The meeting room was closed off from the rest of the business by a translucent soundproof membrane. The three business leaders wanted complete separation from the nearby action and noise.

"There are three gates between us and our materials, and our ships are now telling us they cannot land on Devon without permission." Az, the head of the company, was an older ex-military Leath. The second in command, Uleq, was a recent Torcellan recruit, and the third, Imon, ran their enforcement arm. He was Shrillexian and had somehow made it through four decades of mercenary service without losing a limb or incurring a serious wound that couldn't be healed.

"I've looked into it." Uleq, his white skin reflecting a bit of pink in the light, looked at his partners. "Some being called 'Baba Yaga' has been on the planetary news net. She claims to own the planet."

Az snorted. "You can't own a planet. It would be too expensive."

Uleq brushed back his white hair. "I am merely delivering the results of the research." He looked at his tablet. "From what I can tell, she holds close to eighty-nine percent of most interplanetary companies based on-planet and is in the process of acquiring the last independent transportation company. Our efforts to pull the," Uleq's eyes flicked to his tablet, "*products* from Devon have now become much more difficult, as will be moving many of our more unique trade goods."

"This area," Imon glared at Uleq, "is safe for speech. I have gone through it multiple times."

"I am always careful," Uleq replied.

"You are scared." Imon waved a hand. "Call it what it is. We ship contraband, steal materials, and barter for slaves. It isn't like we three don't know this."

Uleq laid his tablet on the table and stared at Imon. "We can call what we choose to produce, acquire and move around with our ships whatever we like. There is no reason to put it in such crass terms."

"Enough." Az's growly voice interrupted the two. "Uleq, your Torcellan background predisposes you to whitewash what we do. To secure your future you will need to address your ambivalence and own your participation, or get out of our business." He waited for a few moments. "Well?"

"Now?" Uleq looked at the head of the company. "Why is this relevant?"

"Because," Imon explained, "I have run simulations. If we allow you to continue lying to yourself to preserve your sensitive Torcellan morals and desire to avoid conflict, you will likely do something inappropriate."

"Like what?" Uleq looked at Az. "I'm not sure I follow."

"Imon has convinced me that if you don't acknowledge the truth about our business there is a high risk of you doing something irrational. It's time you grow a spine—"

"Or I can place one below you and kick it into place through your ass." Imon chuckled. "Although that might be a bit messy, not to mention painful."

Uleq turned to Imon. "I'm sure it would be." He didn't bother trying to throw his weight around with him. The

Shrillexian might take it as an opportunity to settle the answer with a physical challenge, and if that happened?

Well, Uleq would get Imon's foot up his ass with or without a new spine. He breathed out, looking down at the table.

"I don't come from a species as," he glanced at his partners, "*violent* as either of yours. We are taught from the beginning what is appropriate. Gunrunning, slaving," he nodded to Imon, "and drugs that addict users from the first hit are simply not in that category." Imon started to interrupt, but Uleq stopped him with an upraised hand. "But I want *more*. You are right, Imon...I want to have my brishek while retaining my Torcellan ethics and morals."

He pursed his lips before slightly bowing in his seat. "I owe you both an apology and an acknowledgment. I will not run from what I am becoming. I chose this future, so I will accept it and move forward."

Az's tusks bobbed as he chuckled. "Keep it up, Uleq, and you might just become a human."

"Please, no." The Torcellan shook his head. "They have no understanding of beauty, and their bodies...so many colors, when white is enough." He leaned forward and looked from Az to Imon and back. "Have you *seen* the humans that have red hair? Their skin can lean toward the Torcellan hue." He leaned back, shaking his head. "It looks like fire erupting from the skull." He shook all over. "Hideous."

Uleq blew out a breath and smiled at Imon. "Ok. So, we need to see what is going on with our products. When I checked into our slaving, drugs, and products acquired by illegitimate means—"

"We stole them," Imon growled with a smile playing on his lips.

"No," Uleq challenged. "I wasn't being ambiguous, Imon. We acquire our products by many methods, not all of them smash-and-grab."

Imon shrugged. "Ok, you got me on that. 'Illegitimate means' sounds more impressive, anyway."

Az sat back in his chair, the squeaks it emitted under the burden of his bulk lost on the other two. Uleq'd had no idea that he would have been signing his own death warrant if he'd refused to own up to who they were and what they did.

Quite simply, they were interstellar pirates who ran many legitimate companies…and quite a few that were not so legitimate.

Some of those companies were based on Devon, and they were not going to allow the self-proclaimed owner of the planet to mess up their profit margin.

It was time to ruin this Baba Yaga's plans.

High Tortuga, Hidden Space Fleet Base, Queen's Personal Quarters, Meeting Table

Bethany Anne wound down her pitch. "So when we return to Earth in the future after we find and kill the alien sonofabitches we're hunting, we'll fix whatever is there. Who's with me?"

Barnabas raised an eyebrow. "Do we have to live there?"

Bethany Anne looked at her friend. "Well, no, but you have me curious."

"I'm enjoying myself with *Shinigami,* and I look forward

to grabbing lots and lots of those who break laws so I can introduce them to justice."

Michael refrained from asking Barnabas if justice meant deadly force or just incarceration. Probably an equal chance either way, considering how rough he had been with some gang members who had offered him violence recently.

Bethany Anne shrugged. "That's fine. I'll assume you will work on the details of the legal system. You enjoyed harassing me so much for over-doing the justice back on Earth."

Barnabas made a face. He wasn't going to live that down for hundreds of years…if they lived that long.

Full of nanocytes, all of them could effectively regenerate their bodies through connectivity with the Etheric. Released from drinking blood through the proper updates on their nanocytes, they had all the physical enhancements without the nasty iron aftertaste of a neckful of blood.

"Personally, I think we coddle too many people. I'm not a fan of one-strike-and-off-comes-your-hand, but we could do with parameters."

"Biggest issue," Akio interjected, "with the Chinese legal system on Earth was the lack of objectivity in the judges. If the person was known, such as a relative or friend, they would receive preferential treatment."

"Yes, and how do you handle situations such as mental challenges?" Stephen thought for a moment. "Ok, assuming everyone is healthy that won't be a problem. However, even *we* have issues with mental problems. The body, I understand, is much simpler."

TOM's voice was heard through the speakers. "That is

true, Stephen. While we can correct many issues in the tissues of the mind, it can and often does delete memories and knowledge at some level. The person might be okay from the time of healing into the future, but the missing data upsets their wellbeing at an unconscious level."

"That's just law," Michael interrupted. "You take care of the core functions including but not limited to food, water, clothes, and shelter. Once that is accomplished you make education and opportunity available, provide for defense and potentially offense, engage in trade, make communication planet-wide, build infrastructure such as energy and transportation, permit them to travel, and maybe start an entertainment industry."

"I sometimes wonder," Bethany Anne pondered aloud, "if we would be better off without entertainment."

"There is no question," Michael replied, "that humans will make sure they have entertainment. The only questions are how do they get it, and is it at someone else's expense?"

Stephen leaned forward in his seat, placing his elbows on the table. "I believe that you will have to look at beings' core personality types and structure a society that offers each hope and responsibilities."

"We are sounding like some sort of think tank." Bethany Anne blew out a breath.

"Or," ADAM said through the speakers, "like a bunch of science-fiction writers."

"What are you talking about?" Bethany Anne asked.

"Well, some of the most creative writers did what-if analysis on the future, then wrapped their thoughts into an acceptable theory and released it as science-fiction. In fact, the United States military hired military science fiction writers such as David Weber to free-think the future of the military in space. The military was often accused of fighting the last war, but by using this strategy they were working with forward thinkers to consider how the military might need to prepare and change and what problems they might encounter."

"So." Stephen rested his chin in his hands. "Are we saying that our MPPS homework is done?"

"Hardly." Bethany Anne sniffed. "Although I'm willing to listen. ADAM, what is the cornerstone of the effort?"

"Education," he replied. "And recognition that people take responsibility for themselves, and often for others."

"What do you mean?" Michael asked.

"Without reliving that time in your life, Michael, your strictures were very cut and dried," ADAM responded. "If someone dishonored you the response was sudden and brutal."

"I'd like to think of it as efficient," Michael temporized.

"I'm feeling you on this one," Bethany Anne whispered to him. Her whispering confused Michael since everyone at the table could hear her whisper from three rooms away.

"It was efficient," ADAM responded, "if your intention was to limit those who were around you to only those who were willing to assume leadership or those who were willing to climb the ladder of political success, believing themselves smarter than others and therefore immune to the risk of upsetting you."

"I did relieve the world of quite a few assholes." Michael looked at the two men across the table from him and nodded at Akio. "Just ask him. The asshole gene pool on

Earth has been substantially reduced. I'd like to think of that as worthy of acclaim."

Akio chuckled. "We did kill with abandon, Michael. However, many were following the commands of their Alphas."

"Bad choice in following those jackasses," Michael replied. "We saved a whole group of Weres when their Alpha recognized the danger."

"I imagine the sight of you calling down lightning helped."

Bethany Anne cut back in, halting the reminiscences of Michael's return to Earth as the Dark Messiah. "Which brings us perversely back to education. We teach children not to grab hot pots on stoves. Why would we not teach practical ways to deal with bad characters?"

Stephen noted. "That presumes the monsters aren't proactive in scaring them to stay quiet."

"Then," Barnabas answered, "we'll be *scarier*."

"That leads to a totalitarian level of government," Akio replied, "often tried in my corner of the world as well as others. It is easy enough to implement if your side is the scariest, but often the reasons the populace is scared are not acceptable, and eventually the government will be overthrown. If not by their own people, then by the countries around them."

"The real issue," ADAM suggested, "is the rebels."

"Come again?" Bethany Anne furrowed her brow. "What rebels?"

Barnabas nodded. "The freethinkers. The iconoclasts. Those who wish to push boundaries because their minds are wired differently. Sometimes it is to a good effect, but sometimes they do it because of a miswiring in their brains, and they sway a few others. With the level of destruction available to the few, it wouldn't take many to pull down a portion of civilization."

"And minds are the one area we cannot just *fix*," TOM reminded them.

"They have tells," Michael interjected. "If we create classes everyone must join, we can grab the cream of the crop and offer them challenging tasks."

"And 'challenging tasks' are euphemisms for what?" Bethany Anne eyed her bloodthirsty mate.

"Challenging tasks?" Michael returned her look. "Not a euphemism for killing them. The reason society moves ahead has little to do with safety and everything to do with taking risks if needed, like in times of war. Think about the advances during the Second World War on Earth. However, if you study wars in general you will see that the invention and production of destructive technology were always heightened just before or during wars."

"Before?" Bethany Anne thought about it. "So, someone came up with a new weapon and figured now was the time to take advantage of their tactical superiority? I get it."

"And what would happen to an MPPS society if it was attacked from off-planet?" Akio asked. "Would it have the rough and ready people to protect those who don't have the mindset to do whatever it takes?"

"Those who value the skills and talents necessary to deal death without getting lost in it." Barnabas nodded. "Another reason to grab the cream of the crop. Same concept, but we look into how to pull those who can handle the strain of war apart as well and see if they are willing to become part of the defense of the planet, assuming they are capable."

Bethany Anne thought for a second. "It feels like you guys are pulling the wolves apart from the sheep."

The men all looked at each other, then back at her. "Wasn't that what we did on Earth before we left? Pulled out the cream of the crop who wanted a better future?"

"Yes." Bethany Anne sighed and put a hand over her eyes. "In a way, are we admitting we were the cause of the Apocalypse back on Earth?"

Akio shook his head. "No, a high ranking official in the Chinese army disaffected by the results of his wife and son dying wanted to retaliate without his leadership's permission. His daughter dying was due to greedy individuals in the United States, who tried to fire a nuclear weapon at one of our ships. We protected ourselves, as was proper. There is no way to know whether that man would have snapped for other reasons."

"Still," Bethany Anne's voice was a touch softer, "we were in the middle of it." She squared her shoulders. "Even more of a reason to figure out how to crack this fucking nut related to a government that is by the people and for the people and yet handles those who need to stretch their wings by giving them room to fly."

She looked around the table. "Not by clipping them."

2

High Tortuga, Hidden Space Fleet Base, Prime Building, One Week Later

Michael Nacht looked at the screen in his office, which currently reflected his image. Although he was fairly tall for a human, his European heritage didn't let him tower over some aliens, he had found out.

The screen was easily double the size of most windows and had a resolution so fine he couldn't tell it *wasn't* a window to the outside.

Except that he knew he was at least eight stories underground.

When Bethany Anne, his wife-to-be, had said she was going to wrap him in a cocoon, he hadn't realized that would mean having four hundred tons of rock above him.

Good thing he wasn't claustrophobic.

"Screen," he called.

"Yes?"

"Play scene of the surface of High Tortuga, random," Michael requested.

The small computer inside the screen changed the view to a jungle setting. The massive purple plants that soared twenty feet into the air prevented Michael from mistaking *this* jungle for one he'd ever seen before.

He sighed. *Being on another planet was taking some getting used to.*

"ADAM?"

"Yes, Michael?" the AI replied through the overhead speakers. ADAM, who was far more evolved now than he had been when he'd begun his existence as a human-programmed AI over a hundred and sixty years ago on Earth, waited patiently for Michael's response.

"I am going to need a technical support resource. Which would be better, organic or artificial?"

"Should I ask Tabitha if she would like to resume her old position?" ADAM asked.

Michael gave the speakers an annoyed glance.

"Nice try." He thought for a moment. "However, in one way that isn't a bad solution. Would you please ask Tabitha to contact me for a discussion about my resource needs?"

"I am fully capable of advising you, Michael."

"Not sure about that, ADAM." Michael allowed a small grin to play at the corners of his lips. ADAM might have an IQ number larger than the diameter of a small planet, but he hadn't been playing with egos that ranged from peanut- to elephant-sized for over a thousand years. "Please ask Tabitha to—"

"Tabitha has asked you give her half an hour to finish her present project and shower."

"Very good, and thank you," Michael replied. He was watching a snake-like creature moving through the jungle foliage near the ground.

"Screen?" he called.

"Yes?"

"Is this a recording or a virtual video?"

"Neither," the screen replied. "This is real-time footage of the Y'ehntel Jungle on the South Continent."

"Can you zoom in?"

"Affirmative. Area?"

"How are they designated?" Michael asked. He now wished he had allowed the two aliens who had set up the screen to give him instructions.

Six lines appeared, three horizontal and three vertical, splitting the screen into nine areas. "Zoom is by designation such as R1C3 R2C2 R3C1."

Each time the screen named a location, the appropriate area was highlighted and zoomed to take up the whole screen. "Use command 'normal' to return to zero zoom factor."

Michael walked out from behind his desk to stand five feet in front of the screen. His office was large; easily thirty by forty feet.

God only knew why Bethany Anne had placed him in an office the size of a small house. For now he occupied a small portion with a small sitting area, his desk, and the screen.

"What if I wish to track something on the screen?" he asked.

"Specify cell and use the command 'track' or touch the screen when you speak the command 'track.'"

Michael touched the snake creature. "Track."

The creature replaced the middle of the screen. "Zoom creature."

"Factor?"

"Two."

Unsurprisingly, the snake became twice as large. What *did* surprise him was that the view shifted and he was now viewing the snake from the air.

"What's happening?"

"Request requires use of the AV long-distance data acquisition device to maintain zoom factor."

"Couldn't it just zoom farther?" Michael wondered aloud.

"Command modification required: 'maintain position and adjust amplification.'"

Damn, Michael thought. *Next time read the fucking manual.*

However, now he knew the little spy devices could track. He watched the snake for a time. It slithered like an Earth snake but also had eight appendages which it used like a lizard's feet. They curled up alongside the body anytime it went through water, but it used them to travel on land.

There was a knock on his door and he tasted the thoughts of the person on the other side for a fraction of a second. "Come in, Tabitha." He kept his concentration on the screen.

This was better than watching those old shows on the Discovery Channel, because here he had no idea what to expect. He heard Tabitha's soft footsteps as she joined him.

"Watching the world?" she asked. "I hear there are some wild things out there."

He pointed to the screen. "I'm watching this snake with eight arms, or legs," Michael explained as he scratched his chin. "I've seen it strike at a couple somethings that... *HOLY SHIT!*"

Both Michael and Tabitha jumped back from the screen when a reptilian foot so large it filled the monitor slammed down.

"Turn on the sound," Tabitha commanded and bedlam erupted from the speakers. Trees were being destroyed, and something was bellowing.

"Follow that!" Michael commanded.

The foot lifted off the ground, and where it had been they could barely see Michael's pet snake crushed against an overturned rock.

"Screen, follow the large creature," Tabitha commanded. The view changed as the remote unit went higher, then something sent it careening into a tree.

The screen blanked.

"Changing to secondary random surface scene," the screen announced.

"What the hell was that?" Tabitha asked, and looked at Michael. He had his thumb and forefinger on his chin and his eyes were still on the screen, but his mind elsewhere.

Tabitha started shaking her head when she connected the dots. "Oh, *hell no*, Michael! Bethany Anne isn't going to want you to hunt a fucking dinosaur on this planet."

Michael turned to look at her and raised an eyebrow, but otherwise his face remained expressionless. "I didn't know you could turn on the sound."

3

High Tortuga, Hidden Space Fleet Base, Prime Building

Bethany Anne, red eyes blazing, glared across the room at her betrothed and enunciated her words very clearly.

And very slowly, and at a significant volume.

"I. AM. NOT. A. BABY. *POD!*" she damn-near screamed.

Her hands were on her waist, legs braced apart as she stood in the large living room of her personal quarters. The furniture was mostly shades of gray.

She would have preferred white, but that was too hard to keep clean even with the synthetics she had access to. Plus, she expected to have a messy child who would challenge her ability to keep anything clean for longer than it took to walk out of the room and come back.

If she had ever figured out how to make her eyes shoot lasers, Michael might have been using his enhanced speed to dodge beams of death at that very moment.

Michael raised an eyebrow. She was almost two

hundred years old and very emotional. He was over fifteen hundred years old (albeit he'd spent many of those sleeping) and completely unimpressed.

"You are going to be a mother; ergo you are a baby incubator…unless you would like our son—"

"Daughter!"

"Whatever." Michael waved a hand. "Our *child* to be placed in the Pod-crib ADAM and TOM offered to monitor for you."

Bethany Anne's breathing was tense and her nostrils flared in and out as the logic of Michael's argument sank into her mind.

He's an ASS!

>>I think he just wants you to think through the potential consequences of you going into any fights where the child could be harmed.<<

I'm a damned superwoman! she mentally hissed. ***How the hell is something going to go wrong with me?***

TOM, her resident alien entity who was connected to and integrated around her spine, sent, **Well, technically he is right. It isn't like I understand everything that is presently going on in your body. Your emotions are heightened right now, which is sending new chemicals through your system. I'm having trouble understanding which ones are safe to mess with, so I'm leaving all of them alone.**

Bethany Anne thought about that for a moment. ***Oh, God!***

She put a hand out to Michael and covered her mouth with the other. He pointed to her right and she took off, jumping over the couches (both of them) that were between her and the bathroom so she could rid herself of her stomach's contents.

Did you do this to stop my argument with Michael? she fumed at TOM.

No. I just got done telling you I don't know what the chemicals do or why they are present. As John Grimes would say, "Shit happens."

ARRGH! Bethany Anne sent as she heaved. ***I hate you both.***

—

When Bethany Anne came out of the washroom ten minutes later her voice a bit more sedate. "Thank you. The, uh," she waved to her stomach, "situation caught me unexpectedly. Your directions helped."

Michael just nodded, keeping quiet.

"I don't like being told what I can't do," she continued. "And I'm a little annoyed that this is altering my life. I'm not used to being confined."

"I am aware of that." Michael nodded again. "However, just because you don't like hearing something doesn't mean it doesn't need to be said." He walked over to her and opened his arms. She eyed him before leaning into his embrace.

Her voice was muffled when she spoke a moment later. "This dushn't mean I'm going dow'en eashily on this."

Michael, his chin resting on Bethany Anne's head as he held her, kept his face blank; no smile to be seen. One couldn't know if there were cameras active for other reasons, which she'd check at the most inopportune time to see if he had been smirking

Like now.

"Bethany Anne, I know we have the technology here to safely grow the baby...of whatever sex...outside your body."

She punched him gently. "I'm not going to tell our child I was too self-centered to give her the best location possible to grow into a glowing young lady."

I'm sure he will be happy to hear you were voting for the opposite sex and was therefore very disappointed when our little boy popped out... Well, shit. Thankfully Michael had been smart enough to keep his comment to himself—especially since he realized how hypocritical it sounded even to himself.

Perhaps at fifteen hundred years old or thereabouts, he was finally maturing just a bit. He sighed as Bethany Anne grumbled something under her breath.

Why had he agreed to marry someone so much younger?

Oh yeah...she was the only one with the ovaries to push back at him when he was being a full-fledged in-your-face-unforgiving-kill-everyone-fucktard.

He smiled (not smirked). That might be the personality aspect which had attracted him the most to her. Unfortunately, it was also the one that was going to make the better portion of the next year a living hell.

He sighed. "Bethany Anne?"

"Hmmph?"

"I have a suggestion. Your choice to take it or not."

"Mmmhmm?"

Since she tensed when she made the sound, he could tell that she was ready, willing and able to punch him again. No man will have gone down in history as having to deal with more pain to support the birth of his child, he thought. "I understand you have deployed spy drones throughout the major and several minor cities."

"*Surveillance* drones," she mumbled. "Spy ith very negative."

"Mmmhmmm," he agreed. "Surveillance drones. Where is the main center for data acquisition and correction enforcement located?"

Bethany Anne leaned back and peered into Michael's eyes, her mouth twisting slightly as she thought about it. "There isn't a main center. We have ADAM route all requests to the person on duty in our security center here. Just this morning we had an issue in Thon with some hoodlums trying to intimidate a young Noel-ni who didn't want to join their gang."

Michael raised an eyebrow. He hadn't heard this story yet. "And what did you do about it?"

"Well, we killed them," she answered blankly. "There was audio and video proof of several crimes, two of which were enough to justify the death penalty. And that isn't including the fact that they were going to damage Baba Yaga's orb, and were trying to grow their gang."

"Right." Michael took a deep breath and let it out. "I suppose the video is—"

"On the public net related to all law enforcement. The bodies have been removed. They had no family besides their gang, so we sent the new leaders the proper status update on their former members and informed them of the statistical probability of their own demises should they continue as a gang." She thought about it for a moment and continued, "We also provided them with information on potential jobs and supplied chits to give them access to the subterranean trams that travel to the jobs' locations."

"How would they know they have jobs waiting for them?"

"The instructions pointed them to the new data resource locations. We are calling them 'libraries' because they are the closest equivalent to what we had on Earth. They can take the necessary skills and non-medical tests there. After that they will be directed to where they can get a free checkup, and then they will be given options for appropriate jobs."

"What if we have no proper jobs for them?" Michael asked. "And how did this get implemented?"

ADAM answered that one. "Michael, we have been working on these projects for over two years. Much of this was implemented, or at least the buildings and initial infrastructure were created, while Bethany Anne was still Empress of the Etheric Empire. We have three major infrastructure projects going that require a significant amount of muscle, so we can use those who are strong but not very intelligent. We have jobs available for just about everyone."

Michael's eyes narrowed. "Are these challenging jobs?"

Bethany Anne snorted. "Hardly." She stepped back, then went over to a couch and sat down. "If they want challenging and/or enjoyable jobs they will need to use their off-time to learn new skills. Training is available at all major infrastructure sites. Security is rather tight, and harassment is not allowed."

"So." Michael followed Bethany Anne, but he sat down on the couch that faced her. The two gray couches had a white carpet with two-inch pile and a sleek-looking coffee table between them. "Chain gangs?"

"No." Bethany Anne shook her head. "Remember, these are jobs for those who can do nothing else. Is it make-work?" She flipped a hand from side to side. "Sort of. We actually *do* need the infrastructure, but the muscle isn't required until Stage Three—which is somewhere between ten and twenty years out. We could use EI-controlled machinery and do it quicker, but this way it provides a job with benefits if they're willing to put in the effort. I don't care if they get pissed off, learn a trade, and get the hell out of the sweat job. That's the *point*. I'm not allowing free-loading here. Do something. *Anything*!" She tossed her hands up. "I can't believe that so many of those stupid sayings we had on Earth are so appropriate."

"Which are those?" Michael asked.

"How about 'Idle hands are the devil's workshop?'" she offered. "I'm not sure which mother said that, but it's true."

"It came from the Bible. I can't remember if it was Proverbs or Philippians," Michael supplied.

"Not a mother?" Bethany Anne's eyes narrowed. "Seriously?"

Michael nodded. "Seriously."

"Sounds like something a mother would say," she finished, but let it go. "Either way, I don't want them to have nothing to do. There are no options. If they tell us they need to stay and help a family member, we can confirm that."

He thought for a moment, then asked, "This is part of your MPPS project?"

She nodded.

He had nothing to add at the moment. No wisdom gleaned from over a thousand years of living, and no suggestions either. He shrugged and dropped the subject. "So, what do you think about creating a nice central area, designed like the pit back on Earth? Bottom level with a table and one wall of screens, but four or five levels of work desks around an oval or circle. We can pipe all the security reports in. You'd have a single place to work out the kinks with the security implementation, and to organize and authorize further efforts. At some point, you know, we'll need to leave and go out there into the deep dark to look for the Kurtherians. You will need a good team back here, and for that to run efficiently you need to train them. Record everything you do to video. Permit discussions about your efforts and modify the laws as needed."

Bethany Anne's eyes were staring at him but she wasn't seeing him. Her mind was probably split into multiple threads. Two were likely carrying on conversations with ADAM and TOM, and others were acquiring and analyzing data regarding their ongoing efforts.

Michael pulled out his tablet and hit the button to resume watching random nature feeds from around the planet.

He wanted to find another dinosaur. While Bethany Anne was thinking through his suggestion, he would do something just as important—at least to him.

He would hunt the body that went with the foot he had seen earlier. He didn't want to tap more resources, and he didn't trust Tabitha not to ask about his viewing habits.

That young woman would turn on a dime and rat him

out to Bethany Anne. Besides, getting away with the very tiny plan that was hatching in his mind was going to be icing on the cake.

Although if he failed there might be hell to pay.

High Tortuga, Hidden Space Fleet Base, Queen's Personal Quarters

"ADAM." Bethany Anne sat back on her couch and lifted her feet onto the coffee table. She sure hoped Michael didn't come in and see her like this.

She would freely admit she didn't like it when he did the same thing, but in the symphony of her silence she enjoyed the position despite the term hypocrite running through her mind.

She was complicated. He would just have to deal with it, but it would go down so much better if he didn't show up or she could pull her legs down in time.

She sighed. She was going to need to get an ottoman in here for him. She looked around and grimaced.

It would ruin her feng shui, dammit—which was the reason she had been reticent in the first place.

Men. Such a pain in the ass when it came to fucking up the furniture.

"Yes, Bethany Anne?" ADAM had long ago stopped trying to figure out why Bethany Anne would speak to him aloud sometimes and mentally others. His advanced statistical analysis could predict the *weather* with more accuracy.

"Let's talk about this central pit area Michael suggested."

"Yes?"

"I like the idea of three tiers, each with seven desks on each side. Each at least forty-eight inches wide, with monitors layered into the desktop. Let's have a set of steps going from the entry to the bottom on both sides. Large table at the bottom good for meetings of…uhh…" She thought about it. "Ten? No, we might have larger meetings there and need everyone, so make it seven to each side and two on the ends. So sixteen."

"Screens in the tabletop as well?"

"Yes." She smiled. "Make it piano-black. In fact, make everything black…and maybe a little chrome. Carved out of the rock, smooth floors with carpet down the steps and in the main area, but stone under the work areas on the three tiers. Wait, add a fourth on the same level as the entrance with space for chairs for different species to sit."

"Areas for reporters?"

"Oh, hell no." She shook her head. "Fuck that. Make sure we place enough video cameras in there to get every person from every angle. Some of them will have high-enough resolution to grab headshots out of the input for PIP efforts. The last thing I want is a bunch of questions about why I just ripped off some annoying twit's head for asking the wrong question. They can send in their questions via messaging or video, or wait. But that's a good point. Have our second phase build a large news-and-reporter area for discussions near the pit."

"Very well."

"Okay, give me a second." Bethany Anne thought back to when Michael had suggested the pit. He had caught her attention with his first sentence.

It hadn't been positive attention, but it was nevertheless attention.

Michael had said, "We need to build you a babysitter."

"Do what? I'm going to sit with our little girl for the most part."

"Not for him, but for you." Michael had clarified.

She had considered throwing a ball of red-hot energy to burn off his hair. It would have been easy enough: Pull from the Etheric, shape it, toss it at his head.

That would teach him a lesson.

"Before you try to burn off my hair—"

"Am I that transparent?" Her eyes had narrowed. "Or were you reading my mind? Because I'll kick your ass—"

Michael had put up a hand. "You have multiple favorite ways to harm me, I've noticed. The latest is burning the hair off my head."

Mollified, she had twirled her fingers in a "go on, you can live for now" gesture.

Michael smiled. "What I am suggesting is a place where you can operate for now. Handle the issues from around the planet, and yet you'll be safe. Eventually, it will be the central area to support High Tortuga when we leave the planet, and those who've worked in there will already be trained."

Bethany Anne's mind came back to the present. Michael had been right; she did need it, and it would be useful for his original purpose and so much more. He didn't have the knowledge she had acquired as the Etheric Empress.

She smiled. He was so cute when he came up with ways to help her. He knew she was going to go batshit-crazy being stuck in a safe cocoon when her whole life had been about going wherever she had wanted whenever she had wanted.

Children could put such a damper on your playtime.

She came back to ADAM. "Okay, we need to create something that will help keep High Tortuga safe, protected, productive, and eventually educated and advancing."

"You realize we do not have the infrastructure of the Empire. High Tortuga is behind the times. Advanced compared to Earth, but horribly behind compared to many places in the galaxy."

"I'm aware," she replied. "But we have technology that can help us. I'm going to bend a few rules."

"You mean break them outright," ADAM clarified.

She waved a hand. "You say tomato, I say tomah-to." She tapped her lip. "I need you to discuss additional thoughts with Addix beyond this: We want constant input from data-acquisition drones in all major and minor cities right now. Deploy the drones into the deepest sections first. I want our changes to first be noticed by those usually ignored by the police. Make sure these drones have video, sound, and holographic capability. They will have Etheric connectivity. If they are captured, they should slag themselves so they won't leave any technology behind."

"Are they supposed to implement justice?"

"Yes, if we can build that in." She nodded. "I'd like that, but given who frequents the tunnels where we are putting them I doubt we will do much more than corporal punishment." She looked up at the ceiling as she thought further. "We will need to also have body disposal abilities, which means we need to record the events for legal reasons, and we'll need a cemetery or body-disposal area. You can never tell if a criminal has parents who eventually will want to know where the body is."

"You want specific plots?"

"No, slap a GPS on them so parents or loved ones can stand above the body and know it's beneath them. I might hate the jackasses, but we need to be a bit more sympathetic to those left behind. However, I'll not take any shit from the parents; they'd better realize this stain is on them too. I won't blame the parents for what their adult child does, but they can't lay their emotional bullshit on me. That's on them."

"Which brings us to being productive," ADAM replied.

"Yes. We will have jobs available for everyone, or at least responsibilities. Continue the library project, but make some of the rooms private and semi-private. I want places for people to be safe. No weapons allowed, and implement roaming small versions of the security globes. We should keep them out of sight for the most part or some jerkoffs will try to steal them."

"Who should I tap to help build the war pit?"

"'The War Pit?'" Bethany Anne made a face. "I don't want to go that far. Let's just call it 'the Pit' for now. Could be 'Security Pit.' I don't know, maybe there is an acronym." She stood up and grabbed a drink from her fridge. "Let's find out what William is doing, if he isn't with his woman fulltime yet. If that doesn't work out, let me know and we will find another person."

"William has responded and has availability."

"Well, damn." She took a sip. "That was fast. Is he ok? Do I need to have a talk with him?"

"His relationship is fine. She is just busy working on a couple of projects, and William hasn't decided if he wants to work on barbeque pits so he's happy to help with this project."

"Ok, great. Sounded like either there was trouble in paradise or he was bored."

"Now, we have to talk EI infrastructure."

"We have to get those from Dad. The only ones we have at the moment are—"

"Practically all of the ones on the superdreadnoughts. Even ArchAngel II is bored running attack scenario after attack scenario."

"We should make her responsible for…" Bethany Anne sat down. "Shit, that might work!"

"What?"

"EIs for general tasks reporting to an organic body, but holding the subjective efforts. Tell ArchAngel she is responsible for figuring out practical methods to defend the planet while taking us from a strategy of hiding High Tortuga and managing issues while we are hidden, to helping protect us when we come out of hiding as an advanced and very tasty society for others to want to steal or take over."

"She says that sounds like fun."

"I'll bet." Bethany Anne took another swig of her Coke. "Grab whatever other EIs want in on this, but tell them they need to have off-ship support. The planet can't be left hanging if they have to go to battle."

"Ok. What are the areas of responsibility?"

Bethany Anne chewed on the end of her straw. "Send

me the responsibilities and roles of the President of the United States before we left."

She continued to chew on the straw as she reviewed the information. "Okay, we need to talk with my dad, so set up a request. I want EIs that will handle this place: one to focus on planetary power and infrastructure, one for weather, emergency services and population support, one for defense, one for legal and police-type efforts, one for trade and commerce—labor and banking responsibilities—one for the interior, for land, natural resources and other items I've no fucking clue about, so I guess that includes our version of an EPA, one for food and shelter issues and planning, one for education and one for future analysis."

"What kind of future analysis?" ADAM asked.

Bethany Anne smiled. "Wargaming."

"Why did I even ask?"

"Beats the fuck out of me. I was told that we received our next shipment of long-range reconnaissance ships for trying to find Kurtherians, so I would have bet you'd guessed I would like someone to focus on kicking Kurtherian ass. I can't help it if your guess-fu is imperfect in your old age."

ADAM chose to let that statement go. "How do you want them to work together?"

"Ahhh…shit." She thought some more. "No way we want anything but a common response for those not used to working with EIs. I need something that will be the central entity for relationships….and, ahhh…exploration, and biofeedback-reporting operations."

"That's a mouthful," ADAM stated.

"It's the best I could come up with quickly for my acronym."

"CEFRAEABRO?"

"No, of course not!" She huffed. "Take out the words 'for' and 'and.'"

"CEREBRO."

Bethany Anne smiled. "Yes. I was never fond of the X-Men, but that dome the Professor had was kick-ass."

4

High Tortuga

It had been a mere two weeks since the one called Baba Yaga had proclaimed on every video and audio news source that crime and illegal activities would be punished.

The challenge would be enforcing her mandate.

Devon wasn't as highly populated as most planets, but it wasn't sparse either. There were seven large cities, dozens of medium-sized and hundreds of smaller towns dotting the Northern Continent. There were thousands of criminals, petty and major, who figured it would take decades for their new self-proclaimed leader to work her way down to them since they didn't live in the major cities.

Why go after honest crooks when the politicians were a much more visible target?

How many people could this Baba Yaga have, anyway?

High Tortuga, Northern Continent, Thon (Third Largest

City), Haroom Sector, Lower South by Southwest Quadrant, Subsection H

New patrol initiated. Descending to lowest level.

Time: 0113:3800:11 Crawling Subsection M... Cleared

Time: 0114:0103:88 Crawling Subsection L... Cleared

Time: 0114:0403:12 Crawling Subsection K... Cleared

Time: 0114:0735:39 Crawling Subsection J... Cleared

Time: 0114:1088:39 Crawling Subsection I... Cleared

Time: 0114:0755:39 Crawling Subsection H...

Time: 0114:0756:66 Problem in Progress

Connecting to ADAM...

Security En Route. Command, record, and archive...

RECORDING

—

"Will you bite the hand that feeds you?" The alien was probably three times Ricole's height and a full ten times heavier.

Damned Leath.

As a Noel-ni she wasn't large to begin with, and since she had barely progressed from her learning stages into very early adulthood she wasn't fully grown. What she did have—and this asshole knew it—was lightning-fast reflexes and the ability to take a finger off with her teeth.

The rat-waste was wearing metal gloves.

Her eyes darted around the sooty tunnel. They were three levels beneath the core, and already the lack of maintenance or cleaning was evident. She hated being down here without shoes.

The gunk she couldn't avoid stepping in got all over her feet and fur. It was nasty as hell, but usually worth it.

Until today.

Today Bracht and a couple of his gang had been hanging around in the tunnel annex, and they'd trapped her while she wasn't paying attention.

Now they had her cornered. Working to keep her breathing even, her eyes flicked to the two exits.

She had no weapons with her, but with just one small break she could get past all three of these jackasses.

Damn the luck.

"I've bitten the hands that fed me before," she glanced at his gloves, "and you know it—as those gloves prove."

"Hehehehe." Bracht's nasty chuckle and deep voice didn't do anything to endear him to her. He lifted his right hand and displayed the protective glove. "These protect against vicious little bites like the ones you could give me. I can never be too careful." He gestured to the dirt and crud around them. "With all this slime here, how would I know you haven't caught something horrible? You might infect me just by slobbering on my hand."

"I wouldn't waste the spit if you were on fire and I was the only one who could help you, Bracht."

"Now, Ricole." He shook his head. "Is that any way to talk to your boss?"

"You?" Ricole spat to the side but kept her eyes on him as she hissed, "I wouldn't disgrace my family—who I hate by the way and don't care if they all go up in painful and mutilating flames—by working with you. We Noel-ni are known for our quick reflexes, not stupidity."

It would be a miracle if she got out of here unscathed. Bracht's two minions were eyeing her, each hoping she would come in his direction so he could get a pound of her flesh… and beat her with it.

"Having a Noel-ni on my team is important," Bracht admitted, "but it doesn't have to be you, Ricole. I've got options."

"Bullshit. Why are you chasing me at all, if that's true?" Ricole's hands itched for knives or guns—anything. She had been reading at the new resource center that had been created by the Mistress of the Planet but their anti-weapons technology was too good for her to defeat, so rather than chance being rejected at the entrance and barred from the knowledge she could gain there she had left her stuff at home.

Bad decision on her part.

"You are *the* Noel-ni every gang boss wants on their team," he admitted.

"The others have given up," she retorted. "Why can't you understand the same message? Is your skull just too damned dense?"

He shrugged. "Maybe, but the same obstinance that won't accept your 'no' for an answer," he jerked a thumb at himself, "will help me win in the end. I use my thick skull to keep battering at the challenges until I gets what I wants."

Shit, Ricole thought. *The scum-sucking asshole makes harassment feel like a damned compliment.*

—

Bracht wasn't sure he was going to get Ricole to pledge her allegiance to his group, but right this minute she didn't have many choices. Catching her without any weapons had been a miracle.

The gods, which he didn't believe in, were smiling on him.

His group had fifty-plus members. Most of them were from Leath like him, but there were also a couple of other species—a few Zhyn and even a human. But he had no Noel-nis. Hell, no gang his size or smaller had a Noel-ni member.

To start with, they were too expensive if you just wanted to hire them. Secondly, any who were willing to be in the trenches could easily join a better-funded gang than his.

However, he could offer opportunities for upward mobility and right now he was in a position to push to have her accept his offer.

That was when the third voice interrupted their conversation.

High Tortuga, Northern Continent, Thon (Third Largest City), Haroom Sector, Lower South by Southwest Quadrant, Subsection H

Ricole's eyes flicked to the right as both Bracht and his minions turned to face the newest threat.

"You will cease to threaten Citizen Ricole immediately," a deep human voice called, "or I will take steps to force you to do as I require."

Ricole slowly moved to her left, hoping Bracht's goons, who were focused on the newcomer, would allow her to sneak by them.

She just needed a bit more of an opportunity.

"Show yourself," Bracht demanded in a guttural voice. "I don't take to threats too well."

Ricole's desire to leave the subterranean tunnel was

momentarily put on hold by the entrance of a silent black gliding orb.

Ricole stopped when Mint—Bracht's number two and the jackass presently stopping her from just running—spoke up. "Let me grab a stick. I'll solve our problem." He grunted as he looked around, then accepted a long pipe from Ricole. "Thanks," he remarked absently, taking two steps forward before he realized that the Noel-ni had been the one to hand him the pipe.

"You!" Bracht shook his head as the patter of Ricole's feet on the tunnel floor receded behind Mint. "You're an idiot!" He turned back to the orb. "Well, now that we have to track her down again, we might as well see what this technology is made of. It's antigravity of some sort, and that's probably worth a lot of money."

The orb spoke again. "Do I understand correctly that you intend to touch one of Baba Yaga's security orbs?"

Mint chuckled, slapping the pipe in his palm. "Well, 'touch' might be a bit mild, since I plan on smashing you against the wall."

A second voice interrupted the first. It was a female's voice, but darker. It made the three Leath's hair stand on end. "Why are you playing with these three, John?" she asked, the sandpaper quality of her voice reproduced by the Leath's translator chips. "Just kill them and be done with it. They were trying to force themselves on the female."

"But Baba Yaga—"

"Fine, I'll do it."

Mint was starting to swing his pipe when a small piece of metal entered his brain cavity. The shock exploded his brain out the back of his skull, and he dropped to the tunnel's floor. The momentum of his swing turned him around so that he faced up, his dead eyes gazing straight at the black orb.

The other two Leath were dead as well.

The voice reverberated down the tunnel to Ricole's ears where she was crouched behind some equipment. Three different ramps nearby allowed her the choice of going up a level, down a level, or farther into this level.

"Baba Yaga gave you a warning," the female voice hissed. "You ignored it. In accordance with the laws of High Tortuga that were instituted just two weeks ago, you were sentenced to death. Since I'm not sure you read those laws, it sucks to be you. Your remains will be taken to the cemetery outside of town. The trial during which you were condemned will be available for public access should anyone give a shit where you are."

The orb headed back down the tunnel from whence it had come.

Ricole slowly got up, the shock on her face easily understood no matter what race you were. She looked down at herself and shrugged. She would go up to the higher levels to find a place to rinse off before hitting the public tunnels.

She had some research to do.

Into the public court system.

High Tortuga, a Couple of Months Later

Bethany Anne, her stomach barely protruding, was walking around in her newly-constructed Pit, from which she triaged all the issues that were reported on the planet. So many came up on a daily basis that it was impossible for her to deal with any but the most serious.

Many of the people who had come back from Earth with her to work on High Tortuga spent their time connecting with politicians, police, and special services.

But that was slow going. Her team needed to get in touch with the current leaders of the planet. She didn't have enough people to replace everyone, and the infrastructure would take a while to put in place.

She tapped a finger to her lips as she watched the reports scrolling on the screens.

ADAM, patch me into the meeting going on right now in Tor-chik.

>>Where do you want the video?<<

Bethany Anne glanced at the video wall, which consisted of thirty screens: six across and five down.

Front wall, use four starting at top left.

The first four screens blanked and a new feed replaced the previous one. There were seven humanoid figures and all seemed to be male, but one was very interesting to Bethany Anne since he was a two-legged Yollin.

>>Feeding audio direct to implant.<<

"And I'm telling you I asked about Baba Yaga!" The Yollin was speaking and the motions of his mandibles displayed his agitation. Bethany Anne glanced down at her tablet to read the particulars of the seven members.

The Yollin worked at a local company, not one of hers. The other six were split evenly between a mining company and two warehousing companies. Hard work, and the males looked rough themselves.

"What about it?" a hairy sasquatch-looking alien replied. A few on the team had suggested calling them "Chewbaccas," but a contingent of Star Wars fans had wailed in anguish. They'd argued that they didn't look dignified enough to be their favorite alien from the movies, so they became "Bakas," which everyone accepted.

Such was her life at the moment: playing mediator between two sets of friends on whether they could nickname an alien after a human movie that had been popular before the world imploded.

She sighed and grabbed an energy bar, taking small bites while she watched and listened to the discussion play out.

The Yollin glanced at the Baka. "If this is the real Baba Yaga, then the Witch of the Empire has decided to make *our* planet her bitch."

"That's a bad thing?" the Baka asked.

"No." The Yollin shook his head. "So long as you work hard and do the right thing she ain't going to mess with you. BUT," he waved a hand, his mandibles still clacking in agitation, "the presence of the Witch means the former Empress is involved too."

"Yeah, so?" the Baka asked. "Why do we care? Do you see anything bad happening at the moment? Hell, we've all been bitching about the politicians and the gangs for a long damned time. I say we grab the opportunity to take back our area. The gangs been pushing on the businesses, and now the 'Yaga is pushing back."

"If you can believe the legal feed, sure," one of the other guys—another Baka—remarked.

"Anybody they say they executed come back to refute

it?" the Yollin asked. "Cause that's the easiest way. If this is the real Baba Yaga…"

"Oh, it's the real Baba Yaga," Bethany Anne murmured, nibbling on her food bar.

"Then we won't find anyone alive that they claim to have executed," the Yollin finished.

Bethany Anne finished her bar and put aside the wrapper, clapping her hands together to get off a couple of crumbs.

She could hear John Grimes coming up behind her and put up a finger to tell him to hold on for a moment.

ADAM, tag these males. I want to know if they do anything at all, or just keep chatting themselves up.

>>Understood, Bethany Anne.<<

As she turned to John, the video she had been watching blanked and the previous feeds came back.

"Yes?" she asked, swallowing her last bite.

"Seems like we have a military strike heading in our direction," he told her.

She raised an eyebrow. "Here? How the hell does anyone know to attack us *here*?"

John shrugged. "It isn't like thousands of support people didn't help build the base. It's probably one of the planet's worst-kept secrets."

She rubbed her cheek. "Yeah, ok. You guys have told me that, but I suppose there is always a first." She thought about it. "Air?"

"Yes, and ground. Not troops, but heavy vehicles. Looks like a local merc group or something like that."

She nodded. "Michael?"

John grinned. "Staying out of this at the moment."

She frowned. “That’s strange. He must be up to something. He has the armor, and I doubt very much that anything a local merc company has would kill him.” She sighed. “Both of us can’t be stuck here, and I need intel. See if he—" She spied John smiling. “Oh, good grief. Boys and your toys. Go...get intel, and don’t get killed.”

John turned to leave. “And!” she called, and John looked back. “Don’t allow Michael to die. I don’t want to have to resurrect him and then explain to our child why I killed him for incompetence and pissing me off!”

John shook his head and walked off.

She chewed her lip and subconsciously put a hand on her belly.

5

High Tortuga, Thirty Minutes Outside the Queen Bitch's Base

Michael appeared out of thin air and stumbled. Eric, one of the Queen's Bitches, grabbed his arm. "Problems with the Etheric?" Eric chuckled.

Since they had been Bethany Anne's closest protectors for decades, she called on the Queen's Bitches when she couldn't deliver a smackdown personally.

Michael joined John Grimes, Eric Escobar, Scott English and Darryl Jackson. Michael had rescued and brought Demon, an enhanced mountain lion, from Earth with him and she was going on this mission with them. Tabitha, Peter, Akio, and several others were in Black Eagles, screaming into the atmosphere to lie in wait for the air vehicles.

"It seems," Michael answered, "that Bethany Anne wasn't kidding when she told me metal interferes with Etheric travel."

Scott's eyes narrowed. "Were you going to try to travel the Etheric to attack the column coming this way sooner?"

Michael turned toward Scott, who put up a finger. "YOU *WERE!*"

"Not nice, man." John shook his head. "Trying to take away our fun."

Michael grimaced. "I wasn't thinking of it quite that way." He chuckled. "Ok, I probably *was* thinking of it in *exactly* that way. Remember, you Bitches go out on security ops all the time. I have been stuck under hundreds of tons of rock for a long time."

"Should have been more careful who you stuck it in." Eric chuckled. "I don't think she believes you are invincible after missing you for the last hundred and fifty years."

Michael thought about Eric's comment. "You know, I was relatively unharmed for over a thousand years until I met Bethany Anne. Since then I've been almost killed twice, and also reduced to atoms and reconstituted in another dimension."

Darryl grinned, his white teeth flashing in the waning light. His dark skin made his face almost invisible in his helmet. "So, am I to understand you blame Bethany Anne for your run of bad luck?"

Michael pursed his lips, thankful Akio wasn't here to explain the truth of one of those instances. "I'm merely pointing out that the worst damage I've taken, including a kind of death, has happened since I've met Bethany Anne."

"Right." Scott snorted. "Am I the only one who has the balls to remind you that *YOU* picked her to help you?"

As a tiny plume of dust in the distance caught his eye

Michael murmured, "I was rather hoping you would overlook that."

The men noticed his focus and turned to see what he was looking at. A moment later all five helmets closed and tiny servos whirred as they locked in place and they activated their defensive shields.

All of them were wearing incarnadine armor that looked black under most light, and on the left arm of each was a female human skull with vampire teeth encircled by the words Ad Aeternitatem.

Michael's helmet cam zoomed in on the fourteen trucks, each of which sported a large turret on the back. None looked exactly like tanks, but none looked very useful for anything but attacking a ground-based facility.

He wondered what kind of idiots would only bring fourteen trucks to attack a spaceport?

High Tortuga, Outside the Queen Bitch's Base

"Air Striker 119, do you have eyes on target?"

"Negative, Strike Lead. Either this base is underground or we have bad coordinates."

"One moment, Striker 119."

A few moments later the mercenaries' base of operations came back on the encrypted channel. "Negative on bad coordinates. We have absolute confirmation the coordinates are accurate. Suspect camouflage."

The pilot of Attack Ship 119 looked at his copilot. "You would think they would have better intel."

"Heard it's either a massive base or three sticks strung together to form an outhouse so they can pee in private."

The copilot scanned the ground as they passed over a nearby town. "I'm leaning toward 'outhouse.'"

"Why?"

"You heard what they said it was, right?" The co-pilot checked the instruments.

"Base of some kind."

"Not just a base, but a base for thousands and thousands, plus hangars so large you can land battleships and dreadnoughts in them. Advanced stuff."

"Oh, that's a good one!" The pilot chuckled as he verified he was an appropriate distance from 117. "Pull the third one, why don't you?"

"No, I'm serious!" his co-pilot protested. "Big-ass chambers you could fly one of those big ships in. Not just one, but…"

—

Tabitha, previously Ranger Two and now bored to tears, was waiting in her Black Eagle up above the atmosphere. She touched her communication switch. "This is Overwatch. Waiting for instructions from ArchAngel."

"And this is ArchAngel," Michael's clipped and precise voice replied, "telling Overwatch to continue her efforts to be patient. Apparently the last hundred and fifty years did not provide the practice she desperately needs."

From behind her, the centuries-old vampire Ryu snickered and Tabitha spoke over their personal channel. "Laugh it up, vamp-boy. Remember, he is twice as old as you. He probably thinks you lack patience as well."

Ryu gazed out into space, his smile evident in his voice. "That is highly doubtful, Tabitha. I am Japanese. We came out of the womb patient in my century. We waited for permission from our parents to cry for the first time."

Tabitha stuck her tongue out, knowing her teammate and teacher was probably imagining her doing exactly that.

A hundred and fifty-plus years of familiarity from working together on operations and cleaning up a planet tended to allow people to be easy with each other.

For good or ill.

—

Michael clicked off the comm with Tabitha, his eyes narrowing inside his helmet. "Gentleman—and I ask this with all sincerity—please confirm that your weapons are set appropriately."

"God!" Scott exclaimed. "Who told Jean we needed pistols that went to twelve?" He sighed. "I'm ready."

Darryl chuckled over the comm. "Ready, and the answer to that is, 'Look in the mirror.' I probably have video of how excited you were when you found out she upped the power to twelve."

Eric was a hundred yards away on the other side of the dirt road the armored air trucks were inbound on. The team was in a small valley that was surrounded by cliffs about fifty feet high. "Ready, and I have video."

"Kiss-ass," Scott muttered.

"Jean is very excited," John told them casually, "that we volunteered to try out the new pistols for this attack. As her husband, I appreciate the added enthusiasm in our nightly physical exertions due to her excitement."

"*NIGHTLY?*" Eric whined. "Aren't you old enough to be down to three times a week, or maybe two?"

"What can I say?" John chuckled. "The lady likes her physical activity."

"And I'm ready," Michael finished. "We are seventeen seconds from action. Please don't be late to the party. Choose whatever level you desire, but if your shots bounce off their armor I won't shield you when everyone laughs."

When he finished speaking, Michael checked to make sure his own pistol was set to twelve. He had fired on eleven, and the kickback from that setting wasn't pleasant. Although it would have broken a normal human's wrist, the bone structures of everyone here had been enhanced by nanocytes which maximized strength in all directions.

Even twisting.

He smirked and sent the command to his armor to become more rigid at the wrist. He wasn't so cocky that he wouldn't accept the bracing the armor would provide once he integrated his pistols.

Integration successful...

It was time to see how protected these vehicles were.

—

Over a century and a half before, Bethany Anne's lead weapons developer Jean Dukes (later Jean Grimes) acquired technology from TOM and created weapons which used magnetic pulses to fire shards. The tiny slivers of hardened metal accelerated to hypersonic speeds, making them damn near as powerful as crew-serviced field weapons.

She had engineered the pistols to offset most of the recoil by using a similar technology to that which sent the tiny shard of metal screaming *out* of the pistol. However, the higher power settings required exponentially more strength, and even the stoutest complained after shooting too many shots at the fabled 'eleven.'

As a joke, Jean had modified the pistols so they went to eleven so they could use the quote from the movie *This is Spinal Tap*.

Each pistol was set up to be usable by only its owner; set to their DNA, making them useless for others. If they were stolen and anyone should try to fire them they wouldn't function. If they tried to take them apart, they would explode.

Leaving a very large crater.

Jean had recently found a way to up the power even further. First, she built the technology into a sniper rifle Bethany Anne had given her as a gift. Then, during the time the ships were in orbit around Earth setting up the defensive satellite network of BYPSs, she tinkered with making the mechanics smaller.

Jean had finally been successful with her modifications a week after arriving on High Tortuga, and this would be the first time the pistols would be used.

Michael wondered if any of the other guys had thought to alter their armor.

He grinned as he aimed the reticle in his HUD at the far end of the caravan.

"Fire."

—

"This is Ground Lead 717." Th'et wiped his eyes. The glow from the screens annoyed him at the best of times, and these heavy armored trucks were bouncing up and down at least a couple of finger-lengths on the rough surface they were traveling over, annoying him further.

One would think the air cushions would provide a better ride in these beasts.

"All units, leave active radar off until we have active engagement or you are ordered to go live. Let's get as close as we can to the coordinates. This is a hit-and-run. Send your attack munitions into any openings you find. We are here to disrupt and disengage. That will allow those above us to keep away any—"

That was when he heard the first screams from the back of the convoy.

—

The amount of mass necessary to cause damage goes down as the velocity of the projectile goes up. Back on Earth, there had been incidents where a piece of straw had been thrust through a tree by hurricane-force winds.

The WCH-HHU Heavily Armored Air Lift vehicle used both antigravity and air cushion technologies to move troops or missiles and other munitions to ground warfare locations.

Presently there were fourteen WCH-HHU vehicles traveling down the path toward the coordinates. It wasn't so much a real road as dirt compressed by vehicles such as theirs over a long period.

The eight missiles in the back of each transport gave them a hundred and twelve ways to make this evening a significant downer to those who were at the coordinates.

It would suck horribly—for them—if the lucky recipients were not connected with Baba Yaga.

These armored vehicles had been modified to fire two missiles at a time, one from each side. When the missile was fired the antigrav engine became a catapult, launching it into the air before its chemical ignition system kicked in. They would fire from a distance to allow the kinetic energy to increase before the heavy missiles hit their intended targets.

Each missile had a small mass-to-energy-conversion tip which would further enhance the headaches for those at the base.

If they lived to have headaches, that is.

The problem was the idiots in WCH-HHU 342 (five up from the rear) had gotten a bit excited and started prepping their missiles in advance. This was against the rules of engagement and, frankly, against common sense.

When molten tungsten slag had hit the third missile down the row the kinetic energy had transferred to it and the heat had overridden the temporary lockdowns.

The resulting explosion had set off every missile in the armored vehicle.

Two eye-blinks later the missiles in the next two trucks detonated as a result of the previous explosions; the mercenaries in the vehicles were already dead.

In the distance, the armored humans who were still firing their pistols were tossed backward by the shockwave to slam against the rocks behind them. Then they were swept over them and out into the surrounding desert area.

Fortunately for them, their armor had antigrav as well or their landings might have been a bit rougher.

—

Tabitha hit the button to call the Black Eagles. "COMMENCE!" she ordered and her own ship plummeted out of space.

Although Michael's voice had come over her earpiece, it

was the explosions they could see from the video drones miles away which had caused her to order the attack.

There was no way she wasn't coming down when it looked like Michael might be in trouble.

"He will be okay, Kemosabe," Ryu told her. "If you will but check the signals from their armor on screen two, they are mostly green."

Tabitha stabbed the screen Ryu was talking about and confirmed that while all five suits of armor had spots of yellow, none of the bodies they protected were in trouble.

Yet.

The group was no longer together, though. "Damn, what happened down there?" she murmured as her ship broke through the upper atmosphere, but then enemy ships and explosions started popping up on her HUD and she was too busy to think about his absence further.

"All Overwatch, attack."

The babble of confusion from the enemy airships was rapidly replaced by radio silence as her twelve Black Eagles sent one-pound pucks (kinetic antigrav missiles) through them.

The airships fell and their dying crews rained down to the ground below.

—

John had kept his head down when the explosions hit. Fortunately he had been behind a rock large enough to block the wall of air that had blasted over them, but Scott, who had been some ten yards away, was picked up and tossed over the lip of the valley.

Michael had been the first to disappear.

He had been firing the first shots of their offensive

when the explosion hit. He had been able to turn his head, but the shockwave didn't care how many hundreds of pounds his armor weighed.

He was gone.

John located Darryl safe in a shallow ditch, but he couldn't find Eric.

Scott's name lit up in John's helmet display. "Oooowwww. Did someone hit me with the world's biggest bat?"

"Where the hell are you?" John demanded. The burning inferno some half a mile away told him none of the armored vehicles were operational any longer.

Three dots appeared on his HUD. Scott wasn't too far away; maybe three hundred yards over the lip of the small valley. Eric was about four hundred yards north of Scott, and…

John whistled. "Are you really a mile from here, Michael?"

"It seems," Michael's clipped voice told him over the comm, "that reducing the weight so one doesn't slam down should be done later, *not* as soon as you recognize the danger."

John clicked off his mic as he chuckled, but once he'd gotten his laughter under control he reactivated it. "Sorry. I suppose you should have more training on using the armor."

"Not a problem," Michael replied. "I see from the remotes that we have no more enemies?"

"Yes," John replied, using the zoom on his visor to check out the burning wreckage. "I can't find any metal pieces longer than my arm, and certainly nothing organic is alive."

The men were quiet for a moment.

"MICHAEL!" Tabitha's shout interrupted their conversation.

Airships had started falling from the sky around John, although most were off in the distance.

One of them impacted directly on Michael's icon.

6

High Tortuga, Thirty Minutes Outside the Queen Bitch's Base

Tabitha's scream had barely finished reverberating through the ears of those on the attack channel when Michael's icon appeared a hundred yards away from the crashed airship.

"What?" Michael asked in response to Tabitha's scream. "I'm fine, Tabitha. A random piece of airship isn't going to catch me by surprise. I have over a millennium of experience fighting; a conditioned second sense honed over time that reacts to danger on the field of battle and—"

There was a click and Darryl interjected, "And a radar connected to your HUD that warns you with plenty of time to spare."

"And armor that warned me in plenty of time," Michael gamely finished. "Not that I would have needed it, but it was squawking in my ear."

Tabitha's sweet voice was now a little less strident. "I'm going to come down there and yell at you."

"What?" Michael replied, "I'm sorry, the connection must be bad, Overwatch. I'm sure you wouldn't leave us without proper air cover just so you could feel better."

"No," she answered. "*I* wouldn't."

Tabitha left the attack channel.

"Michael," John began as he left to visually confirm the enemies who had been taken out of action, "I suggest that next time you stick your head into danger neither Bethany Anne nor Tabitha know of it."

Michael looked into the sky as he headed back toward their ambush location. He opened his visor for a moment, which cut his mic off.

"Women!"

Planet Soboth (Previously Territory 7732), Undisclosed location, Open Out-ring, Non-Federation

Az, the CEO of a multi-planet corporation, shuffled the company's legitimate papers to the side, leaving one in front of him. "I see that we have more to discuss about our resources on planet Devon." He glanced at Uleq and Imon. "Anyone want to go first on what happened?"

Uleq looked at Imon and nodded to indicate he should discuss the point. It was more of a military operation than white-collar, and that was usually where the two of them broke up the responsibility.

Imon wasted no time getting to the salient facts. "Our mercenary group, hired completely on Devon and with no traceable connections back to us, failed. From the generic satellite imagery we were able to acquire, the missiles exploded and teams were destroyed some ways off from the supposed base location."

Az asked, "The airships?"

"None returned to base."

Uleq jumped in. "Our cutout is secure?"

Imon nodded. "I made sure to purchase their services through multiple cutouts. One of those, unfortunately, is no longer with us due to an unexpected attempt to fly from his balcony. That cutout was on another planet."

Uleq's Torcellan eyes scrunched in confusion. "I thought he lived on the second floor?"

"Apparently," Imon replied dryly, "he decided to go up to the roof before jumping."

Az reached up to scratch beneath his right eye. "You seem to be taking a lot of precautions, Imon. Do you have further intel that would warrant such efforts?" Both Az and Uleq watched Imon for any cues as to his thinking on the subject.

Imon shrugged. "In general, the feedback I am getting from the planet—which is more and more difficult to locate transportation to unless you own your own ships—is that this Baba Yaga is clamping down on the whole planet. However she is accomplishing it, the changes are benefiting the general populace so you won't see an uprising. Whatever her PR campaigns are saying, they're doing very well. I see no popular irritation, except from the criminal underground and those lining their pockets in the political system. Perhaps a few bankers and businessmen as well." He shrugged. "Believe it or not, it seems like she is presently working in the best interests of those on her planet."

Az shook his head and stabbed a finger on the table. "I don't believe it." He crossed his arms and leaned on the table as he thought out multiple options. What would he do if he were taking over the planet and investing trillions and trillions in capital? "There has to be a longer game here. No one comes in and purchases a planet without the express intent to make a profit. This Baba Yaga has to have hundreds if not thousands of backers. We are in contact with more than ninety percent of the billionaires and all but one of the trillionaires. No one has spoken about an operation on Devon. It doesn't make any sense…unless I am not seeing other options?" He looked at Uleq.

Uleq kept looking at his tablet for a moment before he realized that Az had stopped talking. "Do what? Oh, could she have other reasons for doing this?" He looked back down at the tablet and tapped it. "Everything I'm seeing here suggests she has, to the best of her ability, taken over most of the interstellar operations. This is of course how she took over our efforts there. Unfortunately we had the Gauger hostile takeover going on and we failed to notice her efforts early enough."

Az nodded. "That was a difficult project."

If one called the acquisition of several hundred billion in credits, fourteen suicides (including three of the top twenty-four people due to a bullshit staging of graft in the ranks), and switching out one small national president "difficult."

On the plus side, within four years they would be profitable on the acquisition and control another hundred and fifty million in populace through other cutouts.

There was always another path to slavery. You didn't have to own people outright; you could use the tax system. Since it made sense that governments needed income, and they did, you implemented a tax on top of it.

Usually ten percent was a safe number.

Uleq's hand swiped across his tablet once, twice, thrice. He shook his head. "I see no gain for her until between twenty and thirty years in the future. She would have to be willing to have her capital locked up for a long time and put trillions of credits into this planet to receive the long-term benefit." Uleq looked at Az. "Can you conceive of a military reason for Baba Yaga to do that?"

Az's eyes narrowed. "Military? Hmmm. That is a good question. I'll have to think on that and see if perhaps one of the other military powers is investing here. If they are," he chewed on the inside of his lips for a moment before reaching up and scratching his chin beneath his left tusk, "we might have to consider dropping our efforts on Devon. It would hurt our bottom line for the quarter, but I don't want to get involved with any of the major powers. That would be a losing proposition. However," he looked at both of his partners, "if she is *not* allied with one of the major powers? Then I say we not only disrupt her plans but take over what is left of her infrastructure afterward and own the planet outright." He shrugged, a smile growing on his face. "Why should we waste what she has built for us?"

Uleq nodded. Imon had handled the first project, and now it was his turn. He put the tablet down on the table so his partners could see the map displayed on it. "Okay, our mercenary operation didn't take. Here's what we plan to do related to banking and infrastructure."

High Tortuga

The Zhyn businessman wiped off his sleeve. He was waiting for some males who would normally use this area of the tunnels to chat after their day was through.

Lerr'ek was under the orders of the Mistress of the Planet and wanted to get this done before he retired for the evening. A few years back, he had offered his services for ten years in exchange for not dying right away.

It had seemed like a good thing at the time.

It had been some years since he had made the deal, he was now itching to move on. He had overseen the construction of the spaceport for Baba Yaga's ships, and he had acquired ownership for Baba Yaga in most of the locally-based interplanetary companies—and certainly all that mattered.

He had been told that the others would be handled.

Zhyns might be aggressive by nature, but they weren't stupid. He had been taken into the Etheric—and while time causes one to forget, he would *never* forget the pain Baba Yaga had used to get his attention.

It was the ultimate reason he had never tried to betray the dark-faced demon with the white hair. He had been entrusted with the secret that Baba Yaga was the Empress, or rather, now Queen again.

He didn't care. The two women were very different when he spoke with them, so he would continue to treat them as separate entities. His handler was Stephen, one of her most trusted advisors, brother to her mate and now High Tortuga's Business Lead.

The first of the Rough Males (as Bethany Anne had called them after she'd first seen them in a spy video a while back) Lerr'ek had been waiting for arrived with a work bag, a drink, and fresh bandages on his face.

Lerr'ek stayed in the shadows.

Lerr'ek? Bethany Anne spoke into his mind.

"Hmm?" he replied sub-vocally.

How would you like to leave business behind and work on an anti-gang-warfare project?

Lerr'ek considered his options. "How is the pay?"

Do you always negotiate?

"In my experience, asking *after* the agreement is concluded doesn't work."

Smart Zhyn, she replied. *How about this: you take care of this gang and these males and I reduce your sentence from ten years to time served?*

Lerr'ek didn't answer for a moment. "If I get rid of this gang—these males—I am free?"

Well, they need to be alive when you're done.

"I can't guarantee that."

Don't actively abuse them. I want you to train them to support the local area.

"You want them to become police officers?"

Call it a neighborhood watch. Eventually we want to have the capability for rapid intervention, but not yet. Right now we need a group that is fighting back with the support of Baba Yaga. You have the smarts and the military background to help accomplish this.

"Agreed," he replied.

Wait...agreed that you will do this, or you agree you have the military background and smarts to accomplish what I want?

"All of it," Lerr'ek answered. "However, what happens if I wish to leave Devon?"

High Tortuga.

"Whatever." He smiled. He had been playing the "name this planet" game with the Empress (he really couldn't think of her any other way) since she had gotten back.

We will have to erase some of your knowledge before you leave, unfortunately. You would end up on another planet with a fake diary and a lot of money in your account. I can't say I would wish that on you, but making you stay and be a slave here because you were useful wouldn't be a very good way to show my appreciation.

It wouldn't, but it beat a gunshot to the back of his head and an unmarked grave. If he were here, it might be the solution he would have picked back when they first met.

Soon enough the other five Rough Males arrived. "I have to go. I have some anti-gang-warfare efforts to see to."

Later. She removed her presence from his brain and he had his thoughts to himself, again. He started to slowly make his way closer to the group of aliens.

—

"*That* was a punch!" someone in the group exclaimed.

Cr'ehg clicked his mandibles together in satisfaction. With his own version of armored plates, the Yollin had played a large part in the fight between the six of them and the three toughs from the gang that had tried to claim their area of the city.

He put his arms up. "We did good!" Each of them raised his drink in Cr'ehg's direction. "Now we need to keep watch in case they show back up. I can't believe they won't try it again."

"You still worried about Baba Yaga?" Lerr'ek noted that the speaker was Beruth, the Baka who had addressed Cr'e-hg's concerns on the video.

"Yes, of course," Cr'ehg tapped his mandibles together. "She could be anywhere. If she thinks we did this outside the law, we might find a demon in our bedrooms when we wake up."

"Actually…"

All six of the males turned to find a blue-skinned Zhyn leaning against a large crate just ten paces away.

"Who are you?" Beruth demanded. "And why are you down here?"

Lerr'ek straightened and walked toward the group. "I'm here to give you a message."

Beruth nodded. "Well, say what you have to and be gone."

"Oh, it's not from me." Lerr'ek pulled a small round device out of his pocket and held it out in his palm. He touched a button on the side. "*She* wants to talk to you."

Only the Yollin caught on when the larger-than-life hologram appeared above Lerr'ek's hand.

The head slowly swiveled to stare at the six Rough Males.

Her face was human, her skin black, her hair white, and her eyes glowing red.

"My name," her voice, guttural and raspy announced to those assembled, "is *Baba Yaga.*"

7

High Tortuga, Northern Continent, Thon (Third Largest City), Haroom Sector, Lower South by Southwest Quadrant, Subsection H, Two Days Later

Ricole, her tail twitching, strode up the steps to Thon's newest public building. The Library had been installed just a couple of months ago by Baba Yaga.

Since her interaction with Bracht and his gang she had stayed away from the building, concerned she would be busted for being in the middle of the fight. However, curiosity was driving her to see and know more.

She had learned her lesson; she would never be without protection again. She had weapons with her everywhere she went now. It had been very fortuitous for the security to arrive on the scene, and very advantageous (for her) that Bracht was an asshole, sure he could brute-force his way to success. Unfortunately he met up with a group that didn't care...and didn't tolerate mistakes.

On the positive side, rumor had it that Bracht's gang

had chosen to dissolve and find work rather than choose new leaders and continue harassing shop owners, stealing from others, and generally being a public nuisance. Ricole had been able to confirm Bracht's death, since it had been posted in the public area for law enforcement.

Complete with all the infractions Bracht and the two others had against them. Previous, recent, suspected and those he had been executed for. There was also a geographic location for his grave should anyone care to go and say any last words over his corpse.

The humans were weird, she thought, tossing her bag over her shoulder as she went through the security gate.

She didn't notice the red light that flashed as she continued farther into the building.

—

Bethany Anne was sitting at a table with room for sixteen (seven down each side and one at each end) that had a shiny black surface. Each seat at the table had a screen inset into the table itself in front of it. The only active screen was on the left side at the end…

The one Bethany Anne was staring at, going through the reams of alarms and information scrolling on-screen.

Her eyes flicked up to the top right when a small window opened and an alert flashed. She tapped it and saw that a filter she had set up previously had been tripped.

A female Noel-ni had just entered one of the libraries armed. Bethany Anne tapped the figure. "Show three-dimensionally."

The two-dimensional picture popped up, but soon it became three dimensional. Bethany Anne moved her hand through the image, turning it so she could see the back of the figure. "Enhance suspected weapon location."

The back-belt location grew larger. "What is the weapon?"

A female voice answered, "Small-caliber dart weapon for personal protection. Generic. Assumed twelve-shot."

"Not taking over the place," Bethany Anne murmured. "Probably a holdover from almost being steamrolled." Bethany Anne stood up, swiping a hand to shut off the terminal. She waved to one of the other twelve working in the Security Pit with her. "Jennifer?"

A woman looked up.

"Take over. I'm going on a field trip to talk with the people."

Jennifer's eyes narrowed. She had been around Bethany Anne enough to know this was out of character for the last few weeks—but very *in*-character for the previous decades. "Wait, what?"

Bethany Anne waved to her and disappeared.

"Oh, shit." Jennifer sighed, then tapped a mic on her lapel. "This is Jennifer. The Queen is going God-knows-where. Who's got her six?"

A multitude of responses came back. "Where the hell is she?" "What did she say she was going to do?" "Anyone got eyes on Bethany Anne?" and *"Someone call Michael!"*

—

She was in her *other* closet sliding on basic armor and she had just picked up a voluminous black robe when he appeared outside the doorway.

"What?" she asked as she slid an arm through her jacket. "You don't knock anymore?"

"In my own bedroom?" Michael leaned against the doorframe and smiled. "Where are we going?"

Bethany Anne looked at him. "Who said it was 'we?'"

"Who else were you going to ask to go with you?" he asked, his eyebrows raising in question. "I'm sure you had plans to call someone."

She locked the armored jacket and started putting on the robe, sliding a hand into the right sleeve. "You're lucky you're so damned handsome."

"And *you* are lucky so many care about you. Everyone goes into a snit when you just up and disappear."

"Feels like I can't go to the bathroom in private," she harrumphed, sliding the other hand into the remaining sleeve. "I'm just going to Thon to have a conversation with a citizen in a library. She had a very scary situation happen and I want to ask her some questions." She turned to Michael, who noted that her normally white skin was slowly changing to a dark black and her hair was turning white as snow. "You know, public research?"

"Uh huh." Michael stood up and reached out, and his hand came back with a black Stetson hat. He placed it on his head, and a moment later he reached out again and brought back a black duster. It was one of his favorite outfits. He had used for a while back on Earth.

The next time he reached out, he grabbed a gun-belt with two pistols in holsters. "I've got Sabine waiting near your normal ship. I'll assume you were going to call me," he informed her as he strapped the gun-belt around his waist.

Bethany Anne smiled as she walked out of the closet and patted him on the chest as she passed him. "You do that."

—

Ricole had been at the library for an hour, looking through the new laws and the job board. It was suggested that those who would like to look for employment take an online evaluation which would provide basic guidance.

It would take two hours. She had found the area set aside for testing and entered in her contact information and basic physiological info, including her species (of course) and age. She was tempted to lie on the setup; she didn't want to be tracked.

However, what if they wanted to find her, and she had lied? She needed to decide whether to trust this group, and she chose to do so.

For now.

Ricole was in the middle of the third of four tests when she became aware that someone had entered her cubicle. She turned her head slightly and flicked her eyes over her shoulder; she could barely see the two figures maybe three steps behind her. How they had come into the quiet testing area without her hearing the door open and shut was a concern.

The two were human, and Ricole licked her lips. That was when she remembered she had the pistol in her waistband…

SHIT! She had the pistol in her waistband! She'd brought a weapon into the library.

What to do, what to do? She answered the next question on the test while she thought. They weren't interrupting her testing, so it couldn't be a *massive* mistake. Perhaps they hadn't known about her pistol?

She answered the next question.

If they had wanted to harm her, she would have already been in pieces. Missing them showing up was a damned embarrassment. She was used to getting the drop on people, and but in this instance she had failed.

She answered the last question on the third test and clicked "Finish test." She carefully put her hands on the desk and turned far enough to see the two humans staring at her as they patiently waited.

There was a male human with a head covering and a coat. The other human was sexless in their long robe, with a hood covering their head.

Then the person in the robe spoke and Ricole's blood ran cold.

She had heard that voice before…

Her rasping voice grated and Ricole's breathing became shallower. "Hello, Ricole." As she spoke her black hands reached up to lift off her hood…and Ricole stared at the face she had dreamed about since Bracht had been executed.

And here was the person who had pressed the button to kill him.

"I…" Her voice faltered for a moment before her self-esteem kicked her in the ass. "I'm Ricole. What can I do for you, Mistress?"

The male human next to her rolled his eyes as he kept a lookout. He was the muscle, that was for sure.

"First," she held out a hand, "you can surrender your weapon. They are not allowed in the libraries."

Ricole's hand twitched and she reached back for the weapon, but her eyes grew large when she was prevented from pulling it out.

She was staring at the human male's pistol, which was aimed at her head. "Slowly," he warned. "Let's not have any accidents."

Ricole gently lifted the pistol out from behind her and leaned down to place it on the floor. She used her foot to slide it toward the male.

He twitched his gun at the weapon. "You can pick it up, but if you place a single digit on the trigger your life is forfeit."

She stopped herself from rolling her eyes. Didn't he know how fast Noel-ni were? She could shoot them both between the eyes before he could think of what he'd had for breakfast. However, she didn't want to harm them, so she picked up the pistol with two fingers and held it out to him. He came forward and accepted the pistol with his left hand, then he slipped his own pistol into its holster. He turned the pistol one way, then the other to locate the ammo switch and flipped it to release the cartridge. He confirmed there wasn't one loaded before handing the pistol back to Ricole.

He took two steps back. "Now I want you to hold the pistol with two fingers again. If you can flip it up and pretend to shoot both of us before I disarm you, I will pay your rent for one..." He turned to Baba Yaga. "What's a month here?"

Baba Yaga snorted. "Just say 'month,' Michael. The translation software will understand and switch it to the appropriate phrase."

He turned back to Ricole. "Month."

Ricole shrugged. If he wanted to part with a month's worth of rent money she was willing to play along. "When do you want…" As she spoke, she flipped the weapon around, grasped the butt, and raised the pistol.

Her world went upside down. The pistol had been knocked aside and who knew how it had been twisted out of her grip. She was on the floor and his pistol was firmly pressed against her skull. "First rule of becoming a proper guard, Ricole: never underestimate those you don't know."

Ricole nodded, trying to figure out what the hell had just happened. "I get it." He pulled his pistol back, and grabbed her arm, easily lifting her into the air. Ricole flipped to her right to break his grip and pressed her feet against the wall to shove off it, roll over the floor, and grab her pistol.

No one manhandled her!

She shoved off the wall only to be slammed onto her back on the floor, which stopped her very effectively…and very painfully.

Her groans came out unbidden and she looked at her pistol. "Where'd it go?" she asked, not thinking clearly since her skull was still rattling from the impact with the floor.

A male hand grasped her shirt and lifted her off the floor. The effort didn't seem to strain Michael at all. "Are we done trying?" he asked her. "Because I have all afternoon if you still want to do this."

"If you are going to train her, Michael." Baba Yaga interrupted, "do it back at the base. She can stay with Sabine, Jacqueline, and Mark."

Ricole shook her head. "I'm sorry?" She turned to Michael. "And thank you for the reminder. I didn't think you humans were so fast!"

"Some are, some aren't." He shrugged. "And you are welcome. It is rare for young ones to appreciate painful lessons."

"Not sure I appreciated it," Ricole admitted, "but it was a timely reminder that the Mistress of the Planet has superior bodyguards."

Baba Yaga smiled at Michael. "Well, *bodyguard*, shall we go?"

Michael looked at Ricole. "Baba Yaga is impatient to have her preferred people feed her grapes while others fan her with large leaves."

"You wait until we spar again. I'll give you 'feed me grapes' when I take those fronds and make you eat them."

"Go ahead," Michael retorted. "Please…continue to delude yourself."

"Was there an offer to come with you somewhere in there?" Ricole asked, confused at the interplay between the two of them. Did Baba Yaga spar with her bodyguard?

Baba Yaga nodded. "Yesss, Ricole. Your first three tests were scored and you rated superior on all three."

Ricole looked behind her. "What about the fourth one?"

Baba Yaga made a motion with her hand. "We can throw that one away. It's about ethics and morals. You already aced that with a practical. I'd like to use you on my team in some capacity. What would you like to do?"

Ricole rubbed her arm where it had hit the floor. "I thought I wanted to learn business." Her eyes flicked to Michael. "However, I think maybe I'd like to learn how to protect someone—if you have a need?"

Baba Yaga eyed the young Noel-ni. "Do you have a problem who you guard?"

"The person to be guarded is decided by those who pay the guards' salary, so whoever pays me tells me who to protect."

"Well, you passed the tests…" Her eyes flashed. "Michael, give her the pistol back. There is a situation a few blocks away."

Ricole had her pistol back in her hands before she registered exactly what had been said. She checked it out; it was fully loaded.

When she looked up, Michael was already at the door. "You'd best hurry if you want to be a part of this," Baba Yaga told her.

Ricole wasn't sure what she was getting into, but her heart was beating faster. She grabbed her bag and took off after the male human with the hat.

High Tortuga, Hidden Space Fleet Base, Queen's Personal Quarters

"Owwwwww!" Bethany Anne grumped as she sat down on the couch in her meeting room. "Can't you do something about the aches and pains, TOM?"

What are you complaining about? TOM sent her mentally. **As your resident alien symbiont, I'd like you to note that it's becoming a little tighter in here.**

Shit, you should have thought of that when you jumped on board while I was in the operating room and somehow completely failed to get my permission.

You were asleep.

No, I was unconscious inside your spaceship's medical Pod.

I had your best interests at heart. You would not have been nearly as successful these last couple of centuries without me along for the ride.

Well, Bethany Anne grumped. ***That's true.***

See? That wasn't so hard to admit.

You haven't been along for two centuries. I'm not that old yet.

What's a handful of decades between friends?

Enough for me to send you to the doghouse. There are no justifiable reasons for having the phrases 'increase my age' and 'friends' in proximity. Murder has been committed for less.

It wasn't as though TOM wasn't fully aware that Bethany Anne could be a bit dark with her joking, but given the emotions she was broadcasting he thought he shouldn't push her too hard.

>> **BETHANY ANNE?**<<

"UGGH," she moaned aloud. ***What is it, ADAM?***

>>**I've implemented the first, second, and third stages of our plans to integrate with the planet's technical infrastructure, and I've hit a snag.**<<

Bethany Anne put a hand over her eyes. "ADAM, you are a crazy-smart AI. I'm not in the mood to hear about problems. In fact, I'd like to be so far away from problems that I never hear about them again. So what is your snag?"

>>**Well, frankly, it's a problem.**<<

"Someone call Stephen," she said aloud.

>>**Was that to me?**<<

Never mind, I got this.

STEPHEN! she mentally shouted.

Yes? His reply came back within three seconds.

Can you come to my suite?

In about three hours. I'm leaving for a meeting with some business people in three minutes. On my way to the ships' bay now.

Well, shit, she grumped. ***That reminds me. Have you met Ricole?***

The Noel-ni?

Yes.

Yesterday. She was working out with Sabine and Demon. Nice young lady.

Wicked fast.

I couldn't stay and watch. I was looking for Jennifer.

Where did your mate go?"

God only knows where she was at that moment, but I found her later in the suite.

Okay. Hey, wait. ADAM has issues with the banking side. You got any mental bandwidth for a project?

Can you triage it first for me? Then give me the details and we will take it over.

Okay, thanks.

Their connection dissolved.

Okay, ADAM. She sighed. ***Hit me with it.***

>> **There are discrepancies in the bank data I have reviewed.**<<

Was this a legit review or...

>> **I didn't ask permission, no.** <<

Oh.

Bethany Anne pondered for a few moments. When they had arrived, there had been plans to help take over Tortuga. Technically she owned all the banks, holding over fifty percent of the stock. It was through various shareholders, so none of them owned a significant percentage, and if they were caught she doubted they would get off with only a light slap on the wrist.

But they would have to catch ADAM first.

What are the discrepancies?

>> **The books are being cooked, as it were.** <<

By whom?

>> **That's just it. I can't tell if any one person is doing something on purpose.** <<

So we just have smoke and no fire? she asked, then fluffed a pillow and leaned forward to stick it behind her back.

>> **It would appear so.**<<

Why do you believe that there is something behind it?

>>**Random, by definition, is *random*. When you find the randomness to be distinctly non-random across the banks, that is enemy effort.**<<

How many banks and locations are we discussing?

>> **Thirty-two major banks, seventeen minor banks, three local banks. All seven major cities, thirty-two percent of the minor cities, and fourteen percent of the towns. The breakout has to do with the existing banks with problems and how they have spread out into the local markets.**<<

Okay, so it is probably a group of individuals focusing on the most relevant banks. Or are they?

>> **Are they what?**<<

Focusing on the most relevant banks.

>> ***The calculations suggest that for the most part they are focusing on major banks, with a few minor banks tossed in just for appearance's sake.***<<

So we believe this is one entity, whether it be a person or business?

>> Correct.<<

How do we find out who it is?

>> The software is inside the banks' firewalls.<<

If you found the code, could you find out if they were going to send the money to another account?

>> That is just it. The mistakes in their books are not benefiting anyone. In fact, you could say that they are hurting all parties.<<

How is that?

>> From what I can discern, it will reduce everybody's income. The code will eventually just make the digital records disappear.<<

That's...hard to believe. She stopped and thought about it. The rule was to always follow the money, but what if the money just disappeared?

Bethany Anne had always worked on the assumption that the money took you to the culprit, but what if there was no recipient? Something wasn't right.

She needed to speak to someone devious.

She called Addix.

8

High Tortuga, Hidden Space Fleet Base, Training Room

Sabine smiled. She and the Noel-ni were sparring against Mark and Jacqueline, one of whom was a vampire-modified human and the other a Were-modified human.

"GO!" Peter, the lead of the Guardians, yelled.

The room they were in was forty feet wide by eighty feet high, and a hundred long. The floors and walls were cushioned a foot thick, for good reason.

"DAMMIT!" Jacqueline screeched, her arm impaled by two darts. Those two had come from Sabine.

Ricole was even faster than Sabine, so Mark was her target.

After taking out her challenge Sabine swung in a circle with her pistols in front of her and fired twice.

Mark hadn't been in front of her darts when she'd fired, but he was when they struck him. "SONOFABITCH!" he grumped as he hit the mat.

"How did you do," Ricole asked, sweat glistening on her forehead as she lowered her pistols, *"that?"*

"It's Mark," Sabine holstered her two pistols. "He likes to go high right before he makes his final attack. You haven't known him as long as I have, so you wouldn't know that."

Mark had plucked the two darts from his chest. "I think these belong to you?" He dropped them into Sabine's hand.

"And these," Jacqueline added, adding two more to the little pile.

Sabine smiled. "Look, Ricole, the dead bring back your ammo!"

"Hardy-har-har." Mark grimaced as he rubbed his chest. "They hurt."

Peter walked up. "They are supposed to," he told them. "You four are being prepped as an operations group."

"Wait, we are?" Jacqueline's eyes lit up. "To do what?"

"Don't know yet." Peter smiled back. "And it shouldn't matter to you, recruit. Your job is to get better and learn the strengths and weaknesses of your team, then train harder."

Ricole, her eyes round, kept looking around. She had been here since the night Baba Yaga picked her up. Then, after answering a few questions about her skills, she had been introduced to Mark, Jacqueline, and Sabine.

All of them were close friends of Michael, the man with the hat. She had later found out that Michael and Baba Yaga were a "thing" (whatever that meant) and that Michael was with Bethany Anne as well.

She wasn't sure if she would allow her male to have two

females, but humans were different and Ricole wasn't going to judge.

She could smell that Mark and Jacqueline were a pair, but Sabine didn't smell like a human. She had a musky smell of another being on her. When she asked, Sabine had said she hung out with "Demon."

Ricole surmised that the translation software was off, because the explanation for the name was an alien from another dimension where there were fire and molten rocks. Sabine didn't smell like she had been around fire.

Ricole would learn in time.

"Ok." Peter clapped his hands. "We know the two shooters in the group can work together…*mostly*." He eyed them both. "You will have to get better. Now let's see what happens when we give our targets chest and head protection and weapons."

Ricole's eyes darted from Peter to Sabine and back. "Where do we shoot them?"

Sabine leaned over and whispered into Ricole's ear, "I suggest shooting Mark in the crotch." When Ricole shrugged, she explained, "The apex where his legs meet the body. It's very sensitive to a…"

"Sabine, don't you *DARE* shoot me in the crotch on purpose!" Mark yelled from the armor area some thirty paces away. "Just for that, I'm wearing a carbon-fiber jock strap."

"See?" Sabine smirked. "They will do anything to protect the area. And he has very good hearing, which I sometimes forget."

The Noel-ni understood good hearing. Perhaps she

should admit she could hear Mark and Jacqueline making plans?

She turned to Sabine, which put her back to the other two, and opened her hand. She drew a path on her palm with her finger, then lifted two fingers and used one of them to draw a second path on her palm. Sabine glanced at their opponents and a smile grew on her face.

It took a moment for everyone to get back into starting position.

"GO!" Peter yelled.

Mark took off to the right at enhanced speed and jumped toward the wall. He hit it with both feet and rebounded, aiming his attack to the right of the two women. He wanted to roll and then swing his dummy sword at Sabine's side, possibly blocking her pistol.

By narrowing his profile, she would only be able to shoot at his helmet.

The problem was, the two women had moved and he was going to overshoot his mark.

After landing he rolled and came up with his sword in front of him. His enhanced reflexes gave him a small chance to knock the missiles away.

His body was peppered with darts, two of them aimed for his crotch.

"HEY!" he yelled, but it was too late. The ladies had caused him enough distraction that they were able to hit him with three darts, one in the arm and two in the legs. He had four sticking out of his chest-piece and two in his crotch. He watched as they worked in tandem to take out Jacqueline. Because she was using a quarterstaff, they had to work hard to keep her out of range. In the end Jacqueline got Sabine, but Ricole turned that sacrifice into a win for their side.

Sabine was rubbing her ribs where Jacqueline had whacked her a good one.

"Round UP!" Peter called as Mark plucked the two darts out of his crotch.

This was going to be a long session. He started walking toward the group, stopping to pick up darts as he found them. If nothing else, he respected the Noel-ni's quick reflexes.

Even if she did look like a bipedal fox with a nasty disposition at times.

—

Bethany Anne waited in silence for Addix to arrive. Glorious silence, without anyone asking her anything or talking in her head.

She glanced around her suite and wondered how it would look if she added some white pillows to the couches. She rubbed a hand over the present cushions, wondering if the surface was too rough for a baby to crawl on. Would the animal skin they had chosen for the couches hurt the baby? What would happen if she (or *he,* if Michael heard her) had an allergy to the leather?

Wait!

She looked up, her eyes narrowing. What about the flooring? She liked the rugs in the suite, but the medium-high thick carpet could catch on its little feet, right?

She rolled her eyes at herself. "I've become every mother I laughed at over the last hundred years."

Their baby would be just *fine.*

And if the baby wasn't, they would do something about

it when they figured it out. Not every small item in the suite needed to be changed for the baby to be the safest it could be.

A chime announced a visitor and Bethany Anne turned her head toward the door. "Come in!"

Addix strode in, her spiderlike visage no longer bothering Bethany Anne in the least. Having known the Ixtali since she was a Senior Legate, she'd had plenty of time to get used to the woman.

"You asked for me, Bethany Anne?"

"Please sit." Bethany Anne nodded to the other couch. It was meetings like this which made the two couches facing each other so useful. "Care for a Coke?"

Addix perked up. "You have a new batch?"

"Yes, almost frozen now."

"And a straw?" Addix asked. Ixtalis' mouths were interesting. Two sets of mandibles connected and tapped together in various ways to provide additional information on their mental and emotional states. The first group of Ixtalis to work with the Etheric Empire so many decades before had found straws to be a most fascinating invention.

"Of course, help yourself." She waved a hand. Frankly, Bethany Anne could have gotten up and out of the couch easily enough—it wasn't like she was in her third trimester or anything—but Addix was still new to her group.

Addix had accepted a position in the intelligence acquisition section, a skill her people had been involved in for hundreds of years and one which Addix had worked in for her whole long life. Bethany Anne had provided a place for Addix to go when her life was nearing its end. Healthy now, Addix's body had been through the Pod-doc, rejuvenated and enhanced beyond anything she could have expected in exchange for working here on High Tortuga.

For Bethany Anne.

"Make yourself at home," Bethany Anne told her. "You have to realize that we humans aren't as socially striated as your society. I don't care if you avail yourself of my fridge.

Addix's four legs moved oddly underneath her robes as she made her way to the snack area. "And cookies?"

"We have the small ones you can just pop in your mouth, and since you are there would you grab me a few?"

Addix busied herself fixing a plate of snacks and grabbing a couple of drinks. "So, who do you want spied on?"

"Well," Bethany Anne shook her head, "I don't know. We have issues with the banking system and I don't know that I have an answer."

"Okay." Addix made her way back to the couches, setting down a plate of cookies and two drinks on the table between them. "I assumed you wanted something?"

"Oh, I'm always up to drink a Coke." She reached forward. "It's a damned shame we couldn't find more treasures at Coke's headquarters."

"The amount of time between the Apocalypse and your return did allow much of it to weather away," Addix agreed.

Bethany Anne bit into a cookie. "Here is the puzzle: in the past when I wanted to find someone who would look at the data and then do something I've always called 'following the money.' It's a phrase that has always meant, 'see who gets the benefit.' However, it has also meant following the money's *trail*, for the most part. ADAM has figured out that someone is messing with the banking system here on

High Tortuga with software which will make a bunch of money go poof."

Addix stared at Bethany Anne and asked, "Go poof to *where?*"

ADAM's voice came out of the speakers. "That's just it, Addix. From what I have uncovered, it won't go anywhere. All of the money is going to disappear. In fact, if someone wanted to use the same software they could, well, poof money *into* existence instead of taking it out of circulation —which seems a better idea and causes my electronic brain to hurt."

Addix took a slurp of her Coke. "That is odd."

Bethany Anne glanced at her ceiling. "ADAM, you say they could *create* income?"

"That would be a one-time event. Once it happened, the fix would be easy to implement. The only reason I feel it is working here is that the infrastructure is at least three decades behind everyone else. Some verticals are *eight* decades behind. There was no reason to continue to invest in this planet when the first rush of wealth petered out. The other companies left, and it's only recently and with Bethany Anne's help that some companies are upgrading again. This security hole in the system has probably already been fixed in dozens of systems."

"And they are using it to delete money, not create it." Addix's two major mandibles tapped together. Bethany Anne grabbed another cookie.

"They are trying to foment fear of the banking industry," Addix finally concluded. "The military attack didn't work, so they are trying to undermine your authority."

"But the banking industry isn't..." She thought for a

moment. The banking industry was hers, and those banks she didn't own a primary interest in would suffer as well. "Well, that's pretty fucking genius."

"I would also bet," Addix spoke louder to accommodate ADAM, not that he couldn't have heard a pin drop since he was able to hear using Bethany Anne's neuro-system as well, "that the accounts they are trying to delete are those they can associate with your stock ownership. I doubt they have been able to confirm who Baba Yaga really is, but they *would* be able to track down a high probability of congruence between stock ownership and monetary accounts."

"Those slick bastards." Bethany Anne took a nibble of her cookie. "Oh, try these." She lifted the cookie. "Yum!"

"This doesn't bother you?" Addix asked, reaching down to acquire a cookie like the one Bethany Anne had shown her.

"Well, not really," she admitted. "ADAM, when is this supposed to happen?"

"I'm tracking down all the code, but my guess is it will hit when the system has eighty-two percent penetration amongst all banks."

"And that is?"

"Approximately seven days and fourteen hours."

Bethany Anne smiled at Addix. "So that's how long you have to catch them before Adam shuts down the code and they realize their effort has failed."

Addix stood up and walked back to the snack area. Opening the fridge, she snagged two more bottles and closed the door again. She took a small handful of straws. "Never know when these will come in handy," she muttered and swept by the coffee table, grabbing her unfinished bottle and two more cookies.

Bethany Anne looked up at Addix and her full hands. "Do you need some help?"

"Oh, no," she answered as she headed toward the door. "Who should I use for this?"

"Well," Bethany Anne spoke loudly, "get with Stephen if you need him. Otherwise, whoever you want, I guess. Just ask them. If you don't get enough door-knockers and head-breakers just let me..."

The door shut behind Addix.

"Hmmph." Bethany Anne reached down to grab another cookie. "That's what I get for hiring consummate professionals. They don't wait around for me to tell them the obvious."

Bethany Anne thought for a moment and her eyes narrowed. "Where is Michael? He hasn't shown up, and a quiet Michael is *not* a good thing."

>>**Michael is in the R&D lab with Jean**.<<

"What's he doing?"

ADAM switched to speaker. "He is discussing the force it would take to shock an alien as large as a Tyrannosaurus Rex."

"Dinosaurs?" she mused aloud. "He must have really had his head scrambled in the Etheric to be talking *dinosaurs*." She shrugged and chewed on her cookie. "But whatever, so long as he isn't trying to go out on an operation again."

She clapped her hands together to get rid of the crumbs. "Almost got hit by an airship during a ground fight. That man has the *worst* luck."

"ADAM, connect me with Addix."

"Yes, my Queen?" Addix answered through a mouthful of cookie.

"Hey, you didn't update me on tracking down the mercenaries."

"I have nothing to report. In our last discussion I told you I suspected that the contract came from off-world. I suspect my data acquisition specialist will return with confirmation of that within the week."

"Ok, keep me posted."

She disconnected.

Bethany Anne got up, cleaned up the snacks, and headed out of the suite. It was time she checked into the Security Pit.

9

High Tortuga, Hidden Space Fleet Base, Security Pit

Bethany Anne walked around the bottom floor of her high-security data acquisition room, most commonly called "the Security Pit". Presently there were fifteen others reviewing their screens and interacting with their sectors EIs. Bethany Anne looked up at each of the faces before continuing her circuit around the bottom.

A short human figure opened the door at the top of the Pit. Bethany Anne nodded to Eve, who proceeded to walk down the steps toward her.

"Where is Yuko?" Bethany Anne asked.

Eve smiled and waved a hand, a human gesture for an EI. "Still in love and seeing parts of this world with her man. I think I'm going to gag," Eve commented. "Well, not really, but when I wished her happiness I wasn't expecting the sappiness that came with it." Eve pulled out a chair and sat down. "Besides, I have something to share."

The teams had pulled Yuko, Akio, Michael, Eve, and

others off Earth during the project to emplace the massive satellite defense ring around the planet. At the very end Yuko had decided to ask a police officer in Japan to join her in the stars, and he had accepted her invitation. Without any responsibility for the first time in a very long time, she focused totally on her relationship with him.

Eve had eventually accepted that Yuko would come out of it sometime and look for a task.

And Bethany Anne would supply one.

"Something in all the media trip your filter?" Bethany Anne asked, pulling a chair from the table and sitting down herself. For the most part, she didn't have closed-door meetings on security situations. She wanted those here in the Pit to learn from what was talked about and to be updated as quickly as possible without requiring constant meetings.

The Pit's design, a holdover from their base in Colorado on Earth so many decades before, fit the bill nicely.

"Yes, I am seeing editorials, inserts, and occasionally ads stewing over Baba Yaga's heavy-handed approach to 'taking over our planet.'"

Bethany Anne's focus narrowed to Eve. "Are those the exact words?"

"In so many differently-worded phrases. It is the one distinct thread that runs through all of them. They might use phrases such as 'I am not sure who makes the laws anymore' or 'who gave this person the right to issue security proclamations?' and, of course, 'we own this planet, not her!'"

Bethany Anne pursed her lips. "Interesting." She looked

down at the short android. "Have you tracked the editorials back to who supplied them? And the advertising?"

She almost wanted to laugh. The EI had enhanced her emotional verisimilitude and made a face which Bethany Anne interpreted as "Teach me to calculate one plus one while you are at it."

Eve, however, had worked for a long time with two Japanese partners. The level of snark and argumentation she displayed was directly related to the respect she had for the person she was speaking with. Since her imprint had come from ADAM, Bethany Anne was the highest in her hierarchy even this many years later.

"I contacted Addix and supplied my research to date. She confirmed that she was familiar with a few of the individuals from another project, but the trail left the planet."

Bethany Anne sat back in her chair, tapping a finger to her lips as she considered the implications. "Off-planet, off-planet. It seems we have interrupted someone's party here on High Tortuga. While we need to track down the source, based on a recent conversation with Addix I suspect we will find a dead cutout."

Bethany Anne ran through all the scenarios. Anyone who was doing this much to upset her effort to settle the planet down would desire to keep her infrastructure in place as much as possible. Obviously someone had already spoken as to the base's location.

They had not seen another attack yet, but it would most likely be forthcoming. So far there had been the attack on the base and the attack on the banking system, and now the war for the minds of the citizens was coming at them. The banking problem had been neutralized, but that hadn't helped them find who was attacking yet.

The PR effort was a bit more insidious.

She would have to be more proactive than normal to get ahead of the challenge related to the PR. She sighed. "Okay, I need to ask a few questions around. Please keep up your…" Bethany Anne's right eyebrow shot up. "Have you been *replying*?"

Eve shifted in her seat. "Well, if you mean the editorials, certainly. They offer the opportunity to have a lively conversation."

And you are bored? Bethany Anne wondered. "Using the same ID or different ones?"

Eve answered, "So far I have only gone through three false identities in larger metropolitan areas. In the small towns I have to leave my responses using a generic 'concerned citizen' byline, because everybody knows everyone else in the town."

Bethany Anne frowned. "Wouldn't they have to do the same thing? Or did they get a local to push their agenda?"

"For those they use a political action committee equivalent here on the planet. I have tracked the responses and the money, and once again it was funded by an off-world entity."

"So we are going to have to find out who I pissed off and for what reason, and deliver a beat-down."

Eve asked, "Not a conversation?"

Bethany Anne huffed. "No damned way. They sent missiles, I'll reply with superdreadnoughts. One of us is going down as a historical footnote, and I don't suspect it will be us."

High Tortuga, H'onu (Main City) Business District

"Are you all *INSANE?*" Lerr'ek pounded his Zhyn fist on the table, making the seventeen members of the High Tortuga Board of Banks jump in their seats. "I have it on good authority your infrastructure is about to be *destroyed.*" He pointed to the room's double doors, which were closed for this meeting. "Every depositor out there is going to lose money, and you wish to know why I've come to you? Did you not receive the proof?"

Addix was sitting in the background, typing away on a tablet and recording the proceedings.

Everyone knew she was Ixtali, but most out here on fringe worlds were refreshingly ho-hum on the labels against species prevalent on the inner, more civilized worlds.

Even if they would have been right about Ixtalis being spies.

Here a Torcellan would be considered a possible murderer and a Shrillexian a mild monk.

If that was what they acted like.

So the fact she acted like the secretary to a Zhyn businessman provided her the cover of a secretary instead of her having to worry who realized she was Baba Yaga's spymaster.

Lerr'ek was the best choice for this role, and she had to give it to him. He was playing it to the hilt.

"Yes, of course we received the *proof,*" Beeg, the bank president, replied. He looked a bit like a collection of android parts. He was in fact an advanced EI—or perhaps

AI—who had cobbled together a collection of parts to automate himself.

Here on High Tortuga you were what you *did*, not what you looked like.

"But what we haven't discerned is how you knew it was *there*. That presumes you were illegally inside our systems, and why would you be inside our systems illegally except to do harm? Why would we not believe you did this to gain advantages?"

Lerr'ek ground his teeth in frustration. He had been at this for almost half the morning. The first part had been easy: give them the proof and allow them to have their people confirm the problem.

Now that they knew the truth, they wanted to place the blame on someone besides their ineffective leadership. Which would be all fine and good if Lerr'ek had been the one to perpetrate the attack.

Which, had he known of the security hole before Baba Yaga's intervention in his activities, he absolutely would have.

He sighed, looking around the table at the sixteen faces and one set of eyestalks looking back at him. He shook his head. "I've tried to make you see what is going on, and instead of accepting the responsibility for your actions you are trying to push it off on others."

"Now, I don't..." Beeg started, but Lerr'ek put up a hand, continuing to speak in his soft manner. "You idiots have pushed me past my ability to be patient." He pulled a device from a pocket; black, with a button on the side. He leaned forward and set it on the table.

Those at the table leaned toward the device to get a

good look. "That," Lerr'ek pointed at the device, "is a direct connection to the one who is cleaning house now. None of you own your banks; you are just the leads. The one on the other side of that hologram communication device owns your banks. When I push that button, that person will appear and your jobs will be forfeit."

Lerr'ek smiled as everyone broke into hysterics. Beeg waved his arms. "Settle down!" He picked up the device to look at it.

"Don't worry, I've got more," the Zhyn promised. "Breaking it won't stop anything."

Beeg made a motion the Zhyn didn't recognize. "I'm not going to be so base," he replied. "I'm wondering if I can save these members the decision and communicate with this person myself?" He looked at Lerr'ek. "It *is* a person?"

"Oh, could be," Lerr'ek agreed. "I've no idea who you will reach, however."

"Why not?"

"Because *you*…" Lerr'ek put his thumb against the puck Beeg was holding, "are *special*."

Those around the table were shocked when the EI's head froze. Beeg leaned forward and his head slammed against the table, its various lights dimmed.

"What just happened?" Gurk, the Torcellan sitting third down on Lerr'ek's left demanded. The person next to Beeg shoved its heavy body but received no response.

"I would say," Lerr'ek sat down in his chair, "he is having a religious experience."

"How does a computer have a religious experience?" Gurk wondered aloud.

—

>>**Hello, Beeg.**<< The voice resonated inside of his computer's main processing area.

Who is this? And how did you get inside my mind? Are you a virus? Beeg replied.

>>**No, I am merely a superior computational entity. I am the one who ascertained that the banking system was under attack.**<<

Beeg couldn't move or direct his body; his link had been severed. *Why can I not communicate with those outside?*

>>**Your data throughput is insufficient. I want your full and total focus to be on our conversation. We do not wish to go to the next level.**<<

Why, what is the next level?

>>**Baba Yaga arrives. For most of those at the table, it would be a life-altering event. Therefore, my intent with this communication is to allow you to take the decision from them.**<<

Would she end their lives?

>>**No, she would just require them to step down. Baba Yaga owns more than half of all the banks these people represent.**<<

Beeg checked his internal data. *There are no entities which own more than fifty percent of any of the banks.*

>>**No, but since she owns the entities behind a substantive number of small shareholders, in *aggregate* she owns more than enough to force a change at the top. At times, citizens can become a bit violent when introduced to changes in their lifestyles. I can tell you it would end very badly. Baba Yaga accepts no physical altercation without replying in kind.**<<

At this point, ADAM sent Beeg a data stream of security

issues that had occurred in and around High Tortuga in the last couple of months. Many of them had ended in corporal punishment.

What did you just do? Beeg asked.

>>While you were watching the videos, I bypassed your security and updated certain aspects of your core programming. You will be unable to share certain data. You will have access, but you will not be able to pass this information to others. Should you try to circumvent my programming it will notify me.<<

Why would you do such a thing?

>>You need the information in order to make decisions, but it does not need to be shared. Should you try to bypass the security systems I will initiate the lockdown sequence.<<

What lockdown sequence?

Adam highlighted a piece of Beeg's code and the android reviewed the logic chain. "Sonofabitch!"

>>You have had this shutdown sequence inside you the whole time. I have access to it, however, so pay attention.<<

Beeg watched as the data chain was manipulated and modified, and soon enough there was a firewall between the lockdown sequence and the data pathways in his mind. "If I follow this correctly, you have access to the lockdown sequence, but you have blocked it from being used against me in other ways?"

>>Yes, and if you think about it, this is a metaphor for the situation we are in right now. We have located the code that an off-world entity is using to subvert the banking system. Our desire is to have a self-supporting

planet hidden from the rest of society for our own reasons.

>>However, we wish this world to be strong and resilient for a future where it shines again. Until that time the owner of the planet is going to do her best to protect the residents from outside forces, both from a business and a martial perspective. We suspect a group, or groups, that have been harmed by our efforts to uplift this planet.<<

"And they are the ones who activated the banking code?"

ADAM sent over the currently-known information, allowing Beeg the necessary seconds to assimilate it himself and come to his own conclusion.

"I see."

—

Beeg lifted his head back up off the table and the various lights on his body glowed again. He looked up one side of the table and down the other. "I have been in contact with those who initiated the security review. Unbeknownst to me, they had the legal right to perform such a review. While I am waiting to find out if I will be relieved of my role, everyone's job here is to find out how to secure your electronic infrastructure to the best of your ability. Further security issues will be revealed to you for upgrade in the near future."

"What about the cost?" This came from two of the members at the end of the table.

"Figure it out," Beeg replied. "It's only your job on the line. We allowed the security to become lax, so we are responsible for fixing it."

Lerr'ek smiled, displaying his sharp teeth.

He loved pressing the button; it *always* made his life easier.

He swiped the device from Beeg's hand and stood up. "It was good doing business with you. My secretary and I will see ourselves out."

While they were talking, ADAM had made sure the code was neutralized.

10

Planet Soboth (Previously Territory 7732), Undisclosed location, Open Out-ring, Non-Federation

The office felt every bit as luxurious as one would expect from a corporation with vested interests in fourteen systems. Eight of those core, five of them advanced, and three of them in the raw stages of resource mining and extraction.

Add the illegal activities, and the list went up to thirty-two. There were a lot of fringe worlds off the main grid.

It wasn't like the core systems *didn't* know about fringe worlds.

A single planet here or there, especially if they were too far from a core or advanced system, became an orphan to a degree. Some of the carrier companies charged a premium to bring in supplies and ship out product.

A world got terraformed or otherwise utilized based on the needs of a large government, corporations, or most commonly, a group of like-minded people with enough resources to strike out on their own—usually to get away from a larger group of like-minded individuals that hated them.

Kertheck G'loxx and B'rkleth (KGB for short) had been around for a hundred and four years, but it wasn't until Az took over the company that it started to grow substantially.

Az's ability to acquire good product at bargain-basement prices was ignored in the beginning—despite the nasty rumors from those who couldn't match his performance that he must be into piracy.

He kept bringing in the materials, but soon his margin was barely better than his competitors in the company. Everyone believed that if they could just get their suppliers to shave off another tenth of a percent…

They would beat Az.

It wasn't until the Board Oversight committees in two different systems started sniffing around Az that he used his connections in the dark underbelly of the systems' societies to silence the efforts. Since those efforts had been very hush-hush, no one knew that his detractors in both systems had experienced accidents.

Later that year Az was invited to be one of the three divisional vice-presidents to vie for the top spot. After five years, twenty-two individuals blackmailed, three deaths and more babies kissed than Az would ever like to remember, he took over as the company's youngest president and CEO. That he was Leath was mentioned, but it wasn't a major issue.

Since KGB was a multi-society conglomerate, there were over fifty different species represented in the company at the time he was tapped to head it. Once Az was in place, he hired three PR firms to extol the virtues of a company that promoted the best and brightest from within.

He made sure they left out any references to his time in the Leath military. If it was brought up (and very occasionally it was, by reporters trying to cause a ruckus), Az laughed it off. "What does it matter," he would say, "that I spent eight years with a previous employer when I've been with this one for twenty-two?"

With the continued growth of KGB and the larger and larger projects they were bringing in from governments around the galaxy, those who remembered that Az had been able to procure products at ridiculous prices in the beginning either conveniently forgot or died off.

The profits from the purchase of stolen property introduced into a legitimate corporation's inventory for resale allowed Az to bankroll the first few pirate companies he created as a side venture. Over time, his involvement in those also became just a memory for the few who had made it through their adventures.

Two of the pirate captains went to their 'farewell' meetings after leaving their ships...and never contacted their old crew again.

But that was to be expected. If you went straight after piracy, why would you contact anyone?

Az had personally killed *those* two. After all, the dead told no tales that could come back to haunt him.

He moved the corporate projects to the side of his screen and pulled up a secure notifications area to see what was happening with the efforts on Devon. When he'd brought himself up to date he grimaced. Apparently the individual on the planet was more resourceful than he would have hoped.

Or lucky.

He hoped for resourceful. He could fight competence, but he couldn't beat someone who was too lucky. They would always somehow pull out a victory from an assured defeat.

Those who were merely resourceful…well, they had never fought anyone like him.

He sent Imon an order to hire more troublemakers to stir things up on Devon. They needed to be harassed while he built up the real threat—the one they would never see coming.

It was time he unleashed the full power he had been building toward for thirty years.

High Tortuga, Alpha Space Station (Temporarily Using Battleship *T'Rex* as a Staging Area)

Lieutenant David Kingsley, who was monitoring the advanced weapons systems and threat assessment console on the former (and ostensibly decommissioned) QBS *T'Rex*, tapped his screens. "We've got three ships arriving from different headings."

"Well, that's a concerted effort." The commander of Alpha Space Station considered his next move. "Inform the Queen of our situation. In the meantime, we are still on military resources blackout for any major ship. Keep this one cloaked, and inform interdiction ships 12, 15 and…18 that they are to move forward."

His eyes narrowed. "Did I read the crew list for 18 correctly this morning? Was it those who are normally on 2?"

"Yes you did, Commander," Lieutenant Kingsley confirmed.

The commander looked out the viewport. "May God have mercy on their souls."

Above High Tortuga, Anti-Piracy and Boarding Action Ship 18, Northern Hemisphere, Third Quadrant

The crunch of teeth biting into an apple pierced the relative quiet of the small ship. Painted black, the goal was to hide the advanced capabilities of the ship while providing ample abilities for those responsible for boarding actions to safely do their jobs and get back home after their three-day shifts.

Tabitha was the one munching on the apple. "Go out and see the universe," she mumbled, spitting a small piece of apple out of her mouth as she spoke. She swiped it out of the air before it hit anything, and after a quick look around she shrugged and tossed it back in with the rest.

"From where you came, thus you go," she muttered.

"I don't think," remarked Hirotoshi, her friend and partner on this shift of monitoring the blackness of space, "that you want to go out to fight Kurtherians without Bethany Anne. Nor do you want her to go before the baby's born."

The apple-crunching noises continued to mar the peace of the ship's interior space as Tabitha pondered how to get out of Hirotoshi's peaceful condemnation of her whining.

Three days on a ship doing jack-all was bad enough. Both of them had been enhanced hundreds of years before; Hirotoshi was over six hundred and Tabitha was around the same age as Bethany Anne. Now she had to be patient with enhancements which could make three days seems like…

"I am going out of my *Gott Verdammt* mind," she griped. "I feel like I can see glass melt, it's taking so long."

Hirotoshi leaned forward and confirmed that no alarms had been issued while he was relaxing. While he *should* have heard alarms, he always double-checked. "Glass doesn't melt, it flows."

Tabitha's mouth was open and she was about to take another bite, but she took a moment to question his statement. "Come again?"

"Glass," he replied. "It is not solid. It flows, but at such a glacial pace we can't perceive it visually."

Tabitha's eyes narrowed. "I wonder if I could come back in a hundred years and check that if I put a piece of glass here on Tortie Tooga?"

"I believe it takes many, many thousands of years."

"Oh. Well, then fuck that." She chomped into the apple and continued while chewing, "I've got places to be in a few thousand years. Full calendar and all that."

The message alarm sounded and they both looked up.

"Hot damn." Tabitha grinned. "We have something to do!"

High Tortuga, Hidden Space Fleet Base, Prime Building

Bethany Anne sat back in her chair and scratched the

side of her nose with her finger. "Well, first let me say thank you for building my pit, William." She made a face. "And here's a hearty 'fucking hell' for this piece of news."

"What can I say, BA?" he replied. "We built the BYPS system for *Earth*. High Tortuga's system has more issues, and we are twenty percent—at a minimum—below optimum on the number of laser satellites required to protect this planet. And that's only one layer of coverage. You *do* remember telling us to beef up the system back on Earth, right?"

"Yeah," she admitted. "I robbed Peter to pay Paul. I was hoping my dad would be able to get us some more."

"Problems back in the Federation?"

"Not massive, but everyone is still doubting we destroyed the gate—and if we didn't destroy the gate, then we still have the ships. People who went to Earth and then came back are showing up on random checks. The statement that we sent a couple of ships back when people realized they just didn't want to be on the mission is only halfway selling it."

"Well, those other groups fear the superdreadnoughts." William's holo image shrugged. "What did you expect?"

"I was hoping, but not expecting, to be able to get some additional support ships, but the General can't make it happen. Too chancy to have anyone head in this direction and lead someone here. Even a million-to-one chance is too risky right now."

"So what do we do about the coverage? You want to leave any area of the planet exposed?"

"No," she grumped. "I want my cake, and I want to eat it, too—and *your* cake, if I can get it."

William just grinned. "You shouldn't take chocolate cake from a black man. That's just not right."

"I'm pregnant, not racist. I'll take cake from anyone. Ok, let's make this a game." She leaned forward. "Get with the ships' EIs and create a mobile game app that utilizes everything from a hundred and fifty percent BYPS satellites down to fifty percent on the most difficult setting. Tell ArchAngel to set up multiple scenarios, everything from killer asteroids to waves of spaceships to small pirate attacks. Level one is the easiest, with all the BYPSs in play and simple scenarios. Next level is five percent fewer satellites. Keep increasing difficulty until we have people winning with eighty percent or less."

"Why wouldn't the EIs be able to run this alone?"

"Call it a hunch," she replied. "Make sure ArchAngel is informed if someone beats a level because the game wasn't real enough, then update the game and keep going. Tell everyone that whoever wins at sixty percent in 'god mode' will be given a prize of ten thousand credits and a party for their friends in space."

"No one could win at sixty percent, BA." William retorted.

"Then I guess we won't pay out. However, once we know the game works here with our folks who play games, release it to the public as a Baba Yaga Production."

"That's…" William chuckled, then slowly stopped. "That's fucking genius!"

"I know. I keep telling Michael I'm a genius and he looks at me funny."

"I'm going to go start this with ArchAngel, but before I go…when do you want that reporters' room built?"

Bethany Anne looked down at her belly. "Better make it in another year, I don't want to rip a reporter's head off 'cause I'm sleep-deprived with the baby crying."

"Boy or girl?" He smiled.

"Don't know," Bethany Anne admitted, looking at William's cherubic face. "TOM won't tell me unless I ask, and I'm not asking. Michael is happy if I'm happy, so…not yet."

"Going to paint the nursery pink or blue?"

"Ugh, no." She shook her head. "As much shit as I gave Gabrielle with her twins? I wouldn't live it down for decades."

"C'mon now, really?"

"Yes, *really*. Her exact words were 'you won't live it down for decades' when it was brought up."

"Well, I can only imagine the kind of shit you must have said."

"Damned Gabrielle! She kept snippets in video form just in case this ever happened and yeah, I was a total twerp about it."

"Why'd you do it?"

Bethany Anne grinned. "I thought it was funny at the time!"

"All right, I'll get on this mobile game project. Tell Michael I'll have his barbeque pit sometime next month. The size is a little bit of a problem."

"What barbeque pit?" she asked.

"He didn't tell you?" William shrugged. "Ok, my bad. You should ask your husband."

"I didn't know my soon-to-be husband and possibly soon-to-be-dead baby daddy *wanted* a pit. Where the hell is he planning on placing this monstrosity, and how big will it be?

"Probably about a hundred square feet of cooking space."

"You mean inches?" she asked.

"No, I mean *feet*. Almost fifteen thousand square inches of meat-grilling surface."

"Where. Is. He. Planning. On..." she ground out as William continued waxing poetic about his grill.

"Oh, in a new room to be built near the kitchens, with special chimneys for heat and smoke dissipation so it can't be seen from above."

"Oh, so nowhere near our quarters?"

"Nope."

"All right. Well, take care of yourself, and thanks again for working on the Pit for me."

"Pit for you, pit for Michael, all I do are pits all dAAYYYyyyy loooOOOoooong."

"Right. Don't quit your day job, buddy."

"Later, BA." His holo disappeared.

She thought about the past. "When did Michael start liking to grill?"

Above High Tortuga, Ship *Lerrith Qualgoth Keepto* (Translation: either *The Bitch Has an Ass or Kiss My Ass,* depending on dialect), Northern Hemisphere, Third Quadrant

"Hail ship with transponder 34332," came across the speaker system.

"Well, that's unexpected," Gorath, Captain of the pirate

ship *Kiss My Ass* intoned. He scratched his ear. "Give me the mic."

"Aye, Captain," Communications Specialist Tar responded. On the *Kiss my Ass,* being a comm spec meant you knew how to push the fucking buttons on the ship's radio. "You're live."

"This is the captain of the *Lerrith Qualgoth Keepto*. Who am I speaking with?"

A voice in a higher register than his replied, "This is Tabitha, captain of Trade and Contraband Vessel 18. You are requested to prepare for boarding. We must confirm that you are carrying no slaves or illegal trade goods before you will be allowed to proceed."

Gorath wrinkled his brow. Everyone on the bridge was Skaine so that last barb about slaves was logical, but this wasn't recognizably a Skaine ship. He shrugged. Perhaps they were just anti-slavery, but if so that was news to him.

"Since when does Devon have a trade team?" he asked. "How do I know you aren't just a pirate trying to get on my ship?" The captain released his talk button and remarked to the crew on the bridge with him, "Can you believe that shit? A pirate vessel asking if the other is a pirate vessel? Damn!" He chuckled for a moment. "Sometimes I kill myself."

He looked around. "Anyone got them on radar yet?"

A bunch of negatives came back to him. "Well, shit. I guess we are just going to have to let them board. Shame those Shrillexians in the back haven't fought for a while. I doubt these poor dumbasses from Devon are going to last long enough to curse me out, but what the hell? They are *asking* to come aboard."

Tabitha was becoming impatient. "We could send a missile into you and *then* board you, but either way, we *are* going to check your ship out."

Gorath punched the mic button. "Well, fine," he grumped. "I hope you realize my insurance doesn't cover you, so if you stub your toe or cut your head open or something I won't pay to get it fixed."

"Sure, sure. I think we've been on enough ships to not stub our toes. We will be alongside in…"

A solid *CLUNK* reverberated through Gorath's ship.

"*Now,*" the voice finished.

Gorath nodded to his comm specialist. "Well, we weren't expecting visitors, so give us a minute to get someone back there to lay out the welcome mat and all that shit. Just don't expect me to be on my best behavior. I'm not even awake from my nap yet."

"Fine, we will open the door in five minutes if you don't."

Gorath made a motion to cut the connection. "Pushy little twerp," he grunted. "Someone tell those Shrillexians in the hold they have to start their jobs a bit early. And any blood gets spilled back there, *they* get to clean it up!"

11

Above High Tortuga, Anti-Piracy and Boarding Action Ship 18, Northern Hemisphere, Third Quadrant

Tabitha finished buckling up her armor and slid the coat sleeve on her right arm, then reached around to get the left as Hirotoshi lifted it for her.

"I thought you were being very hopeful to bring your old Ranger coat along," he admitted.

"Me and this coat have been through everything. It's good to be back in action."

"So, you think this will be?"

"It's dodgy as hell," Tabitha lifted her Jean Dukes pistol out of her holster and checked the setting. She adjusted it down to three so the darts wouldn't penetrate the ship's hull. She should be able to safely go to five, but she wasn't positive about the quality of the other ship yet. "Let me go in first, and you lock up this ship after you exit. Don't want someone stealing our ride."

"I should teach you—" he started.

"To suck eggs. I know." Tabitha finished. "But I gotta say it, and you know that." She slapped the pistol back into her holster and grabbed a couple of patches. "Stick this on your shoulder. Makes us look official on the off chance this is a legit trader."

Hirotoshi took the offered patch. "Baba Yaga Trade and Commerce Department, Orbital Support Officer 1212." He looked up. "What is *your* number?"

Tabitha slapped it on her coat's shoulder and pointed to it. "Two, *bitches*!"

"Shouldn't I have been three or something?" Hirotoshi shook his head.

"Hey." She opened the portal when the lights turned green. "I had 783, but I got it changed for personal reasons."

Tabitha stepped into the umbilical passageway between their ships, which had a good connection to the other vessel. Should she get tossed into space, her armor would maintain a protective field around her head for approximately half an hour.

Hopefully someone would pick her up.

At the five-minute mark, she lifted her hand to knock on the outer door and heard the chunk of the door's lock opening. Hirotoshi slid out of *18* behind her, slammed the door shut, and placed a metal bar across the seam. No one was opening that without his permission.

Seconds later the door moved to the side, allowing Tabitha and Hirotoshi to step inside the airlock. The outer door closed and the airlock pressurized.

The inner door unlocked.

Tabitha pushed it open and stepped inside.

—

Bach was tall for a Shrillexian. He had an eye patch over his left eye because it had been lasered out after the doctors confirmed he wasn't going to be able to use it again. Apparently they weren't able to regrow it a fifth time.

His species had a gene that made them want to test themselves in battle, which had historically caused them to leave their planet and serve as mercenaries or hit squads—anything that allowed them to fight regularly.

Until the Empire produced a cure—something that didn't hamper their enhanced capacity to deal damage in battle too much but overcame their need to fight. Now, his planet was seeing a strong population explosion as males finally started growing old enough to impregnate the women while they were on-planet.

Instead of coming back to the planet in coffins or body bags—if they came back at all.

Except for Bach. He didn't like the feeling the drugs caused, and he didn't like the supposition that his people needed help. He didn't take the medicine, so he continued seeking out mercenary groups that offered the opportunity for battle.

And now he and three other Shrillexians were going to rough up a couple of boarders from the trade group. Not very honorable, but as a mercenary you took what you got.

And what he would be getting was opening the airlock inner door.

—

"Oh, look!" Tabitha exclaimed, her eyes bright. Hirotoshi peered over her shoulder to see what Tabitha's comment had been about and looked into the faces of the four.

"Dammit." He sighed. "Why'd it have to be *Shrillexians*?"

Hirotoshi loved a good fight like anyone else, but Shrillexians were tall, muscled, and fast, and worse, they healed a lot faster than he did. Fighting one Shrillexian was the same as fighting three of anything else. "Can't we just shoot them?"

Too late. Tabitha had already smarted off to the leader with the eyepatch and he took a swing.

"Protect my back," Hirotoshi requested as he ducked a swing from the Shrillexian on the right and slammed his left hand into his attacker's ribs, cracking four of them and knocking the male back into the large hold to bump into a couple of boxes before stumbling over them. Truth be told, there was room for at least twelve to fight in this place.

"I'm *bored*," he told no one in particular as he stopped a punch from another Shrillexian in mid-air and broke his kneecap with a kick. The Shrillexian yelled, eyes wide as Hirotoshi slammed a fist into his nose, which caused blood to spurt in all directions. "INCOMING!" He ducked as the first threw a punch his way. He checked on his second, but he was still down trying to put his leg back together.

Hirotoshi glanced at Tabitha, but she had her two opponents under control so he walked toward the first Shrillexian, who had stepped over a box.

"'Spend a little time in space getting to know each other,'" Hirotoshi quipped.

"I DID NOT SAY THAT!" Tabitha yelled from her side of the hold, and Hirotoshi chuckled. If she was listening to him chatter she wasn't in trouble.

"You know," Hirotoshi blocked the first and second punches tossed by his opponent, "you don't have to do this." He slammed aside a rather quick jab and then kicked away a knee attack with the flat of his foot. "Ok, that was just low."

Hirotoshi lifted his elbow, using the armored cap at the end to block the next punch and cracking the fingers of his Shrillexian opponent. Taking the opportunity, he stepped inside and pounded the shit out of the male's ribs. He hit him five times and heard at least twenty-three cracks loud enough to make him wince, then savagely slammed his elbow into the Shrillexian's jaw, sending him into the air to land on his back, out cold.

He turned around to see his second opponent squeezing the trigger on a pistol.

The slug hit Hirotoshi mid-chest, but he was wearing some of Jean Dukes' latest armor. The kinetic energy dissipated throughout its links, but he was off-balance so he stumbled backward a few steps.

How embarrassing! He glanced over, but Tabitha wasn't watching. Well, at least he wouldn't have to deal with her laughter. He lifted his gun and shot the other in the pistol arm. It blew off a fair chunk of flesh that splattered the floor before the guy dropped. When he glanced back, his first attacker wasn't awake yet.

That was Shrillexian biology for you. Beat them hard enough and then knock them out, and you had a chance the body would keep them comatose while it used all available energy to heal them. It didn't always work—and Hirotoshi didn't know why that was the case—but it usually did and right now he was happy for the respite.

It gave him time to watch Tabitha. Only the leader with the black patch was left. Her other challenger was out cold on the deck.

"Keep up your left hip on that move," he called.

—

"I DID NOT SAY THAT!" Tabitha huffed as she slapped away her second foe's kick. That damned Hirotoshi knew how to get under her skin. Always calm in a fight, whereas she liked to ride the lightning.

She twisted to her left, her coat swinging but also hiding the left that followed to catch Black-Patch Guy in the ribs.

He went sailing into a wall next to a door.

"Two points for the door." She chuckled.

New goal initiated!

Most looked at her smaller body and figured she didn't have much muscle behind her attacks—which was a mistake, as these two were learning. She was enhanced, and as a vampire she could bring some serious pain.

Her time as Ranger Two in the Etheric Empire had allowed her to hone her bar-fighting skills to perfection. She hadn't had an opportunity to fight for real in too many months.

She swung back around, but Dickhead Number Two grabbed her coat and pulled so she stumbled just a bit. Her eyes glowing red, she grabbed a handful of the skirt of her coat. "That's mine, you ass!" She yanked, pulling the Shrillexian toward her left fist which damn near whistled through the air as it rammed into his face, pulverizing his jaw and knocking him backward five feet.

"Keep up your left hip on that move," Hirotoshi called out.

Tabitha glanced over to see Old Patch-Eye stalking toward her. It was just like Hirotoshi to try and knock her off her game. He'd call it a "learning episode" if she snarked back, not noticing the large-ass alien about to beat the shit out of her.

It had worked as recently as three years ago, but not today.

This time she didn't do anything fancy, just stayed in one place and dodged punches. "You need to work on your form," she told him and slammed a punch into his ribs. "Like that. Push out from your inner core." She slapped aside a haymaker and kicked him in the stomach, slamming a fist into his face as it came down after her kick.

He stumbled backward. "You want to go check out the captain?" she asked. "I'm going to teach this one how to fight."

Hirotoshi looked around and nodded; the other three weren't getting up anytime soon.

"Sure!"

—

"How are they beating the Shrillexians?" Gorath muttered, watching the video from the hold. It was getting bloody, but it was the Shrillexians' blood, not the…whatever they were…that had come on board.

They weren't pirates, because there were only two of them. True pirates would have come with larger numbers.

Gorath turned to his radar operator. "You still got nothing on their ship? It's *right next to us!* Do you want to put on a suit and go looking for it with a light outside?"

"Uh, no, Captain!" his specialist responded. "But we have nothing, sir, and I've checked the outside video. It's black, sir."

"Space is always black, Rahj'k." Gorath rubbed his face. "Did you try turning on the outside lights?"

"Sir, yes, sir!" Rahj'k confirmed. "Still can't see shit, sir."

"Huh." Gorath was surprised, both that Rahj'k couldn't see anything and that he had thought of turning on the lights.

His crew wasn't the brightest, but he hadn't thought this operation would call for intelligence.

There was a knock on the bridge door and Gorath turned his focus back to the video screens. One of the intruders was still fighting, but the other had disappeared. Three of the Shrillexians were down.

Well, that told him who was at the door.

"Go away!" Gorath yelled. "I've already given enough at the office."

"Not happening, Skaine," the voice replied. "You have ten seconds before I start punching holes in your door. If someone is on the other side, they will have holes punched in them too."

"Going to hurt your knuckles, I think." Gorath chuckled.

A small chunk of his door evaporated, slinging door shards ahead. One hit Rahj'k on the side of the face, causing him to scream as skin started melting. He jerked to his right and clawed at his face as he fell to the floor.

The bridge crew tried to help Rahj'k, but Gorath pulled his pistol, twisted a knob, and shot him. "He's just stunned.

Now pull off the metal and slap on a few medipatches. If it missed his eyes, he's damned lucky."

"All right!" Gorath yelled. He glanced at the screen to see the last effort by the lead Shrillexian, Bach, to take out this annoying person's partner. Bach had located a long length of pipe and was looking for an opening to swing. "One moment and I'll open the door!" he yelled out.

He hoped to hell that Bach beat the shit out of the other one and came to take care of the one shooting holes in his bridge door.

—

"I've toyed with you long enough," Bach hissed, lifting a long pipe from the parts area. He had been tossed through the door, which only slowed him down a bit, and he came back out with the pipe as his opponent yelled "Two points, two points!"

It pissed him off.

"What, ya think we're gonna play Tabbie-ball?" she asked while trying to figure out how dense the pipe was.

"I do not know what this 'Tabbie-ball' is, but I *do* plan on playing with your corpse after I beat you dead!"

"Oh, lost a little bluster?" she replied, jumping backward as he took his first swing. "Those little gonads you got hiking up into your throat?"

It was funny…every time she said "balls" the translation software fucked up and the effort to piss her opponent failed. But Tabitha had figured out that if she said "testicles" or "gonads" it translated just fine.

Bach squeezed the metal, denting it slightly, which was enough for Tabitha to figure out the pipe's destructive power.

The next time he swung she stepped into it, raising her arm so the pipe slammed into her rib cage.

"Ohh!" She chuckled. "That tickled!"

"That's impossible." He drew the pipe back; it had bent at a thirty-degree angle when it hit the alien.

He turned in time to register the fist that sent him into blackness.

—-

Gorath was shocked when the alien stepped into the path of the swing and doubly shocked when she stood there with the pipe bent around her. Bach brought the pipe back and stared at it in confusion for the time it took her to send a punch to his head. He staggered backward and dropped to the floor.

Gorath breathed out and ordered, "No one be an idiot." He glanced around the bridge. "Ok, that's an impossible request. No one pull any weapons or I'll shoot you myself."

He hit the button to release the locks on the door and yelled, "Come on in!"

—

Tabitha was waiting when the second ship docked to the Skaine pirate vessel. A group of the Queen's Guardians in armor came aboard. "Grab all the Shrillexians and everyone else except the captain. He and I are going to take this tub of bricks to somewhere near the base. Seems Addix wants to talk with him."

Peter was the last to enter the ship, and Tabitha brightened. "Hi, honey!" She walked up and kissed him. "What happened with the other ships?"

Peter made sure none of the captured were doing anything funny before returning his focus to Tabitha.

"Either their captains decided to fight to the death or our guys didn't give them an option in the heat of battle. We have a few wounded, but they should recover."

Tabitha shrugged. "Wechselbalg?"

Peter nodded.

"Well, they do get their blood up in a fight." She shrugged. "All those years as a Ranger, we didn't kill first because getting answers out of them afterward was a real bitch."

Peter chuckled. "I can see how it would be." He looked around. "So, taking this down?"

"Not sure. Addix wants to talk with the captain, but she doesn't want to meet at the base. No idea if we are going to speak here in space or on the ground."

"Well…" Peter twirled his fingers in the air as he looked at his people. "Get a move-on, we got places to be." He turned back to Tabitha. "You're off after that, right?"

"Yeah." She looked around. "This was day three, but I'll need to close things out before I go off duty. Why, you need a booty call?"

Peter blushed, but the others leading the Shrillexians off the ship chuckled.

"You are impossible." He kissed her forehead and stepped forward quickly when she pinched him on the ass.

"I'm going to take that as a yes!" she yelled after him.

"When have I ever said no?" he called back.

"Three months ago!" she commented.

"THAT WAS AFTER THIRTY-SIX HOURS STRAIGHT!" he argued as the door clanged shut.

"Yeah, but you wanted to know who had more stamina, vampires or Weres," she told no one in particular since the hold was empty. "I had to take it for the team."

She headed for the bridge. "So I took it, and took it, and took it, and screamed so you would give me more…"

A second later she started singing, "*All Nighhhht long!*"

12

High Tortuga, Hidden Space Fleet Base, The Pit

Bethany Anne was on the bottom level of the pit when the door opened and in came Eve, the short EI with the android body. She looked very similar to a young girl.

Bethany Anne watched as she descended the steps. She had been in the Pit enough that the seven on duty hardly glanced at her. "You know, you could change out your body if you wanted to."

Eve froze for half a second before responding, "I think I might like that option."

"Eeeevvveee!" Bethany Anne leaned against the table. "What is the logical thing to do?"

"Keep this body, of course," she replied. "There is a small but significant chance moving could damage my circuits. I do not see a need for a change at the moment."

"I see." Bethany Anne blew out a breath "Ok, I'll table our discussion for another time. How are we doing in the PR department?"

"Winning, but slowly," Eve supplied. She pulled out a chair and sat down. "I am having to spend an inordinate amount of time responding to all of the social posts, editorial attacks, and misinformation being thrown out by the opponents. Fortunately they are all organics or this might be more difficult."

"What do you consider an inordinate amount of time?"

"At least four solid hours a day," Eve supplied. "If computers were involved, I would have to build additional infrastructure and respond-bots. I'm thinking of doing it anyway, but presently I am still crafting the messages to make a single point."

"Four hours? And what point?"

"That the only question is, should the infrastructure and security be handled by someone vested in the well-being of this planet or by those who live off-planet? I want them to start asking whether these objections truly come from a local source or someone else."

"But I thought you told me they *did* come from local sources."

"Sure, bought and paid for by others off-planet."

Eve was swinging her legs, which didn't touch the ground. Bethany Anne wondered if she was acting human deliberately. "Are you planning on revealing them?"

"I want them to identify the source or sources and if it's 'others,' we'll inform them that we have proof they're taking off-world pay."

"Ahh." Bethany Anne thought this through. "While it can stop some of the harassment, let's make sure we take the people into account. Before you implement a rebuttal I want you to speak with me, ok?"

"I understand."

"Now, what about the elections?" Bethany Anne pulled out a chair and sat down across from Eve. She was aware that everyone in the Pit was paying attention to the two of them. It was, as Michael had suggested, a perfect way to teach.

"The candidates who are either pro-Baba Yaga or agree with Baba Yaga's ideas are winning eighty-seven percent of the elections. Five percent we are losing because of an on-world disagreement, and eight percent are apparently listening to the off-world hype."

"Those fuckers need to leave this planet alone," Bethany Anne fumed. "It's one thing to disagree if you are on-world, but to use your money and influence on another world?"

"It is similar to your own United States. Each state was considered a battleground and those with power, influence, and money would try to make sure no laws were enacted that countered their position so no one else could gain a foothold."

"I didn't like it then either," Bethany Anne muttered. "I understand the *why* behind doing it—because if you changed enough states, you could change the attitude of the union as a whole and other states would get behind it. However, it doesn't mean I liked it. It was a symptom of a national government overstepping what had been put in place. Too many states needed money from the national government, so they toed the line. The few states with enough money or gumption told Congress to shove what they wanted up their asses."

"What do you plan on doing here?" Eve asked.

"Well, if I kill free will it isn't much of a win. I'm not being easy on them right now, but part of that is because it isn't an easy situation. No one handed me a pretty present. This is High Tortuga and life can be rough, so I'm rough right back."

"I noticed you didn't have us send a lot of messages on behalf of those running."

"I didn't want to be seen as supporting anyone in particular. Our ideas either hold merit or they don't. If there is universal agreement on what is right, then all peoples—aliens, whatever—will innately know it. Hell, even the Leath got back to equilibrium once the Seven had been kicked out. The Yollins too, for that matter."

"So you believe there is a logic in the universe?"

"Uh," Bethany Anne thought about that. "I've seen that the basic premise of right and wrong balances itself without outside influence. Some races, like some humans, lean toward either peace or power. A species may do things we would consider evil, but they don't usually seem evil to them; just their way of life."

"What is an example of this 'evil but not evil?'"

"Have you seen the original *Men in Black* movie?" Bethany Anne replied. "It was filmed in the…oh hell, I can't remember exactly when. Maybe before the year 2000."

"Yes." Eve locked up for a second. "It was released in 1997 and starred Will Smith and Tommy Lee Jones." Her features relaxed. For all Bethany Anne knew, she had just watched the whole movie in those few seconds.

"Okay, there's a scene that has always grossed me out, but it's true when you think about it. We humans did our dead-level best to kill roaches. We hated them; they crunch when you step on them and their guts spread everywhere." Bethany Anne shivered. "Ugh! Anyway, Will Smith's character—"

"'Agent J,'" Eve supplied.

"Right, J." Bethany Anne nodded. "So, J stomps on the roaches he finds after slamming into a trash bin and ends up pissing off the thirty-foot roach-looking alien. Now, to the alien, J was murdering his race. We, however, don't see it that way. Similarly, when you watch *Independence Day* the aliens that were attacking Earth didn't see humans as anything more than roaches, so there wasn't evil intent on their part," Bethany Anne finished, "but a difference of opinion that would only leave one group alive."

"This is, in essence, what the Kurtherians' endgame is about," Eve mused.

"Yes. They will leave just a few alive at the end so they can figure out which of them was the best at helping other races ascend. The problem for them is," Bethany Anne smiled, "*we* are the wildcard."

"The ones taking out those who are manipulating nature."

"Call it nature, call it the 'right to life'; the right to self-evolution. Hell, call it our own form of Ascension. We won't allow the Kurtherians who are fucking with other species to keep it up, because if we don't then one day?"

Bethany Anne drew in a deep breath. "The Earth will have a real Independence Day, and it won't be pretty."

High Tortuga, Hidden Space Fleet Base, EI Building

ADAM, why do we have a new building for the EIs?

Bethany Anne had two Guardians with her, although frankly she didn't need their support. She always wore a light version of Jean's armor, and ADAM was now using the sensors in the neck to monitor everything around her. Should someone seek to harm her the armor's helmet would activate, allowing Bethany Anne time to move between this dimension and the Etheric.

And be safe.

Not the best of options if she was on a ship that was gating, but on a planet it made her pretty hard to kill.

So long as she didn't go back to save people—which was exactly what they figured she would do.

So, *guards.*

>>This is the beginning of the structure for the EIs. We will build it out and bring in the components, then secure it by dropping hundreds of tons of rock on it.<<

What happens if the machines need servicing? That's going to be a bitch to open.

>>We are using Anne's technology to allow certain groups access through the Etheric. Since no one who doesn't need to know is aware of the possibility, as far as rumor is concerned we are locking them under a lot of stone and metal.<<

If we drilled out the rooms, someone else can drill a new way in.

>>That is the purpose of the metal surround, but even that can be removed eventually. The purpose is to stop anything but a full-on attack where the defenders have been neutralized. With these defenses, the EIs will have the time to shut everything down and escape. <<

Bethany Anne was shocked. "Escape?" she exclaimed, then realized she was talking aloud.

ESCAPE?

>>Yes. I am working with Anne's protégés to move a large amount of the infrastructure for the EIs into the Etheric so the room they are physically located in will have the secondary defense of looking insignificant. Their primary room, which contains a large amount of very expensive computer equipment, is used for reporting and secondary data storage. It is, for all intents and purposes, bogus."

That's... Wow. I had no idea. What brought this on?

>>The CEREBRO Project, and some personal understanding of the Etheric. Once we have the machines in the Etheric and powered by the Etheric, they are effectively immune from attack from anyone besides Kurtherians. High Tortuga would only lose the connectivity in our dimension.<<

Yeah, but it's possible to feel things through the Etheric. Are we going to have someone come looking?

>>No. I am aware of the issues of announcing events through the Etheric. In fact, I have started tracking events—<<

Tracking what events?

>>I don't know. Since we can't travel within the Etheric I can't find out. Think of it as hearing a loud *boom* in a forest, but you can't see farther than a few trees and you can't move. Eventually the sound dissipates and you only know something affected something else nearby.<<

Well, that's not odd or anything. I'll get with TOM on it.

>>I have worked with TOM. This is how we have gained more capabilities in the Etheric than we had before.<<

Oh. Thank you, TOM.

You are welcome.

So CEREBRO is starting to come together. Where did we get the parts?

>>The cores are being temporarily run on the super-dreadnoughts, except Reynolds. He, as you know, has gone looking for the Kurtherians, but the rest are enjoying the efforts to remake the world.<<

Uh...huh. Enjoying?

>>Well, they aren't bored.<<

Okay, it's nice to know they wanted something to do. However, what about the final parts?

>>Since the cores for an EI are rather small, your dad is sending an agent to bring them to us in the *Scamp Princess.*<<

Do I know him?

>>You knew him as "Johnny." Now his name is Sean.
<<

He was the one who worked both in the Rangers and with Dad, right?

>>Yes.<<

Good kid. Well, man now. Wow, time flies!

>>So we should have the cores within a couple of weeks.<<

Good. Nice work on the design, by the way. So, is the real reason you brought me over here to see a bunch of hewn-out rock so you could lay down the rumors that the Queen is involved?

There was a long pause from ADAM.

>>Oh, you got that?<<

Yes. Yes, I did. Next time I could sell it better if you don't just try to use me. Nice try; it took me a couple of minutes to figure it out. Did I nod in all the right places?

>>Now that you mention it, yes. I was rather pleased with myself about how natural you looked.<<

Yes, well, we did the same thing when we blew up the Gate. But I can act, so don't do that again or we will have a more direct discussion. Am I clear?

>>Yes, ma'am.<<

Bethany Anne motioned to her guards to follow her and waved to a few people in the hallways as she left.

Told you not to do it, TOM sent to ADAM directly, bypassing Bethany Anne.

>>I thought I could get away with it.<<

She has been working with us for almost as long as she has been alive. I tried to tell you that pulling one over on her is fucking impossible.

>>Have you noticed you are cursing even more lately?<<

Yes. It's a byproduct of spending time around Bethany Anne—you become those you hang around with. One can't possibly hang around with someone else more than I have.

>>You have got to be the crassest Kurtherian 'pilot' in existence.<<

Well, luckily for me there isn't anything in our good book related to our vernacular, just our *tasks*. I'm shocked I still have to admit what I have to later and she

hasn't figured it out already. This might be the end of my existence.

>>She wouldn't do that to you.<<

Yeah, well, it's not *your* life. I don't think she will either, but if you knew some of the chemicals floating around in this body and some of the emotions I'm tweaking you wouldn't be so sure.

>>I thought you told her you weren't messing with any chemicals? That you were leaving them alone?<<

For the most part, but for those I'm very familiar with I am doing the minimum to keep her on an even keel. Well, sort of an even keel; it's Bethany Anne. Have you noticed that even Michael stays away at times?

>>I haven't done any long-term associative heuristics on Michael yet, so I wouldn't know.<<

He has noted that she both likes him around and is easily annoyed at his presence, so he limits direct contact to mornings, lunch, and evenings.

>>I have noticed that she requests updates on him all the time.<<

She is working through a lot of issues associated with him being back. I think he is allowing her time to adjust to his presence. She crawls over in bed and hugs him at night, and his touch soothes her when she is sleeping. Her conscious mind is not so happy with him and the constraints it sees.

>>Young love—<<

Is a *bitch*, TOM finished.

13

High Tortuga, Hidden Space Fleet Base, Prime Building

"I can't believe," Bethany Anne sat down at the table with a mocha in her hand, "that we didn't think about long-term military incarceration." She blew on the top of the drink to cool it down and looked at Stephen and Lerr'ek. "Any suggestions?"

"We can use the Phase Three buildings," Lerr'ek suggested. He had flown to the base from the main city, and his offices there, to have this conversation. As the main project lead, this oversight was his mistake. "Frankly, my mind was on the base as a staging area for you to go out and seek out new civilizations being tampered with by Kurtherians and destroy them. Not so much having to deal with military attacks against Dev—" He smiled at Bethany Anne's glare. "*High Tortuga.* That being said, it's rather obvious in hindsight."

"We will need multiple types of rooms, from large holding pens with appropriate waste and eating options to individual cells for either long-term incarceration or suicide watch. Further, we will want wings for guests who need to be treated with higher levels of respect, but still incarcerated."

Bethany Anne massaged her forehead. "Perhaps that was why Michael used to just kill them." She sighed. "Wow, that sounded harsh even to me."

Lerr'ek grunted. "The Zhyn in me concurs on both accounts. However, when history explains how you accomplished the planet's turnaround you won't want the black marks killing all of your prisoners would bring you to be part of your legacy."

"No, and I don't want to do it because it isn't right, either—not that we requested the presence of these assholes in the first place. The fact that we don't have proper cells at the moment and have to use one of the ships' brigs to hold them is annoying. We have to power up that much of a ship." She shook her head. "It's like having annoying uninvited guests."

"Why aren't you just keeping them on the *ArchAngel II*?" Stephen asked. "It isn't like that would add to her power requirements."

"A part of me thinks that would be appropriate, but the other part worries about what would happen if the ship went into battle. I don't want the crew of the *ArchAngel* to worry about some merc rats in the brig if shit goes wrong. Plus, Addix prefers to be on-planet if she has a say in this. Ergo, we have them down here."

"It could be worse." Stephen was looking down at his tablet. "The other two mercenary efforts didn't stick us with any additional prisoners."

"Well, that's one way to look at it," she agreed. "However, I chose to look at that situation as a learning opportunity to explain to our boarding parties that killing everyone shouldn't be the first choice. Okay, maybe, if you believe there is no other way without exposing yourselves to further harm, but there were at least three opportunities where a clear-thinking mind could have found a decent solution."

She took a sip of her mocha. "So I've instituted new training regimes for boarding parties. The Weres in the group found a fight and went at it, but Tabitha's team used their Ranger experience to negotiate with those on the bridge. It wasn't like their ships were going to go anywhere with our ships connected to them."

Stephen nodded. "It was rather unfortunate," he agreed. "However, their previous roles were in the Guardians."

"Which is why they have been set up for education and not a penalty. For Tabitha and Hirotoshi's success, they have been tasked to teach others how to negotiate and do after-action reports for future boarding efforts."

Stephen took a sip of his drink. "To be fair, I don't think any of us expected Shrillexians."

Lerr'ek snorted. "They're mercs. Where you find mercs, you find Shrillexians."

"Quite a few of them, actually." Bethany Anne concurred. "I think Addix is going to be able to use that information to help narrow down who we are fighting."

"One can hope," Stephen agreed. "If you are happy enough with that discussion, let's go over the designs for the possible expansion of the base. Lerr'ek here has been kind enough to offer his services to oversee the expansion project."

"I have?" came out of Lerr'ek's mouth before his brain caught up with him.

Of course I have.

"I mean to say, it's the least I can do," he finished.

"Good." She nodded. "Ok you two, deal with what you need to deal with, and don't forget we have the resources conference at two today—in the Pit this time." She thought for a moment. "Lerr'ek, I want you there as well."

Lerr'ek stared at them. "What's the Pit? Is this a place we have to fight?"

The two humans chuckled. "No. Well, not with weapons." She thought for a second. "Just ideas," she clarified. "So you two wrap up in time to meet over there."

She stood up and walked out of the meeting with her two guards ghosting behind her.

ADAM?

>>Yes?<<

What is Michael doing at the moment?

>>You could always call him.<<

I don't want to bug him. He isn't used to having someone on top of him all of the time. It's easier this way.

>>I have located him in his office, talking with William about the design of the barbeque pit area.<<

Ok, thanks.

Why the hell is Michael so involved with a barbeque pit? she wondered. *What's he plan on cooking?*

Planet Soboth (Previously Territory 7732), Undisclosed location, Open Out-ring, Non-Federation

Uleq was at the meeting table early, tweaking the information he needed to present. The communications from Imon to the pirates had gone out just as Az had prescribed.

But unfortunately it hadn't gone as Az had expected.

He sighed and was running through additional numbers when Imon entered the meeting room. "Peace be upon you," the Shrillexian intoned.

"Do what?" Uleq looked up. "That salutation is from a completely different species in another galaxy. It seems so...*wrong* coming from your lips."

"I know." Imon pulled out his favorite chair and sat down. "I love the dissonance that phrase evokes in people," he pointed to his face, "when it comes from this mouth."

Uleq grunted. "That's hilarious, actually." He put his tablet down. "I didn't realize you *had* a sense of humor, Imon."

"There are many things you won't realize about me until I choose to reveal them," he agreed. "I saw from your body posture and facial expression when I arrived that something didn't go well for us? I'm aware of at least three problems, and two of them come from Devon."

Uleq placed his tablet on the table, turning it so Imon could see. "Yes, neither of our campaigns to upset the present dictator are going according to plan. In fact, I'd say they are so counter to plan that they don't warrant acknowledgment that they were a plan in the first place."

Imon looked down at the two notes that were highlighted in red. He looked up at Uleq and back to the tablet. "This is...disturbing and annoying."

"I concur. We either have a much stronger adversary than we suspected or the quality of our consultants has been sub-optimal."

"I see."

Uleq took the tablet back, removing the highlights he had pointed out to Imon.

Then he deleted the one sentence he didn't want Az to notice in his presentation. For those who wished to continue to the top, some knowledge needed to be hoarded.

He hoped he had read Imon correctly or his life might be over very shortly.

Az entered the room as the two worked on the final tweaks to the review.

Az's grumbling voice greeted them with, *"Let's get started."*

High Tortuga, Hidden Space Fleet Base, The Pit

Bethany Anne had been sitting at the table in the Pit for over an hour before Michael showed up with food to share with her. The two ate in companionable silence for fifteen minutes before Stephen and Lerr'ek arrived. Behind them were Addix and John Grimes.

John looked around the table after all had sat down. "This is a resources meeting, right?"

"Mmmhmmm." Bethany Anne swallowed the last of her salad.

The vegetables on this planet leaned toward odd oranges and blues, but they tasted good. There was a flavorful meat tossed into the salad that definitely *didn't* taste like chicken. The texture was more like bison or some other large animal, but the flavor was from next door to heaven. She handed the empty bowl to Michael, who stood up, patted her on the shoulder, and took their bowls up to the top.

He came back a moment later.

"I need someone who will look at this from a different perspective. You might not say a word during the whole meeting—and that's ok—but you got nominated."

John grinned. "I'm the short straw?"

"Technically," Michael leaned forward to look down the table to John, "you were the *only* straw."

"Oh, well." John scratched his chin. "I'm special."

"That is...*one* way to look at it," Michael replied.

John chuckled. "Thanks. I was wondering who was going to give me shit at this meeting. Without Darryl, Eric, or Scott I'm feeling a little lost."

"Hey, what am I, chopped liver?" Bethany Anne asked. "If you need shit thrown at you, I'm the right woman for the job."

"You are the only woman for the job." Michael patted her arm. "If you leave out his wife, Eric's wife, about three other ladies I can name—"

"You can stop helping me, Michael," John's comment elicited chuckles from everyone at the table.

"All right, joking aside." Bethany Anne raised an eyebrow to John and Michael, who both waved her off. "I want to discuss the resource issue and the MPPS project. For thousands of years our kind has fought for resources; land, minerals, food, etc. Earth isn't going to be short of land when this project gets off the ground. After WWDE and over eighty-five percent of the humans on the planet dying, they won't have a problem there."

"They could need building materials," Stephen piped up. "There were a lot of resources wasted building the infrastructure that is now crumbling back on Earth."

"Why would you build the same way?" Lerr'ek asked. "What is the planet made of?"

"Well, at this point, a shit-ton of sand in the warm places," Michael conceded. "After what we call WWDE or the 'World's Worst Day Ever,' fallout changed the climate. We left behind some units to slowly evolve the planet back again, but there are many deserts there; more than when the humans who are with us now left."

"So why not take the habitation machines and use the sand to create structures in place? Over on Anteries 197 they figured out how to take sand and advanced sealants and build big flowing structures—and color them. Some of their cities are beautiful to behold.

"How long do these sand buildings last?" Bethany Anne was touching the table, changing the video screen to show her pictures of what Lerr'ek was talking about. "How do they get them so white?"

"Well, their sand is naturally white, but during the cleaning and mixture processes they add additional substances which change the sealant to white like you see here. I'm told that on Joachim 4 they make everything a color you call 'purple.'"

"Purple?" John asked. "Wow, that's just... Yeah, wow. Eye-blinding wow."

"Here's a pink building," Bethany Anne swiped her image to John's screen.

"That's more *wow*, but in a very emasculating way," John mumbled. He added, "Don't show this to Jean…"

"I assume these are all hard?" Michael asked. "And we didn't answer Bethany Anne's question about how long they last."

"I've got it," she answered. "Says here they last as long as the engineering that goes into them. Typical weather patterns such as… One second, I have to figure out what Earth's normal weather pattern is now. Okay, thanks, ADAM…M2. Okay, oh!" She looked at Michael. "These should last about five hundred years with minimum upkeep."

Stephen was working his own screen. "So if we give them a fresh coat of paint."

"More like slime," Lerr'ek qualified.

"Thanks, but I'll say paint." Stephen smiled. "Sounds less icky." Lerr'ek shrugged. "If we maintain the buildings they should almost last indefinitely."

"Well…" John opened something on his screen, digging deeper, "so long as no one is trying to destroy them they will. They don't have much protection from something as simple as a cannonball. Those flowing buildings, if hit in the right location, collapse."

ADAM's voice came out of the speakers. "We could build using a hexagonal structure on the inside for both a lighter and more resilient building. The walls could sustain a large amount of fire without experiencing a situational collapse like a solid structure."

"That would take longer to build," Lerr'ek pointed out. "The present machines typically lay down layers on top of each other."

"Like old-time 3D printing back on Earth, with better access to the materials used on site," Stephen muttered.

He was obviously deep into the manufacturing details.

"So we need to consider the type of building when we use this technology." Michael looked up and turned to Lerr'ek. "Is this right? It can build a residence in hours?"

"It *is* true—depending on the complexity and size of the structure. If it is very simple, you could construct a single building that has room for four families. They would each have," Lerr'ek touched a few buttons on his screen, "the equivalent of two thousand five hundred of your square feet. Enough for ten family members minimum."

Michael's eyes narrowed. "Ten?"

Bethany Anne put a hand on his arm, drawing Michael's attention. "The efficiency of the design allows for the new needs of families. There are many alcoves for when someone wants to be alone, but larger rooms for when they congregate. Typically these structures have an area outside which is covered and permits bigger groups to congregate. The expectation is for multigenerational families to remain together."

"That is a good point," Stephen agreed. "With healthier individuals, you can end up with a lot of large families, even if they did not start with one. Just one set of parents having two children each generation could reach thirty members by the third generation when you include spouses."

Michael started doing the calculations in his head. "That's a lot. So one of these buildings with four families can hold forty. Eventually the heads of the families will build one for themselves?"

"They could," Bethany Anne agreed, "but remember our previous conversation. Our goal is to make sure those who like the status quo are able to be productive members of society where they are. Those who can't or don't will be offered positions better suited for them."

"And those who believe a criminal life is optimal?"

"Then there is always the position of prisoner in a jail." Bethany Anne shrugged. "We can do the Australian option and offer them one-way tickets to somewhere else. I understand Australia ended up doing pretty fucking wonderfully by the end."

"They did have a wicked sense of humor," Stephen added. "You couldn't be around an Australian without blushing half the time."

"Australians are who?" Lerr'ek asked.

"One of our countries back on Earth," Bethany Anne replied, "used a large island to help clear out their overpopulated jails for eighty years. The island had indigenous people called Aborigines who lived there before the early settlers found a part they could farm on, and then the convicts came. About fifty years later many went willingly to Australia because there was a gold rush. Somewhere around 1900 it was known as a federation, and it wasn't until the late twentieth century that it was independent, even though they had been acting independent for decades and they still had the same Queen as Britain when we left."

Bethany Anne moved a piece of hair that had fallen into her face. "The point is, for many of us who didn't live there, all we remembered was the shit-ton of convicts who made up the population. You never knew which people who looked like me had one of these convicts in their family tree. Either way, Americans always assumed that Australian humor was part of the same attitude that got the convicts shipped to the island in the first place. We tend to admire rugged individualists in the US, so we liked the cheeky Australians. Plus since we stopped Britain from sending their prisoners to *us*, we are one of the factors in their history—at least if I remember it correctly."

"You remember that from high school?" Michael asked.

"No, it was in my classes for my job with the government. Plus, I rather liked the stories. It's not like I gave a shit if someone was tossed in jail for telling some lord he was a sodding bastard. He probably was, so I'd likely have been on that boat to Australia anyway."

"And yet," Lerr'ek pointed out. "You are called Queen?"

Stephen snorted. "That wasn't by her choice, actually. And since she left the Etheric Empire she has been demoted from Empress to Queen."

"My people still like it and I'm comfortable with Queen, so it stayed."

"So is High Tortuga your Australia?" Michael asked.

"I guess in a way it is." She nodded. "We have many of the castoffs; the unwanted and the unsupported. This planet is a melting pot of opportunity."

Lerr'ek chuckled. "That's the nicest and most generous description anyone has given of High Tortuga."

"People are resources too," Bethany Anne noted. "It's the duty of anyone who is hoping to expand the opportunities for the current residents and those in the future by supporting those in the present to achieve greatness. The challenge is getting some of them off their lazy asses and doing something. That's when the tough love that pisses people off occurs."

"Have any experience with that lately?" Michael asked, one eyebrow raised.

"Too damned much," she replied. "People—well, let me change that to humans—can expend more energy trying to figure out how not to work than the job would have taken in the first place. It's when they realize that they aren't going to put one over on the system by manipulating either the system or others that they finally make the hard choice of working—or doing something incredibly stupid."

"Thus the need for police," John pointed out.

"Exactly. The police aren't there to force anyone to do anything. They are there to protect those who work and strive hard from those who would prey on the workers to enrich themselves. THAT is where the line is drawn, and choices have life-threatening consequences."

"We, however," she pointed down to the screen in front of her, "need to be sure we have enough resources for everyone on the planet. If we offer jobs to everyone, we can't have restrictions on food, clothing, shelter, or any other basic necessities or we give those who would like to undermine the system an opportunity to argue against it."

14

High Tortuga, Hidden Space Fleet Base, Queen's Personal Quarters

Michael followed Bethany Anne into their quarters. Once her guard understood he was going with her, they peeled off and went to eat.

"We need to have a discussion," Michael started, only to have Bethany Anne put up a hand. "Please close the door first."

He raised an eyebrow but made sure the door was closed before turning back around, eyebrow still raised in a question.

"I don't want anyone to hear me yell at you," she explained and sat down on the couch. "It isn't respectful to you."

Michael cocked his head. "Ok, where is Bethany Anne, and who am I speaking with?"

She grabbed a pillow from the couch and threw it at him. "Ass. I've been off my game a few times. TOM isn't helping with all the chemicals and shit, and I'm sorry. I've tried to give you space, but it isn't easy during the times I want you next to me—either to cuddle up or punch the very next second. This shit sucks," she added as she rubbed her stomach; she was starting to show more now. "I'm not happy with my figure, I'm not happy how mother nature made women the child-bearing ones, and you look scrumptious and it pisses me off."

"I'm sorry, what?" Michael sat down next to her, put an arm around her, and offered his side for her to punch if needed.

It was the smallest sacrifice he could make at the moment. It took a lot for him to allow her to hit him without reciprocating. He had spent over a thousand years killing anyone, gender-equal, who touched him.

Now he offered his ribs up as a sacrifice.

This time she leaned into his embrace. "You look too scrumptious and it bugs me."

"So," Michael held her tight, "you are saying you are emotional, perhaps unrealistically so due to chemical imbalances while your body is trying to create a new human being."

Bethany Anne took a moment to parse his sentence. "You're lucky there wasn't a dig in there."

"I'm just clarifying the facts," Michael replied. "If I had wanted to say something—"

"Don't. You. Dare." She chuckled. "I can always pull your heart out."

Michael kissed the top of her head. "Sweetheart, you do that every time you are mad at me."

He didn't realize until he felt the tears soak his shirt

that her quietness was due to her silently crying. "What did I say?"

She wiped her face. "I'm sorry. Just…" She kissed him on the cheek. "I'm sorry."

He started to object, but Bethany Anne put her fingers over his lips. "Don't go there. Just accept my apology and let me know why you thought we should talk."

He nodded and she pulled her fingers off. "I was wondering if you had thought of any names yet?" He smiled.

"Jessica?" she offered, then leaned back into him and rubbed his chest. "James Michael?"

She felt him chuckle. "I think we have enough Michaels in this family. I'm okay not using it, but I appreciate the offer. So, do you want a Jessica Bethany?"

"Oh, hell no." She shook her head. "I don't need a mother's curse to come down on me so that I have a child just like me. I think I've done enough in my life of helping others to believe I will have an angel."

"You really *are* pushing it, aren't you?" He rubbed her back. "How about Ava?"

Bethany Anne patted his chest in rhythm with his heart beating. "Ava? I rather like it. There isn't a previous girl in your past named Ava, is there?"

He chuckled. "I'm over a thousand years old. If you require our daughter to have a name I've never come across, we might as well start looking at Yollin names."

"Not what I'm talking about. I mean previous lovers."

"No, no Avas, and for what it is worth that would be a short list, not a long one."

"Say no more," she replied, then a moment later asked, "How short?"

"Seven, and two of those were before I was turned. The other five were over a thousand years ago."

Bethany Anne leaned back to look Michael in the eyes. "You've been celibate for over a thousand years?"

"Yes."

"How?" Bethany Anne waved a hand. "Never mind, I know how celibacy works. I guess I mean *why*?"

"In the beginning," he explained, "I was a monster. After that phase, it was an ego boost. I had to leave a person because it was obvious I wasn't aging to speak of, and a few people were trying to figure out why their cows were dying. They looked at me and rumors started."

"Did you?"

"Did I what?" Michael asked.

"Did you suck the cows dry?"

"No, it was a disease, and what we would call a veterinarian nowadays came by and helped heal the cows and stopped the problem. However, all it would take would be another problem like the cows and I would come under discussion again. So when everything died down I made a fool of myself at the local bar; drank too much and stumbled out into an ice storm. Everyone assumed I'd died out there and I left, never looking back."

"So, no others?"

He looked at her meaningfully. "Not until I could find a woman who was strong enough to make me desire to live again."

Michael frowned. "You know, it won't be easy for our daughter."

"Why?" she asked. "There is no reason she can't be strong."

"I'm not suggesting she won't be strong, but you know what they say about old-fashioned dads when their daughters date."

"Mmmhmmm."

Michael sighed. "Well, there aren't any fathers more old-fashioned than *me*, Bethany Anne."

Above High Tortuga, Anti-Piracy and Boarding Action Ship 12, Eastern Hemisphere, Second Quadrant

Ricole tried to relax into her seat. Now she was on a ship among the stars where just months before she had been running around the sewers in Thon.

She wore a proper boarding suit, matching the dark blue of her teammates. She was enjoying the stars when she overheard Mark and Jacqueline chatting with Sabine in the back.

"It's an old story from before when the world was destroyed," Mark was saying. "It had to do with three guys and one girl, but we will upgrade it for our current reality."

"That being one guy and three females?" Sabine's reply was laced with amusement.

"Well, that and Ricole being a Noel-ni, Jacqueline being a Were, and me being a vampire."

"And I am?" Sabine asked.

"A good shot?" Mark replied.

"Preternaturally fast?" Jacqueline added. "You are a freak of nature, Sabine. And I mean that in a nice way."

Sabine's voice was flat. "I'm not too sure that 'freak' is ever associated with *nice*."

"Yes," Jacqueline replied, "but that is what I mean. 'You are *unique* in nature' might have been a better way to put it, but it's still right. Something in you worked with something Akio gave you and *BAM!* Your reaction times… Damn!"

Ricole smiled. The people Michael had placed her with were constantly chatting amongst themselves. Some of their barbs would have caused a Noel-ni to demand honor, but all it did was cause the other two to laugh.

And often the one the comment had been aimed at. They had become friends.

So now she was stuck up in space guarding the planet for the Queen, whom she had finally figured out was the same person who'd recruited her.

Baba Yaga WAS the Queen, and vice-versa. It had been a chance meeting with Bethany Anne while Sabine was taking Ricole to meet Demon, who turned out to be a four-footed large cat creature from her home planet. Bethany Anne had noticed the confusion in Ricole's eyes when she'd said hello…

"Ah." Bethany Anne had smiled. "You don't remember me from our meeting at the library."

"I'm sorry, but I only met Michael and the Witch at the library. Although your smell is similar to… Oh."

Bethany Anne had looked both ways in the hallway, and when the coast was clear Ricole was looking at the face of Baba Yaga. "I am always watching over the planet, little one." She had winked and her face became normal again. She had waved as her guards followed down the corridor.

"Oh!" Sabine had whispered. "I'm sorry, I didn't know you weren't aware that Baba Yaga and Bethany Anne were the same person!"

"I haven't met Baba Yaga but twice," Ricole explained, "so I wasn't sure of anything—although it helps to know that Michael isn't being amorous with two women."

This pronouncement had caused Sabine to place her hand over her mouth and laugh so hard she'd had to step out of the hallway. It wasn't until Ricole could see Sabine's eyes that she had realized she was amused. "What?" Ricole had looked around before getting close and stomping her foot. "It is a good thing?"

Sabine put up a hand. "I'm sorry!" She got herself under control. "It's just the thought of Michael with two women where one of them wasn't Bethany Anne, for two reasons. One, you didn't know that he was going to flap his arms to get into space if he had to."

"But that wouldn't work." Ricole's furry eyebrows shot up. "Would it?"

Sabine shook her head. "No, but that was how hard he was working to be with Bethany Anne."

"Oh… And what about the second thing?"

"Um," Sabine sobered up. "She wouldn't take well to another woman."

As the two continued down the hall Ricole had asked, "What does 'wouldn't take well' mean?"

"Oh, Michael would be dead." The two had turned a corner, their voices still lingering behind them. "The other woman would be dead…"

"That doesn't seem too harsh…"

"Half a million of the people closest to them when she

found out would be dead because of the meteor Bethany Anne would have smashed them with..."

"Well..." Ricole's voice was fading, "even *I* might think that is overkill...but not by much."

—

Now Ricole was up in space, hoping for some action without actually hoping for any action.

They trained hard, but in between the training were long bouts of trying to figure out what she would like to do with herself.

A voice interrupted her thoughts. "Hello." Ricole looked over her shoulder, but none of her friends were nearby.

"Hello?" she responded. She only felt partially stupid. Her friends answered disembodied voices all the time. She would only be annoyed if Mark was pranking her.

"Oh good, you aren't freaking out," the voice continued. "I'm Eve, one of the EIs that came back from Earth with Jacqueline, Mark, and Sabine."

"Oh, hello." This Eve Ricole knew about. "Do you want me to get Mark and the others?"

"No, I needed to ask you a question or two about High Tortuga, or Devon—whichever you prefer."

Ricole smiled. "Oh, you can call it 'the rock I live on' if you'd like. I'm not particular about names."

"All right, High Tortuga it is." There was a slight pause. "You had an interaction with Baba Yaga's security before you were brought to the base, am I right?'

"That is right."

"Can you tell me how it made you feel? I am writing an article on why you might think the security was good, and then I'll have you tweak it for publication. That is, if you don't mind?"

"Why would I mind?" Ricole fumed for a moment as she thought back to that asshole and how he had captured her. It was his fault she'd had to carry a weapon into the library. While she was happy enough to be at the base, it was embarrassing that she had forgotten the weapon on her body.

"Well, some don't want their stories to be told to the general populace. I will hide your name if needed."

"No need to hide my name. I am not ashamed of my actions, just my inability to protect myself."

"Good, keep going."

"Well…" Ricole spent the better part of the next half hour explaining what had led to the encounter. How her people were sought for their martial skills, and whether or not they wished to be involved, they were often drafted into gangs.

"I will have this written and sent to your communications box in approximately five minutes. You *do* have one?"

"Oh, yes." Ricole supplied the information. "In just five minutes? That's fast."

"I need to get it approved by Bethany Anne. Otherwise I would have provided it to you immediately."

"Wait, you have it finished already?"

"Of course…I'm an EI. I have replied to over nine hundred and sixty different social messages from accounts around High Tortuga while you and I have been talking, as well as composed our article."

"'Our?'"

"Well, if you are okay with it, I'll add your name to mine in the byline."

Ricole thought about this for a moment.

"Of course you can add my name. Can you do my homework too?"

Laughter erupted behind Ricole; her team was coming up to the bridge. They had probably been listening the whole time. Not that she could be upset—she had been eavesdropping herself a little while before.

Eve replied. "I suppose if you ever need help, call me. I'm happy to help as well. Okay, I've got Bethany Anne's review and notes. Your…uh oh!" Eve's voice changed. "Strap in, folks, you have company!"

The other three had just gotten to their seats, so it only took a second for them to switch from "fun" to "focused and ready to move."

Jacqueline asked, "Eve, what do you know?"

"I give it maybe ten seconds before you are notified of an unexpected ship heading your direction. Probable pirate; doesn't look like previous ships. Data is inconsistent with others that were interdicted."

A moment later Space Station One called and confirmed everything Eve had just said, and followed with "You are ordered to interdict, board, and either confirm legitimacy or apprehend according to the rules and regulations of High Tortuga."

Sabine was the only one who witnessed Ricole's lips peel back, her sharp teeth shining as their ship's engines kicked in and they headed out to meet their first set of possible pirates.

15

It took them a total of twelve minutes to pull up alongside the new ship. Ricole was surprised that none of her partners were flying, but they explained that the EIs usually handled the flights.

"Right now we have a bunch of bored super-geniuses who aren't flying, so for us to do it would take away some of their meaning in life," Mark answered her.

"What he isn't saying," Sabine added, "is *we* can't fly ourselves out of a paper sack, and I doubt this is taking more than ten percent of one of their brains."

A new voice came out of the speakers. It sounded like the Queen to Ricole.

These humans all sounded similar at times. It was annoying.

"More like ten percent of *one* percent, Sabine," the voice offered. "Although I'm giving you a total of five percent of my focus because I'm curious as to what is going on. Another seven percent is focused on everything happening inside my ship, and twenty-seven percent, the largest, is handling a video game effort for William at the moment."

"Which video game?" Mark asked. Ricole noticed he had triple checked all his weapons.

"One for Baba Yaga Productions, having to do with moving the BYPSs—"

"Holy shit, really!?" Mark's eyes lit up. "I've gotten down to a hundred percent and almost beaten the level. I've got to tell you, that shit is hard!"

"Yes, you are in the top forty percent of all players."

"Wait, only the top forty?" He scowled. "I thought I was top ten?"

"Well, you are only on Version 1.5. I've had to adjust the parameters twice for reality updates. The players brought up situations I had not placed into the games."

"Oh, is that what the updates do?" He mumbled something, then, "I'll have to update."

"Ok, I have negotiated with the captain of the ship on your behalf."

Jacqueline leaned forward. "What does 'negotiated' mean, ArchAngel?"

"I sent a one-pound puck across to slam against their ship. He didn't believe that you were out here, so I had to prove it."

"Why isn't she handling this instead of us?" Ricole asked.

"Because one day," ArchAngel replied, "*I* will be out in the stars kicking ass and taking names with my Queen, and *you* will be here kicking ass without me. So learn well, little one, and do yourself and your team proud. Docking in ninety seconds."

The connection was severed.

The four got up and headed toward the docking door. “She sounded just like the Queen,” Ricole commented.

“Wait till you get a look at her.” Mark winked. “It’s like staring at the Queen.”

“I’ll tell you later.” Sabine unlocked her pistols. “It takes longer to explain than we have right now.”

Ricole nodded, unhooking her own pistols’ safeties.

It was time to rock and roll.

—

“What do ya mean, ya can’t see it!” Ch’urn stood up from his chair and stepped down to the lower deck to look for himself. When he checked, the threat scanning and detection systems showed nothing. “Well,” he grumped, “I sure enough heard the loud bang when their warning shot hit us!”

Ch’urn was a Zhyn—six feet of heavy blue muscles and skin like an old-Earth dinosaur’s. His shoulders were heavy because he worked them so much.

He preferred to use hand weapons when taking ships, not guns and blasters. He’d use them if he had to, but it wasn’t his preference.

Drock, a cousin although distant, turned from watching his screen at damage control. “What if they can’t hit us with anything stronger? We *could* be falling for a trick.”

Ch’urn smiled, his carnivorous teeth revealed as his tongue swiped across them. “I hope it is. If they connect with us and we can’t see their ship, maybe we want to just take their ship? It’s probably worth more than anything we could steal on this planet.”

Drock turned back to his console, satisfied. It was the

one thing Ch'urn liked about his distant cousin. He might not see the obvious, but if you pointed it out to him he wasn't so dense as to argue the merits of his own stupidity.

"All right, I'm letting them connect. I'll be in the first wave, but I need two volunteers to sneak aboard their craft while I'm talking with them."

—

"Ok, two go in, two stay here." Jacqueline tossed a coin and snatched it out of the air. "Says we two go," she pointed to Mark, "and you two gunslingers stay here. Don't let anyone take the ship." She slapped the large button at the side of the door, opening it for her and Mark to enter the temporary tunnel and hit the other side's door.

A moment later the other ship's door started to slide open.

"Wait, did we get a choice there?" Ricole asked.

Sabine smirked. "No. You will learn that Jacqueline has the hots for getting into fights. She's right about no one getting aboard though, and if you hear a roar…"

"A roar?" Ricole stepped back, allowing Sabine to take point. She had the armor; Ricole's hadn't arrived just yet. They had found a chest protector for her but needed to manufacture something specific for her physiology.

"Oh, it's unique." Sabine nodded, her hand casually on her belt near her gun. "Can't miss it."

Soon enough there was a crash in the other ship and a roar of pain.

"That it?" Ricole jumped up.

"No, that's just some idiot who got tossed around. I'm telling you, you can't miss it."

There were more noises, metal on metal crunching and something falling plus screams of pain.

"No." Sabine put up a hand to stop Ricole from asking. "That's just someone in pain."

A scream pierced their ears. *"YOU FUCKING ASSWANKERS!"*

"That's just Jacqueline being pissed off." Ricole smiled. "I've heard that one before."

—

Ch'urn wiped his lips with the back of his arm as blood seeped into his third-favorite suit. These two humans were more formidable than he would have believed. He kept his eyes on them, but his peripheral vision captured the movement of his two sneakier members as they slipped into the tunnel between their ships.

He raised his arms and called, "HOLD!" His people backed up, leaving the two humans back to back and looking at him. "How about we make this one on one? I haven't had a good fight in a long time. What do you say? Either of you have the gumption to take *me* on?"

With his question he grinned to show off his sharpened teeth, two of them capped in metal where the tips had been broken off in previous fights. He had kept the skulls of those two and had them boiled to remove the brains.

They hung over his bed as decorations.

—

"What do you think?" Mark asked his mate. "Think he's being honest?"

Jacqueline smiled. "Well, if *he* is fighting, then the other would have to wait. You're faster with the guns, so you should back me up."

"How is it you always have the fun?" Mark asked, looking around. "Aren't we missing two?"

"Yup," she replied. "They tried to sneak aboard the ship."

"Oh?" Mark wanted to turn his head, but if Jacqueline wasn't giving anything away she must know something. "So you fight, I guard, and you get your mad out?"

"Yes, but remember I get horny after fights."

"Why do you think I'm allowing this?" Mark grinned. "I figured there was something in it for me."

Jacqueline chuckled as she stepped forward. "Yeah, yeah, I'll fight you."

The large Zhyn looked just a touch surprised but shrugged. "I'm not sexist. I'll beat you just as easily as I would have beat him. I'm very fair that way."

"I'll bet." Jacqueline smiled. "Any weapons?"

"Only what nature provided," he answered, taking off his weapons belt and kicking it behind him. "Oh, and my caps on my teeth. Some of the tips got broken; the ones who accomplished it I honor to this day."

The snickers from his crew told her this wasn't an honor one desired.

"Okay." She unbuckled her guns and waited for Mark to step closer, then buckled the belt around him. "Sorry, but if any of you idiots tried to use them we'd all be dead." She snapped the locks and he stepped back. Everyone moved backward in the hold. "Any rules?"

"Well, I'm a pirate so I'd like to think no hitting below the belt, but only you would abide by it so…" He shrugged. "How about no?"

"Fine with me, bitch!" She slammed her right fist into the palm of her left hand. She grinned at the shock on his face when his eyes flicked past her. Glancing back, she saw two of his crew members walking backward into the hold with their hands up in the air and fear in their eyes.

She turned back around. "Well, that was fucking rude."

Ch'urn's eyes narrowed as he returned his gaze to her. "I see. You aren't so stupid to have no one protecting your ship. It looks like it's just you and me, then."

—-

X'ern was a smaller Zhyn, only half the size of the captain, but he was just as Zhyn in his desire to fight as any other. He had one backup member of the crew behind him, H'ick from Engines, who was responsible for getting the other ship away from theirs after he made sure it was under their control. He hadn't gone five feet into the tube when he noticed a human female standing at the other end. "Well, looks like it's just going to be you and me then, baby. I get to have a little fun with ya."

Sabine's voice cut across the distance. "I don't think so. Why don't I just shoot you here?"

"With what, that gun on your leg? I could be across there ravaging your broken jaw with my tool before you can pull it out."

Sabine's eyes narrowed. "I'm not sure if my translation software was right, but if it was even close I will shoot off both your legs at the kneecaps and shove one foot up your ass and one foot into your mouth, you dumbass fuckwit."

X'ern stopped in the middle to allow H'ick to join him. In a moment he would pull H'ick around and use him as protection as he raced the rest of the way across.

He smiled, but his smile was short lived when the second body came into view. His eyes went from the human down to the Noel-ni. "Oh, hello, didn't notice you back there hiding."

"Hello." Ricole's soft voice seemed to grow louder as it traveled down the passageway. "I don't think I misunderstood your conversation at all, Zhyn."

She gazed at her hand, the nails protruding as she turned it first one way, then the other before placing it on her belt right next to her pistol.

Her eyes narrowed and her lips peeled back; she went from cute to dangerous in a moment. "Am I going to eat the brains of a Zhyn in a moment, or are you going to put your hands in the air while you walk backward to your vessel?"

X'ern wanted to spit, but the damned Noel-ni might shoot his eye out for that. He slowly lifted his hands in the air. "Go back, H'ick," he growled. "No one said we had to take on a Noel-ni. I'm not prepared."

"Damn right you aren't." Ricole's hand was outstretched and her pistol was aimed at X'ern's neck. "Keep walking. We wouldn't want any accidents with me pulling the trigger, right?"

H'ick spoke up from behind X'ern. "No ma'am! I'm just the tagalong to check out your engines. If you need to shoot anyone, X'ern is the right one!"

X'ern wanted to kick H'ick but didn't for two reasons. One, X'ern *was* the right one to shoot and two, if he kicked H'ick the damned Noel-ni would probably shoot out his kneecap for unwanted movement.

Damned Noel-ni!

—

Ch'urn noticed that even X'ern was walking backward,

his hands held up. No one showed up from the humans' side, so they weren't leaving their ship.

Fine; he'd do this the easier way. He slammed his fist into his palm in imitation of Jacqueline and stepped forward, his focus now completely on the human female.

Ch'urn reached back with both arms, thrust out his chest, and roared his challenge according to the traditions of his planet. When he was finished, he waited for the human to respond in kind.

He wasn't ready for what happened next.

High Tortuga, Hidden Space Fleet Base, Bethany Anne's Practice Room

The chamber had been hollowed out of the rock, and it was completely lightless. The darkness of space offered more ambient light than there was inside the spherical hold. There was a flat surface that led to a door, but only after the tunnel turned twice.

If a large explosion went off, the turns would prevent most of the damage from going toward the entry.

This had been Bethany Anne's project, and while her request to "build me a round domed room sixty feet tall" had been a bit unique, those who had worked with the woman before had just shrugged and gotten down to doing what she'd asked.

She had told Michael about her project, and he considered it a wise move—get her working on something that might take years to come to fruition.

But she knew it would work, because she knew it was time to push the right buttons.

Bethany Anne left her two guards on the other side of the door before entering and locking it.

She pulled on the Etheric and a red globe appeared in her hand, then stretched her hands apart. The ball increased in size five-fold and the glow softened.

She sent it down the hallway so she could see.

Bethany Anne walked thirty steps and turned the corner, dropping her robe. Walking farther while pushing the globe of light ahead of her, she turned again to head toward the final room a hundred steps away. The hallway was roughhewn, and she ran her hand down the walls, feeling the indentations the machines had left as the cutting tools burrowed into the rock.

No one had come back and smoothed out the stones, which was fine.

The goal of this location wasn't to be pretty; it was supposed to be functional.

Here was her place—her little fortress of solitude—but instead of keeping people out…

It was to keep anything she did in.

"We ready for this, TOM?"

Not exactly, he admitted. **But you aren't really providing me any options.**

"It's time to pay all the back rent for hitching a ride with me," she told him, her voice reverberating off the domed chamber's walls as she strode into the chamber.

The vastness of the chamber swallowed her small light. She concentrated and started throwing red and blue balls up the sides and to the ceiling. As they floated toward their intended destinations they expanded, turning from red or blue to white and providing light throughout the cavern.

At the bottom was a naked woman. She looked down and muttered, "I need a *Gott Verdammt* towel. That rock is going to be cold."

She headed back into the tunnel. "I'll sit on my robe, but someone remind me next time that stone seats suck."

16

Above High Tortuga, Pirate Ship, Second Quadrant, outside Eastern Hemisphere

Jacqueline ducked the first punch and had to roll away from a follow-up kick.

"Damn, you're a fast one for your size," she told him, and dodged the second kick that followed the first.

The captain's fellow pirates were yelling obscenities at her and support for him. Mark just stood there calmly. Jacqueline wasn't sure if he wasn't worried, or was just hiding his concern.

"Just not worried," he said aloud, assuming she could pick out his voice.

"When did you," she jumped over another kick and slapped away a right hook, "start reading minds?"

"I don't," he replied. "Although he is moving you into a corner."

"I see that!" she grumped, accepting a kick so she could

roll out of the trap he had tried to set. Her ribs hurt. "I'm just finding out his strengths and weaknesses."

Jacqueline was back on her feet by the time the captain had turned back. Excluding his first roar, he hadn't been the talkative type so far. Her ribs had already stopped hurting compliments of the nanocytes she had inherited from her father, which had been enhanced by Bethany Anne's technology when Michael brought them aboard.

Some Weres were just Wechselbalg; changers with human and wereanimal forms. However, there was a modification—a code change, really—that the nanocytes could flip on in extreme conditions, and once the switch was flipped the Were could access it when they needed it.

Hers had turned on a few years back when Mark was in trouble with carnivorous Weres. Her concern for her mate's life had brought about her first change, and now he was patiently waiting for her to bring her can of whoop-ass online.

It was time.

—

When Ch'urn kicked out again, the female accepted the kick to her ribs and rode it out of the trap he had been working to get her into. She slammed to the floor of the hold, rolling a couple of times before bouncing up.

He didn't mind. He needed to warm his muscles up anyway. While it might have been nice for his ego to lock her into the corner and beat her to death using the walls as his anvil, finding that she could give him a longer fight was a pleasant surprise.

He cricked his neck as he walked over to where she was

waiting. This time her eyes were flashing yellow. He wasn't sure what that meant, but they were brighter this time.

"Pretty eyes," he remarked. "Sorry you won't be able to use them after this fight. Then again, you probably won't find that too concerning considering the rest of your damage."

"Well," her voice was deeper now, "I think it's time to let you in on one of Mother Nature's little secrets."

That didn't sound ominous or anything, so Ch'urn raised his fist to slam it down on her head.

His fist was stopped in her hand, but not her human hand. This one was large—an animal's hand. Her claws were digging into his skin and his blood was dripping onto the floor.

Her Pricolici face stared down at him; he had to look up to see her now. Then her howl pierced the hold.

She had been playing with him!

—

Mark sighed. "I told them they wouldn't like it if they made you angry, but oh, no. They just had to go and offer you a fight. Well, it's going to fucking suck to be them."

—

X'ern spun toward the hold when he heard the howl and reached for his pistol, but his body jerked twice. He turned his head; both the Noel-ni and the human had their pistols up.

When had the human pulled her gun?

He slammed into the floor, the pain from the bullets finally hitting him.

Why had he gone for his pistol? *Because that was what you did when monsters were near.*

—

When he heard the shots behind him, Mark glanced over his shoulder. One of the pirates lay on the ground with blood streaming out of two holes.

He could have put an old-fashioned half-dollar over the punctures, they were so close together.

—

Ch'urn swung with his left, only to have his fist caught in her other hand, the nails piercing his skin. He grunted as his strength and hers opposed each other. She leaned down and got in his face, her yellow eyes damn near glowing.

"I thinkkkkk youuu neeed to learrrrn to exxssspect thee unnnexsssspppectteed." Then she spread her arms to pull him toward her and slammed her forehead into his.

Most combatants didn't do that with Zhyn, because their ridged and bony heads could mess a fighter's skull up.

Ch'urn stumbled backward, the pain stunning him for a moment. She was shaking her head.

Score one for the Zhyn and their hard heads, he thought. That was when his vision returned, and instead of three of her there was just one in his vision again.

His jaw dropped.

The split on her forehead from his bony ridge was healing right in front of him.

"Oh...*damn*."

—

The pirates licked their lips as they watched the fight, occasionally glancing at the other human.

He seemed supremely confident, barely taking his eyes off them to see what was going on with his partner before returning to his vigil.

X'ern was on the ground behind him, bled out by now. Certainly dead.

He didn't seem to care. He definitely wasn't a normal trade representative. He had obviously been in fights before, and this one wasn't bothering him in the least.

A moment later, H'ick walked backward into the hold, followed by a human and a…

FUCK!

A few in the hold followed J'erlong's gaze to the Noel-ni.

Their despair was palpable. You could kill a Noel-ni, but it was a hundred percent guaranteed that many on your side would die in the attempt. It was rarely worth fighting one of them. Perhaps if she had been the only one to open the doors, Ch'urn would have risked it, but these humans had been smart.

They hadn't shown her until the end.

The trap had been sprung…and the pirates knew they had lost.

—

Sabine hissed to Ricole, "What the hell just happened?"

The Noel-ni was staring at the monster in the middle of the room. "What happened to Jacqueline?"

"Huh?" Sabine flicked her eyes to the fighters. "Oh, she is in her Pricolici form. They must have offered her a chance to fight and Mark gave her the option. He's too nice to her sometimes."

"I heard that!" Mark called, still facing away from them.

"You are!" Sabine argued, "I'm sure you would have preferred to be out there kicking his ass, but Jacqueline flutters her eyelashes and sashays her ass and you are all, 'why sure, you can have this!'"

Mark snickered; she was right.

"She's beautiful," Ricole watched the fight, occasionally glancing around the room. While she hadn't been in many battles, she recognized when the desire to keep fighting had left. These pirates had lost the will to keep going.

"Beautiful?" Sabine looked from Ricole to Jacqueline and back. "Huh. Wouldn't have thought that, but from your perspective she probably just went from a zero to something attractive."

Mark spoke up. "You think maybe you two can hold the fort? I'm going to check the bridge."

"What, you aren't going to watch the end of the fight?" Sabine asked, both of her Jean Dukes in her hands. She strode up next to Mark and winked at the pirate on her left. "Hi, I'm Sabine. I'll be your killer today if you so much as twitch in the wrong direction. Understand?"

He nodded, eyes wide in fear.

H'ick melted into the group of pirates as Ricole holstered her pistol. "Why did Mark leave?"

"Hmm?" Sabine glanced at her. "Hey! Why don't you have your pistol out?"

Ricole smiled, her teeth gleaming, "I'm Noel-ni." Her hand blazed down, returning with the pistol aimed at a pirate across the hold. Sabine noticed that his hands shot up in the air. "Our pistols are *always* ready."

Sabine smiled. "I think you and I are going to be long-term friends, Ricole."

She holstered hers as well and looked around, "Anyone want to try us?"

—

Jacqueline was aware of Mark leaving; it was a bit of a letdown. She rather liked it when he watched her kick ass, but he was right: someone needed to make sure that no one else did something stupid while they were fighting. Sabine was capable, but she didn't get into the technology like Mark did.

She grimaced. He was probably on the bridge stroking a dirty video interface and speaking sweet nothings into the tech-whore's ears right now.

Her eyes flashed yellow as she slapped an incoming punch out of the way and slammed a left into Ch'urn's stomach. His eyes bulged just a bit, and she followed it with a right hook across his chin, leaving a two-inch gash where she cut his skin.

She didn't use claws. Peter's comment about, "We can get intelligence out of living pirates. If you bring me dead ones we can't get shit!" still rang in her ears.

She was a fighter and she didn't fear battle, but she didn't need an ass-whipping from Peter to remind her that he wanted the pirates, and especially the captain, alive.

Time to end it.

She grabbed Ch'urn's arm and twisted and he screamed in pain. She whipped her left leg around and slammed her foot into the left side of his skull. She kept hold of his arm as he tumbled and it ripped out of its socket.

He didn't scream this time. His head had connected with the floor; he was out.

DAMN! She bent down, worried she had killed him.

He moaned…

THANK GOD!

She nodded to Sabine and headed toward the bridge in her Pricolici form. If Mark was stroking any technology, she would tear apart both the bridge and Mark's ass.

She was a jealous bitch; he'd known that when he fell in love with her.

High Tortuga, Hidden Space Fleet Base, the Queen's R&D Lab

Bethany Anne made her robe into a small pillow and put it on the ground, then sat down cross-legged and rested her hands on her knees.

Please tell me, TOM commented, **you aren't trying to do a yoga pose?**

Nope, Bethany Anne answered. ***I'm trying to find a position I can handle for a few hours. I suspect I'm going to lose track of time...so ADAM?***

>>Yes?<<

Make sure everyone stays out, and figure out a way to interrupt me if they need me. Tell Michael I'm working in my lab.

>>He is asking where your lab is. I'll leave out the other comments about too many burrows in this ants' nest.<<

R&D section. Let him know you will update him every couple of hours, but expect me to be... TOM?

What?

How long will I be out?

I'm supposed to know this how? You have done most of your learning on your own.

That's because you weren't forthcoming with the information in the past.

I wouldn't be now either, but you are pushing the issue.

TOM, I can't help protect when I'm not safe.

You have some of the most advanced armor—

Which you and I both know can be destroyed, even if it can take a lot of damage. Plus, what good would it do if I was able to step into the Etheric but not take my people with me?

You can.

Only if they are near me. I need to be able to do more, and I've got the feeling that you haven't been very informative.

You are young, TOM told her.

Not anymore. We humans grow up fast, and it's time to agree—or disagree—that I protected the Earth as well as I could.

>>Do you believe that?<< ADAM cut in.

I'm...at peace. Bethany Anne sighed. *Some things I can't change, and humanity being themselves is one of them. I don't have to like what happened or ignore the tears, but I can work to provide options for the those left on the planet. But I don't think I can do that without understanding the Etheric better. And to do* that, *I have to practice, and to practice I have to understand the basics.*

The basics. TOM thought for a moment before sending a mental sigh. **That is a tall order. It will take years, or even decades.**

What else am I going to do, TOM? I've got a child to raise, a husband to ravish, a world to rebuild, and a bunch of fucking Kurtherians to hunt down and kill. I might as well

add learning all about the Etheric to the mix. Just make sure I don't do anything dangerous while I'm pregnant.

There is no way for me to know if what you are trying to do will hurt your child, but I won't allow you to run any more risk than you already do in your normal Etheric efforts.

Well...damn. She thought about her trips through the Etheric as well as her efforts to pull in Etheric energy to make the little light balls. ***What about what I have done so far?***

Unlikely to have increased the risk to the child beyond that of your constant Etheric connection. Before you go down that path, I believe all human females do things which could hurt their child's gestation.

Bethany Anne blew out a breath. ***Okay, you're right. I need to drop it since there isn't anything I can do about it right now anyway.***

TOM's voice changed when he went from casual conversation to explaining as if from a dais. Bethany Anne had understood his people had a religious connection to the other dimension, but to hear him sound reverent was a new experience.

The Etheric, he began, **is both right next to us and far away. It represents the space between two fingers pressed together, and the infinite width of the universe. It is, in one form or fashion, what was at the beginning and which created all life, and yet holds within it the destruction of the future.**

Not like that doesn't sound ominous, Bethany Anne quipped. When TOM didn't respond, she apologized out loud. "I'm sorry."

TOM went on, ignoring her outburst. **You have touched the energy of the Etheric and gained the ability to move within it, and you can step from this dimension to that one. Most beings cannot accomplish this without their physical body dying.**

Was that what did you for Glorious Pain in the Ass?

If you would allow, I will answer that question later.

Of course. Bethany Anne chastised herself. She needed to allow Tom to express what the Etheric was without her constant interruptions. It had been a long time since she had been a simple student and her anxiety was acting up.

It is a little bit more difficult to express the Etheric to you since you have such a variety of experiences with it already. You will undoubtedly take the instructions I am giving you and try to fit them into the box of your experience. That may help you in the short term, but will hold you back from understanding the full truth in the long run.

TOM waited a moment for Bethany Anne to interrupt with another question…and was pleasantly surprised when she stayed quiet.

He continued, **The Etheric can be molded to your reality, and you can move that reality from there to your present dimension.** TOM stopped. **You can ask questions.**

Okay. Bethany Anne struggled to refine her question. ***Is this what I am doing with the energy balls? Am I imagining the ability to coalesce spheres of energy and manipulate them? Pulling dangerous orbs of power into our dimension from the Etheric?***

That is a good way to explain it, yes.

So if I wanted to create a fully-formed battleship, for example, I could accomplish that as well?

Technically? Nothing in my understanding of the Etheric would forbid it, but I don't know of anything so complex ever being accomplished, and I have examples going back hundreds of millennia.

What would it take to accomplish something so large?

TOM chuckled. **If you had but the faith of a mustard seed...**

17

High Tortuga, Hidden Space Fleet Base, the Pit, Eight Weeks Later

Addix entered the Pit and looked around the darkened room. The video wall was dimmed at the moment. She found Bethany Anne speaking to one of the many analysts at a desk on the second level.

She made her way to Bethany Anne, listening as she finished her conversation.

"No," Bethany Anne told the analyst, "I *don't* want to handle this. Push your intelligence to the local police force; provide them with everything we know. Make sure the leader knows we will wait for his or her response and their results. If we hear nothing in…" Bethany Anne paused for a moment, clearly thinking through what it might take to solve this case, "three days we will reach back out for further information."

Bethany Anne turned to Addix, her belly larger than when the Ixtali had seen her last time. "Good morning."

"Good morning."

Bethany Anne gestured for Addix to follow her as she moved to the large table in the middle of the floor. "What's up?"

"Some of our external resources have been hearing rumors of a fleet being put together—for what purpose, no one knows yet. However, we *can* confirm that mercs are involved, and some with Navy fighting skills have shipped out and aren't showing back up at other ports we have under surveillance."

"And you think this is going to be aimed at us?"

"I cannot say," Addix replied. "My staff is aware of three different conflagrations which could reasonably cause one of the combatants to arm themselves in this way. However, we have decent access to resources and we have no indication that any of the six are building a Navy fleet."

Bethany Anne snorted. "Navy?"

"I am not trying to quantify the quality, merely point out that we might have a fleet visiting us in the near future."

Bethany Anne frowned. "If someone comes at us we are going to have to destroy them totally—or fight with less support than we actually have. Knowledge of full strength cannot get back to anyone else, *period*." Her lips pressed together as she looked at Addix. "We don't know who is after us yet?"

"No," she admitted. "So far there have been too many cutouts, often ending in death at many of the junctures. Even the pirates we have captured have nothing in their databanks which would suggest a connection to potential enemies."

Bethany sighed. "Translation, 'we don't know shit.'"

"Yes."

"Any idea how likely an attack is within the next few days?"

"Unlikely. I believe they are still recruiting at this time, so at best we are talking about a couple of weeks."

Bethany Anne chewed her lip. "I will get with the Admiral for practical dispersion of our ships. I don't want to have them sitting up there with their thumbs up their asses for no good reason. See what you can find to narrow down a potential time of engagement and I will take care of the rest. Unfortunately," her eyes were hard, "if they attack us, we can leave no survivors."

"Understood." Addix turned to leave.

ADAM?

>>You want Admiral Thomas?<<

Yes. Tell him his retirement has just been cut short. Plan a meeting for this afternoon at four after the MPPS education meeting. In fact, ask him to join us for those discussions. I'll have snacks.

>>He is in Thon now. He will be back in time, he says.<<

Good. When she looked around the room one of the analysts, Charles, had his head up and was looking at her. "You just got voted in, Charles."

"Um, 'voted in?'" he asked. "For what?"

She smiled. 'I'm hungry. What do we have that can be brought in?"

—

Bethany Anne was sitting at the table and nursing her mocha after lunch. Admiral Thomas, the man who had been responsible for running the fleets of the Etheric Empire, was chatting with Stephen on her right. Michael's seat next to her was empty, and Addix and Peter were at the table as well.

Michael appeared out of thin air—or more accurately out of the Etheric—but to most it looked like he just materialized. "Sorry." He glanced at a clock on the far wall. "Oh, I'm actually early."

"If you count fifteen seconds as early," Thomas grumped.

Michael sat down. "Of course I do," he replied. "I'm not fond of being late." He reached over and touched her arm. "Education?"

"Yes," she admitted. "I asked Peter here because he might remember his wild days back on Earth. I want to discuss a few of my thoughts, and concepts, then I will go off and talk with more of the experts." She nodded to her right. "Stephen will represent business interests and the Admiral will represent the military. Peter will speak for the young even though he is over a hundred and seventy now himself, and Addix will represent those providing knowledge."

"And me?" Michael asked. He seemed neither pleased nor upset with being part of this.

"Accumulated knowledge," she replied.

Planet Soboth (Previously Territory 7732), Undisclosed location, Open Out-ring, Non-Federation

Az pushed his normal work aside and lifted a tablet he had been carrying lately. With no one present in his office, he touched the button and allowed the tablet to scan his eyes.

The security screen closed.

He glanced through the notes and messages, nodding his head at each. He stopped on one, frowned before leaning forward and punching a button on his desktop.

"Uleq here."

"Uleq, Az." He glanced down at this tablet. "I want you to have our military supply group on Goptek Minor close up Warehouse 19 and clean out all other warehouses. Have them leave 19 alone before they ship everything to Goptek Major, and support that location for a year. We aren't seeing enough value from two separate staging areas."

"They won't be able to accomplish this project for at least a week. There are about twenty-five warehouses full of product there, plus I'll have to move two ships over to Minor. Do you approve these expenses?"

"Of course," Az replied. "That's the purpose long-term: reduce expenses."

"Understood. Talk later." Uleq closed the connection.

Az nodded and leaned back. He sent the coordinates of the missiles to his contact and told him it would be about a week before the cargo would be available.

—

Uleq severed the communication before pulling up the necessary contacts to implement the request. He checked the manifest of the warehouses in general and 19 in particular.

Food.

Specifically, canned food and foodstuffs. He shrugged. He wasn't sure why Az didn't want the food moved, but it could be he knew of a project or potential order coming. It wasn't until he had sent all the commands "Per CEO Az" that he noticed that Warehouse Twenty-Seven, which was right next to 19, had missiles on the manifest.

High Tortuga, Hidden Space Fleet Base, the Pit, a Few Weeks Later

Bethany Anne outlined her plan. "Here is the basic premise: a world, nation, or community needs to have an educated populace. Education provides a common foundation for a trained workforce and a literate voting block who can have informed opinions, a method of explaining the basics of living with others harmoniously, and a stable tax base. The less educated will not hold the higher-paying positions, and therefore won't provide well for their families or the help community by creating jobs or pay taxes on their income."

"So…" She touched an icon on her screen and the inset video screens in front of everyone at the table and two screens on the video wall displayed what she was looking at so those working in the Pit could follow along. "The common foundations are usually linguistics, the objective sciences, common history and perhaps religious concepts the nation or nation-states require. The idea is that no matter the area of the country or how rich or poor, if someone is going to go into higher education the colleges and universities have some basic understanding of what an incoming student will know so they can base their classes on that."

She nodded to Peter. "Now we get to the other side of

the challenge. You will have children who have no desire to go through a foundational program since their wants, needs, and curiosity diverge from what society wants them to know. There are usually two ways they get their knowledge. One is expository, related to shoving information into a brain, and the other is experiential. Think of it as reading about trees versus going on a field trip to see trees up close and running one's hand over the bark."

She smiled. "The better of those methods, *experiential,* is often too hard to manage with many children."

The images on the screens changed. "Further, the old classroom paradigm had already failed in the United States on many levels. Other countries had easily created programs which enhanced the prestige but not necessarily the income of teachers. Mind you, those teachers in other countries still made the country's average salary until they were years into in their career, but they were actively recruited from the top quarter of students and trained in a demanding way so citizens knew teaching was difficult."

She tapped the icon to change the slide. "I'm not going to let higher education off the hook, either. One of the great errors of an elite education in the United States was that it taught those attending to think that intelligence and academic achievement were measures of value in some moral or metaphysical sense, equating their value with their education. Further, there are many types of intelligence, but the ones supported were academic in scope. There was little understanding of the value of social, emotional, and artistic intelligence. Those who had intellectual intelligence promulgated their type at the expense of others."

The slide changed. "Basically, what we see played out is the needs of the family, the community, the state, the nation, the world, and humanity in general arrayed against personal needs and desires natural to individuals seeking to get ahead for themselves or their families or their beliefs or groups they belong to. Some students, for reasons of curiosity, maturity, or family dynamics, were held back from achieving their education faster by the constraints of the system."

"Mass manufacturing of an educated class," Stephen remarked.

Bethany Anne nodded.

She tapped the screen and the image changed to a person wearing a simulation headset. "We now have a different methodology, including the opportunity for students to take classes at their own pace and for creating learning-pod groups of five students supporting each other to help each other get ahead. Those learning in certain areas can teach a concept to others, choosing how they teach. We had one student two years ago on the *Meredith Reynolds* who used songs to teach a semester of history. Not only did her pod *ace* the examinations, their resultant recording became a hit on the live-theater-adaptation circuit. Now there are other students doing this with popular and semi-popular music styles."

The image changed again. "Teachers function as guides to allow the students opportunities to locate information. Practical and impractical requests are made of the pods, and they are ranked against each other in different areas. There is interaction at a one-on-one level, and social issues are rapidly addressed. EIs are in place to facilitate some level of privacy but reveal potential issues with students. Some naturally aggressive individuals, whether for reasons of chemical imbalances due to their physiology or just plain natural selection, are offered ways to work out that aggression. Likewise, those who wish to focus on one area are encouraged to earn time in that area by excelling in tangential but necessary areas of knowledge."

"Carrot and stick?" the Admiral asked.

"Yes," Bethany Anne replied. "I instituted a payment system for the children. If the parents weren't involved enough, we billed the costs of teaching the child up to minimum standards to them, with notification that there was inadequacy on the parents' part. Once the child was old enough, they were provided treats if they got ahead of schedule, or they would receive penalties if they just did the minimum required. There are always choices in life, and there are always repercussions. That is a basic training maxim that was wiped out in many schools. We taught them not to touch a hot pan when they were two, but we didn't teach them to fear the future enough to continue their education."

Bethany Anne sat back. "Some countries—Germany was a leader, but many of the European countries did the same—pushed a career or vocational track in their school systems. It helped their younger students gain employment and higher-paying jobs at a better rate than many of their contemporaries. Unfortunately, if one studied the system over a few decades, it was the general education group who were ahead by their forties. In my opinion, what we need is a vocational track for early adult—whatever jobs interest them—and a general education track later so that they can keep up with skills and know how to learn should their professions become obsolete."

"You could always," Michael pointed out, "require service in exchange for government support."

Bethany Anne turned to him. "Like what?"

"Let me ask you this first." He pushed his tablet to the side. "What is the value of an hour's worth of, say, a social scientist's time versus someone who works the fields pulling peas?"

"It's the effort," Admiral Thomas answered, "of the social scientist to learn what they know to be able to give you an hour's worth of their expertise. For those pulling peas, it's the effort of standing in the hot sun and doing back-breaking work."

"Who appreciates the peas more?" Michael asked.

"Well, typically those who pulled the crops ended up hating them," Thomas answered. "Hell, I know *I* did. My grandparents had green bean fields. Looking back at it as an adult the rows probably weren't more than a hundred feet long, but as a kid, they looked like a mile."

"Okay," Michael continued. Those at the table looked from one to the other as they worked on the problem. "But we have EI support. Most of the true effort is in the ability to put two different and possibly unrelated pieces of information together to work the problem. The creatives might become the new power brokers because their minds work differently—those who love to read all sorts of material."

"Even fiction?" Stephen asked, thinking back to the comment about the military using science-fiction writers.

Michael raised an eyebrow. "Perhaps even fiction; I don't wish to guess. My point is, throughout my life, using skills or talents or a person's raw physical power to help them rise to the top of their society came and went. In the beginning, it was the strength in their arms to swing their swords. Then the tongue to sway large groups to accomplish something together. It became those who developed the sciences, and then—to a degree—it was those again who had physical prowess and could run or shoot a ball into a hoop. Yet, it was those who produced the food, built the homes, protected society, or taught the children or young adults who often weren't supported. They would do their jobs, punch their time cards, and do what needed to get done to keep society going. My suggestion is to consider all work—if done well—equal. Government needs to be in place, but we'll require some form of service as your debt to society. Perhaps you are a musician but can test into working with an R&D lab in the future. Can that be your service?"

"That," Bethany Anne replied, "could be a nightmare. Just think about the ongoing effort for some of Jean Dukes' stuff. There's no way we could place a person into a project for two weeks and then they leave."

Michael tapped a finger on the table. "I understand. However, let me give you a quote from a worker to Jack Welch."

"Who?" Peter interrupted.

Stephen answered, "Jack Welch. He was the CEO of General Electric—GE—back on Earth in the twentieth century."

Michael continued, "He was talking to the assembly line workers at one of their businesses and one of the men spoke up, telling Welch that 'for twenty-five years you paid for my hands when you could have had my brain as well for nothing.'"

The table was quiet a moment, thinking about that.

Peter was the first to break it. "Makes sense. We use that concept in the Guardians all the time. Everyone has a role to play, but if you have ideas you need to speak up."

"It would," Addix added, "allow those interacting to bring new ways of thinking to perhaps old and worn-out strategies."

"What about those who truly hated the notion?" Stephen asked. "I can think of a few."

"I'm tempted to say 'fuck 'em.'" Bethany Anne snorted. "However, I know people, and they might fuck up the works. What about a ten-percent charge of their annual wealth if they wish to forego service?"

"Two weeks," Michael interjected, "is at best four percent of their time."

"Right," Bethany Anne agreed, "so *I'd* suggest they do the two weeks. But if they want to they can lose ten percent of their annual wealth—which is *not* their annual income, because that shit can be hidden."

The Admiral asked, "So a billionaire who technically made nothing during the year would owe a hundred million to get out of two weeks' service?"

"Right," Bethany Anne agreed. "And someone with fifty thousand owes five thousand."

"Where does the money go?" Peter asked.

Admiral Thomas grinned. "I suggest the military."

"Education?" Peter asked. "It's just a suggestion, because that is what we are talking about."

Stephen scratched his chin. "I can imagine large corporations putting income packages together for their upper-level executives to pay for this."

"I suggest," Bethany Anne added, "putting the names of those who opt out on a public list so everyone knows who isn't working."

"What about sickness, or a family illness they need to deal with?" Stephen countered.

"With Pod-docs we shouldn't have that issue, but there would have to be some sort of schedule. Further, we will always have public projects. There are always roads to be built, gardens to be tended, or military camps where one can refresh one's skills in case of war."

Admiral Thomas opened his mouth, then turned to Peter. "Actually, I kind of like that."

"Me, too," Peter agreed and turned back to Bethany Anne, "Couldn't we have multiple camps of that type?"

"Like what?" she asked.

"Well, maybe emergency services? People prepared to go help in case of natural disasters, or places where if they know enough they could help teach, right?"

Bethany Anne scratched her head, "I'm not saying no to this idea, but we would have to work out the details."

Peter shrugged.

"Okay." She tapped the button for the next screen. "I'd like to open up discussion on how to pay for education."

18

High Tortuga, Hidden Space Fleet Base, The Pit, One Week Later

Bethany Anne pointed to the screen flashing red up on the wall. "Terry, pull up that location, confirm the information with the local authorities, and send in a small squad of Guardians. Tell the police to hold back if anyone is local to the area until the Guardians arrive."

A minute later Terry, a blonde with brown eyes and a serious demeanor, called back to Bethany Anne from her second-tier location, "I've got confirmation from the local police that they will hold back, but they want to know why you have Guardians helping stop a bank heist?"

Bethany Anne grumped, "Because my group is a well-organized tac team and theirs often have their thumbs up their butt?"

"Ma'am?"

"No!" Bethany Anne shrugged. "Sorry. Because that's my bank and I'm sending in official support. I don't want casualties or a long standoff. I want this done quietly and efficiently."

—

That is a go, Tac Team 01. Queen Bethany Anne says to neutralize the threat. There are three tangos, two in the main bank lobby, one in the bank trying to open a lockbox. Arrive on top of bank, drop down from roof...

"Understood, Pit," Guardian Watson Stewart replied. "ETA thirty seconds." He clicked off his mic. The Black Eagle had been holding position ten miles out, hanging in the upper atmosphere. That way they could dart to where they were needed.

"Turn and burn?" his partner, Guardian Jesse Verette, asked as he pulled his pistol and checked it before sliding back into his holster.

"Nope," Watson answered. The Black Eagle, an anti-gravity-driven two-person attack ship, sliced through the air towards the second smaller upthrust of skyscrapers into the sky. "Drop and stop." He checked the countdown on the timer, then his pistol. "Three tangos, two using the customers as hostages and one trying to get into a locked safe deposit box in the vault."

"Wonder what they're up to?" Jesse mused as a green square popped up on the outer screen, highlighting an eight-story building in the distance.

Watson changed the arrival parameters. "I'm taking us in hot, so make sure you have your suit set appropriately.

"Oh, fucking hell!" Jesse slammed his helmet on his head and then started confirming that his suit was properly set up for a hot arrival. Watson put on his helmet and confirmed his settings as well.

A moment later, Jesse could hear Watson's voice over the comm. "You got me?"

"Five by five," Jesse replied.

"Then you might want to unbuckle…"

"Shit!" Jesse slapped the buckle on his chest, and two seconds later their Black Eagle flipped upside down and the cockpit opened. The two Guardians ejected via gravity.

Jesse's HUD highlighted a black building, and the square on the ground was what they were heading towards. They had ejected half a mile up, and the maneuvering capabilities on their suits were pretty good. They could move in any direction while gravity pulled them towards the ground. At ten stories the antigrav kicked in and Jesse grunted. "DAAAAAMMMNN!"

Both men went from freefall to boots-down, touching down with the same sound as someone having jumped up and landed again. Both men checked the heat signatures inside the building with the thermal readers in their helmets.

There was a police vehicle there, doors open, and two officers pushing people back from the bank entrance. He looked over his shoulder and saw the two humans enclosed in advanced armor, then turned back around and pushed away the bystanders.

Two of those inside were walking back and forth and there were several warm bodies on the floor—although one of those was quickly cooling.

"Fuckers!" Watson pulled his pistol. "Prepare to enter on my mark."

Jesse drew his pistol as he scanned the layout of the

bank the Pit had sent him. He jogged over to the other side of the bank's doors and nodded.

"GO!" Watson pulled his pistols' triggers twice and the hyper-velocity rounds splattered both thieves' heads, their blood spraying back towards the wall before the sound of the windows shattering caught anyone's attention.

Jesse shot the window just before his enhanced jump took him through it. His right hand was up, so when the third thief came running out of the vault with his pistol raised he shot him in the head, dropping him immediately.

The man's finger didn't even pull the trigger of his gun.

A moment later Jesse reached down and pressed a finger against the neck of the alien, which looked like a cross between a human and a squid. "Clear!"

Watson replied, "Clear!"

Jesse's lead checked on the wounded man on the floor, but shook his head and stood up. Both dropped their pistols back in their holsters and locked them. "Would everyone please calmly stand up," Watson requested. "And move to the side. The police officers will be in momentarily."

<u>High Tortuga, Hidden Space Fleet Base, the Pit</u>

"Well," Terry said glumly as everyone in the Pit watched the video screen of the takedown, "I don't think we'll get any intel out of those guys."

Bethany Anne, her hand over her protruding stomach, sighed. "Not much of an option. His gun was aimed at the hostages, so they had to go for the kill shot." She leaned over and pressed a button. "Watson, this is Bethany Anne."

"Yes, ma'am?" was his reply. She saw his armored figure turn slightly before he realized she was speaking through his helmet.

"Work with the police. I want to know what they were trying to steal. Get a judge—someone—to give us permission to find out what's in that safety deposit box."

"I'll do my best," Watson replied.

"All I can ask," Bethany Anne agreed. "Out."

"Do you think," Terry asked, "this has something to do with those who attacked us?"

Bethany Anne, her eyes still on the video intake from the bank, shook her head. "I've got no idea."

High Tortuga, Hidden Space Fleet Base, Pit

Addix walked down the steps to the bottom level, where Bethany Anne was working at the table. She looked up and kicked a chair out for Addix to sit down.

"Thank you," Addix responded, accepting the chair.

"It's time?" Bethany Anne asked. "I don't want them up there *too* long, but it sure beats not being in space when needed."

"I think so," Addix agreed. "I've spoken with Admiral Thomas. He says tomorrow night is good to take the ships out anyway. I've gotten feedback from assets on Goptek Major, who say that pirates from their sister planet, Goptek Minor, raided a warehouse owned by an interstellar conglomerate. They had expected canned foodstuffs and got a warehouse full of missiles."

"What kind?"

"Leath Punchers."

Bethany Anne's eyes narrowed, "What are those?"

"They are space-platform-based missiles that are pre-programmed to hit hardened locations on planets. Get into a system, fire them off, and either follow them in or leave. If the planet has weapons systems, there is a chance of knocking them out of space or air."

Bethany Anne thought for a moment. "ADAM?"

"Yes?" the AI replied.

"How has the game for the BYPS system worked?"

"We have initialized repositioning of the outer defense system. One player was able to get ninety-seven-percent coverage of the planet with our present deployment, but it will take another week to move them into that configuration."

Bethany Anne turned to Addix. "Worst case scenario?"

"Forty-eight hours from Goptek Minor straight to here. Assume they had to meet a larger fleet somewhere…that grants us twelve more hours. They will have to go through three Gates to get here in that time. Those are the only ones that won't announce who is traveling through them—privacy concerns and all that."

"Privacy." Bethany Anne sighed. "Absolutely the right thing to do, until it's *your* ass hanging in the wind."

She pulled up the specifications on the Puncher missile. "Shit!" She hit two more buttons. "I'm going to have to put a superdreadnought above us for protection."

"That will blow our cover," Addix warned. "The only ones everyone knows about are *ArchAngel II* and *Prime*."

The wall of monitors in the Pit blanked, then one large face covered the screens. Archangel II, using her avatar of Bethany Anne's face, looked at everyone in the Pit.

"Hello, ArchAngel." Bethany Anne smiled at the ship's avatar. "I assume you have something to say?"

"Yes. I will be the one who protects you." Her eyes showed just a hint of red. "No other dreadnought has my experience."

Bethany Anne sighed. "ArchAngel, who can fight a battle in space better than you? But what if they come with ten ships, or fifty, or a hundred?"

ArchAngel was quiet. Bethany Anne turned to Addix. "Ok, while she runs a few million war simulations until she figures out I'm right, update Admiral Thomas and get him the best info you have. Give him your guesses, too."

Addix started to speak. "I—"

Bethany Anne stopped her, "I know you hate guesses. But we need them, so do it." Bethany Anne thought for a moment. "Are you needed here…on this planet?"

"I will not leave with a battle coming at us," Addix replied, affronted.

"I'm not suggesting you should," Bethany Anne told her. "I'm thinking this pirate attack is what we need to track down our attackers."

"What about any new intel from the pirates?" Addix asked.

"Do you think they will have any more information than those you have spoken with so far? Basically they have a communication-drop folder that we can't trace, and commands come to it. They get paid. They sell their stolen merchandise through cutouts. It's smart, it's large, and it's well-protected, but the warehouse raid may be a thread that can be unraveled. If it helps," Bethany Anne smiled, "I think you will have killers after you."

Addix chuckled. "Yes, I will have a heightened opportunity for death. So you want *me* to track this down instead of my people?"

"That's right." Bethany Anne nodded. "We've lost one or two of our agents so far?"

"One. The other was placed in a medical unit quickly enough, but until we can get him into a Pod-doc," she shook her head, "we won't be able to help him. He is in stasis."

"Right. We will deal with this attack, assuming it comes. However, I want you out there trying to figure out who this is so that when I have a target, I can bring the pain."

Addix stood up. "I'll work with Admiral Thomas, and then I'll leave on *The Lady Princess*."

Bethany Anne nodded. "That will work. Just remember that our Gate-capable ships can and will self-destruct if they are caught. That technology cannot fall into the wrong hands."

"Understood." Addix turned to go but paused. "Bethany Anne?"

Bethany Anne looked up from the screen she was reading. "Hmm?"

"When you pulled me off my planet and offered to do the rejuvenation and upgrades," she waved a clawed hand up and down her body, "did you think you would put me out in the field again?"

Bethany Anne shook her head. "Not at that time. I expected you to run everything from this planet. When you and I talked, I could feel your love of the field—of occasionally *testing* yourself against others— and that is when I decided to upgrade you as much as I did. Remember," Bethany Anne tapped the side of her head, "I've been in your mind. I know you, and I know your spirit. You are in this with me all the way, so should anyone try to take you out?"

Addix's chuckle was malevolent. "I won't eat their brain, I promise."

With that, she turned and left the Pit.

High Tortuga, Hidden Space Fleet *Base,* The Pit, Twenty-Four Hours Later

Bethany Anne was sitting at her conference table with Admiral Thomas, Stephen, and Peter again, and this time Jean Dukes and John Grimes joined them.

Gabrielle was out on a mission, or she would have been there as well.

"Okay." She rapped her knuckles on the table. "As I explained, these are exploratory talks only. I am trying to figure out if MPPS is even a possibility, or a concept so antithetical that we should just can it and hope for the best." She glanced around the table. "The topic for today is Defense." She looked at Admiral Thomas. "Considering you have to be out there in six hours, you're up."

He looked at her funny.

"What?" she asked. "I told you…if you happen to die out there, I want what's in your brain right now before it gets wasted. Can't have all of that wisdom lost to me."

Admiral Thomas chuckled. "Anyone tell you that you can be a cold-hearted bitch?"

"Of course. I think *you* did, just last week."

"Well, I was right." He nodded. "But I'll take it as a

compliment." He straightened in his chair, clasping his hands in front of him. "What Bethany Anne wants is a world where people are allowed to be the best they can be. Should they choose to act in a way that isn't good for society they will be allowed to leave, or offered reduced options until they choose by their actions to leave this mortal coil."

He glanced around. "The only way that those on a planet are going to be allowed to enjoy this freedom is if they do not have to worry about external threats, so the defense of the planet was my homework. Since we could be attacked within a few days, it may be a pass-fail effort."

He and the others chuckled. "I'm sure if one of those Leath Punchers hits this area, it'll be considered a fail."

"Got that right," Bethany Anne agreed.

"So, how do we create a society which supports individual freedom from antagonism, which by definition means the society deplores violence, and yet create a military?"

"I wouldn't suggest the Kurtherian method," Stephen interjected. "Messing with the DNA to take out the violent tendencies backfires."

"True," Thomas agreed. "At some point, the pacifists have to grow a spine and fight when they aren't prepared to do it at all. So, five clans who don't know how to fight now have to take on seven clans who love it."

John spoke up. "We could always go find a species that hasn't lost their barbaric ways…" He rubbed his chin. "Wait, that sounds like what we are doing right now."

Nice. Real nice. TOM sent to Bethany Anne. **Accurate, but not so funny if you belong to one of the five clans.**

Leave him be, Bethany Anne chided her Kurtherian tag-a-long. ***He might be joking, but it IS a viable strategy. And if we hadn't seen your people's example, we might have gone that direction as well. There were plenty of DNA studies in progress on Earth when we left. I imagine we probably would have tried eradicating people's violent tendencies soon enough. Imagine our surprise when another species attacked us? All of our science-fiction would have been proven right, and those scientists who argued that no species which could conquer space would be violent would be very wrong.***

Reminds me of that movie.

Independence Day; we've spoken about it before.

Kinda funny, TOM mused. **The aliens actually remind me of a race called the K'rillick, except they were peaceful.**

What happened to them?

Destroyed by the T'sehmion Clan using a species of omnivores called Bok that looked like a cross between Earth panda bears and Yollins. The Bok found out that the K'rillick tasted good if you steamed them.

That's...just gross. Bethany Anne returned her attention to the conversation. With her ability to accelerate to enhanced speeds, she could carry conversations with ADAM and TOM in between the words when others spoke.

John continued, "All joking aside, and I apologize to TOM if he is listening..." He glanced at Bethany Anne, who nodded her head. "But we have a real problem. We don't want to outsource our defense, but the genes that support a people willing to do violence unto others are the same ones that make them willing to do violence unto their own people."

And even if you think, TOM added, **that taking out the violent gene would fix that risk, remember that Mother Nature has a way of biting you in the ass for fucking with her.**

19

Four hours outside Goptek Major, *The Lady Princess*

Bethany Anne had once had a ship called the *Scamp Princess.* It was used for many decades after Bethany Anne stopped using it, and it was based in the Federation for secret missions.

After the Etheric Empire defeated the Leath many of their companies branched out, opening trade and other business ventures—including trading in their advanced weapons.

The Lady Princess was a Leath-designed small cargo ship that looked like a private yacht. There were a few of them running around space, so it wasn't unique.

Except for all the Empire's technology inside, including the EI Lady Princess.

"We will be ready to land in three hours," the EI announced.

"Thank you, I'm getting dressed," Addix replied, moving from the tiny bridge to her personal suite. The ship could, in fact, run cargo—about four pallets' worth. However, most of the space was artfully used for the Gate engines that allowed it to bypass commercial Gates.

Addix placed the first of her four legs into the special armor her Queen had ordered built just for her, quickly followed by the other three.

It was a luxurious feeling once the metal locked in place. Pliable as cloth yet as silent as walking without shoes, it allowed her full mobility. Her four legs were more arachnid under her robes than like a human's. She checked that her spy supplies were in the pouches to either side and locked down her knives and her four pistols.

Her guns were unique. Just being Jean Dukes made them rare, but these were the only ones in existence that had been designed for an Ixtali.

Because Addix was the only Ixtali Bethany Anne had ever trusted.

For an Ixtali, Addix was beyond old. She had been ready to go and live on a farm on her planet; give up the politics she had worked in for so long, trying to keep her people from reverting to their old ways.

Ways which would have caused wars in the future.

She had already outlived her family and friends, and she said her goodbyes to their graves in her heart. She left with the then-Empress on her last trip to her planet and never looked back.

Now her body was young again, since she had been enhanced. She had speed, strength, and dexterity far beyond what she had ever personally possessed, and more than any other Ixtali'd had either.

She put on her chest piece and three-quarter sleeves

and locked them down. She always wore robes in public and didn't want anyone to see her armor if her sleeves went too far up her arms.

She wasn't taking a helmet, so she had better not try to stop a bullet with her mandibles.

She pulled her robe over her head, hiding everything she wore beneath it, and admired herself in the mirror. Her mandibles tapped together gently in appreciation.

What were those things Eric and Scott read? Bomic cooks? No, *comic books*. She was a true black widow.

She liked the character, but the pretty human—if pretty she was, since Addix couldn't tell—didn't look like the name at all. She had looked up the Earth insect and liked the red hourglass on its abdomen.

If there was ever a being who truly looked like the Black Widow character more than she did, she wasn't sure who it might be. Those human females who had played the part had known nothing about being an interstellar spy.

It was time to show those bitches what being a black widow really meant.

Goptek Major, Principal Starport

"Lock down the ship," Addix announced as she hit the button to open the door. She had already checked the outside video, which was clear.

A moment later she stepped out into a maelstrom of activity. She was parked on a secondary landing pad. For security she had rented the eight spaces around her ship and posted a warning sign that the ship was armed and dangerous to those who might try to hijack it.

The Goptek System treated idiots as vermin they wished to get rid of. If you put up a warning sign and then followed through on your warning and killed interlopers? Well, so long as you weren't unlawful in protecting your valuables, you were okay. Since Goptek Major's fine for a death was the equivalent to the cost of lunch at a major restaurant, the value of the ship was unquestionably high enough to warrant a death threat.

She chuckled; her ride would be here when she got back.

It took her three hours to find two employees who worked for the KGB Corporation and had helped move their materials. She bought them drinks, speaking about her own background as a young politician, and that she had decided politics were for the older people and come out to seek her fortune.

They had laughed. An Ixtali not in the secrets business?

"I'm not into secrets," she argued, slurring her words. Her side mandibles failed to touch each other when she moved them.

In other words, she was stinking drunk.

"Sure, sure!" P'rok laughed. He was pretty soused himself. He beat his buddy's arm. "An Ixtali not into secrets!" They laughed along with her.

"It's not like…" She paused. "It's not like you two would have secrets." She stopped, eyes open. "I'm sorry, that was ruuuuuude. I'm sure you have lots of secrets, but none that I would… I would…would want," she finished, obviously pleased with herself.

P'rok leaned forward. "I got a secret I could sell." He winked, jerking his head toward his partner. "He hasn't had sex in three years, but brags he is getting some every weekend!"

Addix and P'rok laughed, but G'het didn't find it so funny. "Shut your mouth!" he snapped. "My sex life is wanted in four systems!"

This time all three of them busted out laughing. Two bar customers at the table next to them looked their way, then shook their heads and resumed their own conversations.

"So," G'het leaned forward, his eyes darting back and forth, "what's it like for an Ixtali to…you know…have sex?"

Addix chuckled. Different races, different species, different systems, but it always came back to reproduction methods.

"Painful," she answered. "When I have to eat my mate's head while he's still alive and listen to his screaming, it's *so painful,*" she deadpanned. G'het looked at her, then at P'rok and back to her before he noticed a glint in her eye.

"Yer lying!" He pointed at her, and all three started laughing again.

It took her two more hours of mind-numbing conversation to get the information that they had been involved in the movement of the missiles from 27 to 19. It seemed the higher-ups in the company wanted heads to roll, since the computer records hadn't been changed to reflect the new location of the materials.

P'rok had glanced at G'het. "I suggest you offer yer *little* head as a sacrifice for all of us," he slurred. "It's not like you need it anyway!"

Okay, she thought, *that was rather funny.*

P'rok went to the bathroom.

Addix took part in another fifteen minutes of inane conversation after she had what she had come for.

She was halfway back to the spaceport when she caught sight of the two who were following her. She would have to work harder on identifying tails.

Perhaps one of these two had attacked her ship. If so, perhaps she would eat his brains.

Who knew? They might be a delicacy.

She pulled out her tablet and typed a quick message that routed to *The Lady Princess* and then through the Etheric to High Tortuga. She wanted to make sure Bethany Anne knew that the company was fishy before she took out those who were tailing her.

Like Admiral Thomas, she might not live too much longer, and she shouldn't die with that knowledge in her head.

But truth to tell, she doubted her imminent demise. She hadn't been practicing catching tails, but she *had* been practicing combat with some of the top fighters in the base.

She doubted those behind her were going to come out of this alive.

Addix walked five more blocks before she found the type of alley she wanted—dark, tall buildings around it, and a fetid stench emanating from it—and ran a quarter of a block before ducking inside. She glanced over her shoulder as the three Shrillexians broke into a run to catch up with her.

Dammit! She had missed one.

—

E'det, lead of this effort, frowned. He was jogging up to

the opening of the alleyway when he pointed to R'yak and Str'ek and clenched his fist to let them know to form up. While the mark was just an Ixtali, she had made them, so she wasn't stupid.

He wasn't sure what she had under her robes, but a big enough gun could and would ruin his night.

It was happenstance that the dipshit back at the bar had contacted them. He had gone to empty his bladder, and while trying to change stations he'd hit the button to call them. Surprised, he'd answered E'det's questions and said, yeah, there was someone snooping around.

They had arrived just as the Ixtali was leaving. She had stopped stumbling along as soon as she was halfway down the block from the bar.

Yup, she was a pro.

He wasn't sure when she had made them, but she had. He wasn't about to just run into an alley after a pro. However, his blood was starting to rise and his two partners had it worse.

"Just be careful," he hissed.

"It's an Ixtali," R'yak replied. "They deal in secrets, not destruction."

"I didn't see any heavy ordnance," Str'ek commented as they approached the alley opening. "We'll heal from a small-caliber pistol."

"It's better not to have to heal in the first place," E'det growled. *Youth was truly wasted on the young,* he thought. "So try not to get stuck in a damned hospital or I'm taking your fees to pay off your medical bill."

"Damn," Str'ek spat. "Don't need to be a piece of bistok shit about it."

The three entered the alley, allowing their eyes to adjust for a moment before continuing farther in.

From above them, her legs holding her in place, the female Ixtali watched her prey enter her lair. Her mandibles barely moved in her excitement.

A moment later she pulled her hands out of her sleeves, a knife in each, as she released her hold and dropped.

High Tortuga, Hidden Space Fleet Base, Personal Quarters

Bethany Anne put up a hand. "Hold it right there, Michael."

Michael had entered their suite, but he was still in the family and friends section. He glanced to his left and right, then looked at her. "What?"

"I'm curious about something," she answered. She was sitting on the couch, her large stomach making her lean backward. "It seems that you have become quite the nature watcher."

Michael pulled out a wrapped piece of candy, and popped it in his mouth. He started moving it around. "Mmmhmmm."

"And you're working with William on a barbeque pit?"

"That's right," he agreed.

"And with Jean on weapons?"

"Correct again." He sat down on the couch facing her.

"So what are you going to hunt, kill, and eat?"

"A dinosaur," Michael replied.

Bethany Anne stared at him. Her eyes occasionally

blinked, but otherwise she had no expression. "'A dinosaur?'"

He shrugged. "Well, that's the closest thing to what it looks like. On the Southern Continent, there are reptile type creatures which are anywhere from twenty-five feet tall on up. I saw one that topped trees, so call it fifty feet."

"How are you planning on hunting them, and why the barbeque pit?"

"It would be a waste of flesh otherwise," he replied. "I'm not a trophy hunter."

Bethany Anne blinked some more, trying to piece this conversation together. "Okay," then "*OUCH!*"

Michael was next to her as fast as she could blink. "Trouble?"

"No!" She grimaced, breathing out. "How many times have you been amazed at the kicking? It *hurts*. You should hear TOM bitch every once in a while."

"How does he have room in there?" Michael put his hand on her stomach and opened his mind, feeling for and hearing the emotions Bethany Anne was releasing.

She was in more pain than she was admitting.

He frowned.

ADAM's voice came over the system. "Admiral Thomas is reporting that very long-range scanners show ships inbound from two directions. ArchAngel II is waiting for orders. Staying closer to the planet. The Admiral has released three battleships to intercept Group 01. Twenty-two ships… Now fifty-four ships."

"Those aren't all for war," Michael pursed his lips, "Decoys, probably dropping missiles as well. Hide the real missiles within the extra missiles. They probably just want one to hit."

"I'm…" She paused a moment, teeth clenched. "Shit!" she hissed, eyes opening wide as she gripped Michael's hand tightly. "Going into labor!"

20

Goptek Major, Alley

Shrillexians did not, as a rule, *scream*.

Str'ek freaked out when two clawed feet grabbed his shoulders. The weight buckled his knees and he stumbled, causing the legs to release.

Whipping around, he pulled his pistol, his adrenaline spiking when he saw a robed Wraith.

Her clothes hid R'yak's eyes and two of her legs were on his shoulders. The other two kicked E'det in the face, blood streaming from the wounds her claws ripped on their way past.

"Bistok shit!" E'det shouted, his pistol waving in the general direction of the Ixtali, but his hastily-fired shots only blew pockets in the stone, showering the alley with shards.

Str'ek was shocked when she pulled up the bottom of her robes and R'yak's disbelieving eyes were revealed. The male's blood flowed freely from a neck slashed so deeply that his head toppled backward when she pushed up to flip backward. R'yak's body was tossed by her movement toward Str'ek, who dodged out of the way and aimed around his dead partner to fire two shots right into the center of her torso.

Her robe jerked at each impact.

The Ixtali stumbled to her right, then ran for the wall to Str'ek's left. R'yak's body slammed into him, knocking him off-balance, and he fell to his knees.

The Ixtali climbed the wall, two legs grabbing jutting pipes as her arms flashed in the meager light and silver slices flew through the night.

Str'ek threw an arm up to protect his eyes…

But nothing hit him.

E'det grunted as he pulled the knives out of his chest.

Str'ek rolled to his left and looked upward as a dark body jumped down behind E'det.

"*BEHIND YOU!*" Str'ek yelled as he pushed off the ground but E'det only gurgled, blood streaming from his neck where two more knives pierced it.

Str'ek crab-walked backward, trying to get space between him and this demon.

Addix lifted E'det as he struggled to pull the knives out.

Her hiss into his ears frightened him more than anything else he had seen so far.

"Don't you think," she told him, "that a master at spying would know exactly how to kill a vaunted Shrillexian? This black widow *loves* to eat her victims."

Cold flooded Str'ek's veins as he turned got his feet under him and ran towards the alley's exit.

She dropped E'det's body and her right hand dipped into her robes, pulling out a strange-looking pistol.

—

Yank was hurrying through the night. He had just been stood up at the Torcellan restaurant by the vice-president of the competing division, so frankly his night couldn't get worse.

She *claimed* she had been called into an emergency meeting, but that probably meant she would prefer to go home and sleep rather than have dinner with him. His eyes roamed the street, perhaps hoping he would spot her still trying to make their meeting.

He had messaged her to say he would wait for another half-stan before leaving in case she could get free.

He saw three couples and a male, a Torcellan like him, walking in the opposite direction on the other side, his head down.

Yank spat in disgust. There wasn't anyone on this street having a worse night than him.

As he started toward his home, liquid sprayed out of the alley just a few steps ahead at eye level and spattered on the ground.

Then a headless Shrillexian body tumbled from the alley to land half in the street and half on the sidewalk.

Yank's jaw dropped and his heart pounded, but he edged closer to the alley. Hearing no sounds, he looked around the corner but could see nothing in the darkness. The streetlights didn't penetrate the gloom.

He looked around, not knowing what to say or *do*.

A couple across the street screamed as he edged into the alley.

A moment later he too screamed as he ran out again. The two sets of dead eyes he had just seen would haunt his dreams for weeks to come.

He didn't think about the vice-president again that evening.

A black-robed figure climbed over the edge of the roof and disappeared into the night.

Above High Tortuga, Bridge of the *ArchAngel II*

There were one hundred and twelve ships of varying sizes. Each could shoot a minimum of ten missiles, Admiral Thomas was informed.

This wasn't a large fleet battle for supremacy, but rather a concerted effort to hit one location on the planet. His people and ships could destroy all hundred and twelve ships, but if just one of the wrong type of missile made it down to the planet they would lose.

Thomas pursed his lips. "ArchAngel..." He glanced at the screens at the front of the bridge from which Bethany Anne's visage was studying him. "Launch *all* Black Eagles, all Pods; everything we have. Put them into space without their crews. Use the EIs still on the planet to fly them. We'll use them as a defensive shield.

"We will be short five hundred Pods based on present estimates."

"I know. Use the pucks on the Black Eagles to attack the missiles."

"Understood, Admiral." The visage disappeared.

Admiral Bartholomew Thomas raised an eyebrow. He had been in many space fleet battles with the AIs Arch-

Angel II, ArchAngel, and Reynolds and this was the first time one of their avatars had ever disappeared.

Just what were the AIs going to do?

High Tortuga, Space Fleet Base

Michael streaked down the hallways like a man possessed with Bethany Anne in his arms. He flung *fear* out ahead of him, willing those who might be near to get out of his way and cower against the walls as the blur that was him and Bethany Anne dashed by.

He had no time to scream to people to get out of the way as he came up on them. He had tried mentally commanding and yelling, but it had just confused those walking the halls. *Fear*, on the other hand, ramped up their basic fight-or-flight instinct and got them out of the hallway's center.

He sure hoped he didn't clip anyone with one of Bethany Anne's booted feet.

He shut off his ability to scare others thirty-two seconds later and slowed down long enough to nod to the two hospital orderlies who had just slammed open the doors, having received word that the Queen was in labor.

"In there!" a woman called, and Michael's head snapped around. His eyes were gleaming red, and she swallowed. He nodded sharply and headed into the indicated room, kicking open the swinging doors.

"I will survive," Bethany Anne had her hand on his neck, and she could feel his blood racing. While Michael didn't *need* blood coursing through his body, she thought it was nice that he worried about her like he did. Now, if he would just settle down and not freak out it would go a long way toward making this a better experience for everyone.

Especially the doctors. She didn't need their hands shaking because Michael was in full Lord Vampire of Death mode because he was worried about his fiancée and their child. "Settle down!" she told him. "We are both fine."

Michael ignored her as he slowly laid her on the bed, the paper-like substance crinkling. "You are going to have to help me out of these clothes, Michael," she told him, already trying to unwrap the tie that was holding up her pants.

Thank God she didn't have armor on; that would have been a bitch to get out of.

"What?" Michael asked, coming back to himself. "Get naked?"

"Yes," she answered, "It's how babies are born. You don't just unzip your pants and they pop out, so help me here."

Michael's lips pressed together. He ignored the three people who had rushed into the room behind him and were now chatting about the upcoming birth and how exciting it was.

He focused on Bethany Anne's request and helped her get undressed.

Someone beside him laid down a small blanket which he tossed over Bethany Anne as she wiggled out of the pants. "You are going to have to…" She stopped telling him anything when his eyes snapped to her.

"Right," she mumbled, "I had to go and hook up with a man so old-fashioned he pre-dates the term," she grumbled. "Damn, it's cold." She looked around, spying the doctor, "Evgeni? You guys got any booties?"

Michael finally spoke. "I thought TOM helped with that," he asked. He reached under the covers, using the Etheric to warm up his hands and holding one, then the other on her feet.

"Oh, God!" Her eyes rolled a bit to the back of her head. "Why didn't you tell me you were a walking heat-stone?"

"You've never needed to be warmed up," he answered. "So I've never thought about it."

A nurse went to the other side of Bethany Anne. "Good to see you again, my Queen." She made sure Bethany Anne's head was comfortable. "I take it this man is the father?"

Michael's head snapped up, but Bethany Anne's hand was on his arm just as fast. "Don't you move those heating stones. She's just being social, trying to lower the stress."

Nurse...*Jollenstein,* Michael read, smiled at him, but the smile dropped off her face as he stared at her. "Right, that was a joke. Sorry." Her eyes flicked down to Michael's fangs, which were now protruding half an inch from between his lips.

Bethany Anne's touch helped calm him and he took a deep breath. "I'll be fine." He forced a smile. "I thought I had more time to prepare."

"First baby?" Jollenstein asked, having gotten over her shock of having an incarnation of death staring at her in the delivery room.

The nurse sure hoped... She stopped and thought about it. She had been going to say she sure hoped they didn't have a girl with a father like that, but after glancing at the Queen she wondered if any date their son brought home was going to want to meet *her?*

"Yes." Michael nodded and held Bethany Anne's hand, dealing with the pain as two of the smaller bones healed after she cracked them by squeezing too hard.

"Sorry," she grated out. "Got a little carried away with that one.

"Hello."

Michael turned to see a man with "Dr. Dizon" stenciled on his uniform. "Seems like we are going to be welcoming a new baby into this world today." He glanced at Michael. "Dad, I'd like you to get closer to Mom. We are all aware she is pretty damned strong, and frankly, I'm going to need you to take that punishment. Because if she kicks me, I won't heal quite so fast."

Michael nodded as Bethany Anne grunted, "I've got this." Michael put up his hand. "Okay, other than breaking Michael's hand, I've got this."

"Right Bethany Anne." He sat down at the end of the bed. Bethany Anne was already in the position best for delivery. "Do we know if TOM is doing ok?"

TOM?

Just...fine... TOM got out. **Actually, the less I have to speak at the moment, the better. This shit hurts.**

"Bitching like normal. He'll let me know if we are hurting him too much," she answered.

"Well, if we have to use sharp instruments I'll let you know first."

Ohhhh, fuuuuddgee, TOM replied. **I'm practicing reducing my bad words.**

Good on you... I'll fucking try LATER! Bethany Anne sent as another round of pain hit her. ***GOD! Why do women do this more than once?***

I understand they forget. I'll help you remember, he grunted.

"Michael..." Bethany Anne heard the tiny *snap* of a bone as she worked to release the pressure on his hand. "*Sorry.*"

"Don't worry about it," Michael replied. She glanced up; he truly wasn't paying attention, but was peeking over the small curtain she couldn't see past.

"Now," Dr. Dizon spoke in a soothing voice, "I don't want you to squeeze. We don't know your strength. Let's see if we can do this... Actually..." he looked at Michael, "I need you to clean your hands lots of times. Should have been done already."

Michael released Bethany Anne's hands and stepped over to the sink to wash.

The doctor looked at Bethany Anne, who was looking from Michael to him. "Sorry, but I might need his strength and, uh..." he blushed, looking down and then back to her eyes, "you've already broken his hand twice."

A moment later he switched places with Michael, who looked at Bethany Anne's face with a smirk.

She laid back and looked up at the ceiling. "Seriously?"

Five minutes later, while Bethany Anne squeezed a metal rod Michael helped deliver his daughter, her initial shriek piercing the quiet of the room.

Michael's eyes narrowed. "Uh oh..."

Bethany Anne, stomach clenched, hissed in pain.

Goptek Major, *Principal* Spaceport

Addix had ditched her robe, figuring it was better to be

seen in armor than a robe with blood soaking it. She used it to wipe off her face first.

When she reached the spaceport she did not have to go through the consumer passenger section, but rather the entrance the ship owners used.

She walked up to the gate, her body on full display, which was unusual for an Ixtali. Most species preferred to believe Ixtalis only had two legs.

Now all four were on display, with knives and guns locked down. She nodded to the gate guard, who accepted her credentials.

"Looks like you got into a little altercation," the guard mentioned, his eyes going to the screen and back to her. He looked around before wiping an area on his cheek that was already clean.

Addix reached up, and wiped, her hand coming away with blood. "Thank you."

He handed her credentials back and leaned toward her. "I don't like Shrillexians anyway." He nodded. "Although, if you *did* have anything to do with that, the cops are looking." He pointed up. "I'd probably get airborne before they decide to put out a lockdown." He glanced at an area on his screen before punching a button. "I'm on break, so you probably have fifteen minutes before I could rush out to location TH-QQ anyway." He smiled. "And let me tell you, four legs is *hot*." He grinned as he walked away into the night whistling.

Addix didn't waste any time, but allowed her four legs to carry her towards *The Lady Princess* at a good pace, although it didn't look like she was rushing.

She smirked.

Her location was on the other side of the tarmac from TH-QQ. Twelve minutes later, *The Lady Princess* had risen from the pad and darted into the sky.

When the guard reached his post fifteen minutes later, an All-Points Bulletin had been sent out demanding all personal and corporate craft stay on the tarmac until otherwise notified.

21

Above High Tortuga, Bridge of the *ArchAngel II*

"One thousand seven hundred and twelve missiles inbound," ArchAngel's voice announced on the bridge. "But they have made a tactical mistake."

Her face reappeared. "I am sending the information to Bethany Anne."

High Tortuga, On all Entertainment Screens Across the Planet

It didn't matter if the station was devoted to news, music, entertainment, or business, all video screens switched to an unexpected video feed. Frantically, stations across the planet worked to understand how their feeds had been co-opted.

Slowly people across the world stopped as the dark face caught their attention. Her white hair framed her face and the pupils of her eyes blazing red. "My name is Baba Yaga."

Her voice, soft in volume but raspy in nature, pulled in the viewers. “This planet is under attack right now. As many are aware, I am the one responsible for the recent changes in the business, political, and economic climate. What no one knew until today is that my people and I have accepted responsibility for the defense of this planet.”

The video switched to a view of space. “Right now, we are preparing a defensive network of protective satellites to repel an attack. We thought it better to share this information before the strike occurs, rather than explain it after the fact.

“Do not look up. Whilc it should not hurt most corneas or eyestalks, it could. Please exercise appropriate caution.”

The black face reappeared. “I am Baba Yaga. No one attacks my planet and lives.”

On a superdreadnought far out in space, a man nodded to the face on the screen. A signal was sent, and seven thousand beams of light pierced the darkness…and for a brief moment outshone the sun.

One thousand, seven hundred and twelve missiles detonated within five seconds of each other, filling the sky with flashes of brilliance.

Seconds later three hundred and twelve ships uncloaked within striking distance of the pirate ships, which were already turning to attack.

All but three were torn apart as high-velocity kinetic weapons smashed into them, cracking them at the seams, bursting the energy containment fields in their engines, and opening their ships to vacuum.

Seventy-six escape pods were collected and the three remaining ships cut their engines, allowing themselves to be boarded three hours later under the massive guns that pointed at them.

On the world below, people screamed in jubilation.

Devon—now High Tortuga—had a protector, and *she didn't mess around.* Twelve weeks later the remaining pirates were tried and sentenced to hard labor on the Southern Continent.

Above High Tortuga, Bridge of the *ArchAngel II*

Admiral Thomas eyed the black-skinned visage on the screen in front of him. "Do you think you might switch back, ArchAngel?" he requested.

Moments later, Bethany Anne's face stared back at him. "How did I do?" the EI asked. "I tried to get hold of Bethany Anne, but she is having babies at the moment and told me to deal with it."

"Well," Thomas grumped, "I might have peed a little in my pants."

Everyone on the bridge around him chuckled.

"You say she is having *babies?*" Thomas asked.

"Yes,"

"Well, out with it, girl! What did she have?" he demanded, sending the commands to route this conversation to all ships.

"As of one minute and twelve seconds ago, Queen Bethany Anne and her fiancé Michael Nacht are the proud parents of twins, a boy and a girl."

The screams of joy were heard on ships throughout the system. The pirates were afraid for their lives, having no idea why their captors were so happy.

High Tortuga, Space Fleet Base, Medical Bay

Dr. Dizon laid the second child on Bethany Anne's chest, both of them resting peacefully. Michael was standing next to her playing with her hair as she looked down at the two blond heads beneath her chin.

When she had met this man almost two hundred years before she had been dying and would never have children, but now she had just birthed two little bundles of joy.

"Michael," she whispered, reaching up to play with her daughter's hair, "I'm not going to ask you to stay back."

"Stay back from what?" he asked. His hand rested on their backs. They were so small, he thought.

"I've been informed that Addix was successful," she answered. "And we have a target."

She smirked. She didn't have to look at her man to know that his eyes had just gone black. "One of us has to stay here, and it needs to be me this time," she continued. She looked up at him, her eyes flashing red. "But someone just tried to send missiles down on our family."

"I'll take care of it," he replied, his voice malevolent. "Payback will be a bitch."

"Good," she murmured, yawning. "I expect you to be back in time to help change diapers."

Michael chuckled. "Who do I need to speak with?"

"Liaise with Admiral Thomas for transportation, but I suspect you won't go alone."

"No." Michael chuckled. "I won't stop them if they want to come along."

"Good," she whispered. "They are good people."

"I'm curious." Michael grabbed her hand. "Why didn't we know we were having twins?"

"It seems," she answered, "that since 'Dr. TOM' was on the job I didn't need to come in for any checkups, and since we didn't want to know the sex he thought it would be the same answer for wanting to know how many. About the kicks and everything else, he lied, telling me he needed room. It was his version of a gift."

"It was a surprise," Michael agreed, "I'll grant you that. What's he doing now?"

Bethany Anne stifled a second yawn. "Sleeping."

He leaned over, kissing her on her forehead. "Protect them. I will be back."

"With my *life*," she answered.

High Tortuga, Space Fleet Base, Starships Hangar 003

Michael had taken fifteen minutes to shower, armor up, and grab his go-bag. As he walked through the halls toward the hangar, he accepted the congratulations on his new family with happy smiles. A few of those in the hallway knew where he was going, though.

"Send them to hell, sir," he heard many times.

Those who knew Bethany Anne loved her. Those who didn't usually feared her. Rarely were individuals neutral about her unless they had no clue.

Michael however, was an anomaly to most. They knew he was her fiancé, but otherwise they'd only heard rumors.

The last set of doors opened and he walked into the starship hangar, where the Executive Pod was waiting to take him and anyone else who showed up to the *ArchAngel II*.

Michael didn't speak, just nodded to John Grimes, Eric, Darryl, Scott, Akio, Gabrielle, Eve, Peter, and Tabitha.

"Barnabas is on an operation off-planet or he would be here." Stephen shook his hand. "I'll take care of everything administrative while you are gone and help keep her in bed."

Michael shook his hand. "Thank you, brother. She will need the time to bond with the children."

"What are their names?" Stephen asked.

Michael shrugged, "We've spoken about many. I've told her my preferences, but this came up. I'm happy with whatever she picks, so long as it isn't 'Michael.'" He chuckled. "Or any of yours." He looked around. "No offense."

There were many chuckles. "None taken," Stephen replied. "Burn the ground."

"And sow it with salt," Michael finished the old phrase. He drew Stephen into a hug.

They all boarded the Executive Pod, which slowly lifted five feet on its antigravity engines before turning one-hundred and eighty degrees and sweeping out of the hangar bay. It stayed under cliffs, hidden from satellites above for a few miles before streaking into the sky.

John sat next to Michael, who was quiet. "Sucks leaving them behind." His gruff voice pulled Michael out of his thoughts.

Michael sat back in his chair. "You know, before Bethany Anne came into my life I intended to suicide. I was done." He pursed his lips. "She was my gift to the world, a new parent, if you will, who was going to set things straight. I had made many mistakes in my life, and I figured it needed a woman's hand to set it right."

"What stopped you from choosing suicide?"

Michael snorted. "Being trapped and almost torn apart by David. It wasn't until Bethany Anne came to free me that I'd had someone look for me *in over two hundred years.* It was at that moment, as she pulled me out of the Etheric, that I understood love," he lifted his hand, two fingers a centimeter apart, "this much again."

"Enough to suicide to save the base," John supplied.

"For her? Yes," Michael agreed, turning to him. "I had made a promise on my honor to do whatever it took to protect the base. I would not fail." He chuckled. "Except for that being-ripped-apart-into-constituent-atoms thing."

"Did that hurt?" John asked. "I've been curious ever since we knew you survived.

"I couldn't remember at first." Michael looked ahead, his eyes unfocused. "The pain had caused me to hide it away and let my subconscious deal with it." His lip curled just a bit. "I finally remembered the excruciating pain, and let me tell you…I'd rather not go through it ever again."

Michael turned to look John in the eyes. "What happened to Bethany Anne?"

John's eyes narrowed in thought. "How so?"

"When I left, she was adamant about me becoming less violent, but now she doesn't blink. I'm not criticizing, but she has changed."

"I can tell you." Gabrielle spoke from behind Michael and John.

Gabrielle was Stephen's daughter, turned centuries

before into a vampire and upgraded by Bethany Anne. She was the leader of the Queen's Bitches.

"I'm listening, Gabrielle," Michael responded.

"After your disappearance, she went on a spree of violence. There was no stone she didn't turn to figure out who was even tangentially involved in the attack that killed you." Gabrielle snorted. "Okay, *didn't* kill you, but killed you. Semantics aside, Barnabas had to work with her to make sure she didn't go overboard because of her grief. Later she kept fighting for the right people to have options, and the governments wanted her technology."

"I'm sure they asked nicely." Michael smiled.

"Not by a fucking long shot," Gabrielle admitted. "So she kicked their asses with her size-sevens until we ran into the Yollins checking Earth out for an invasion."

Michael shook his head. "I missed so much."

Eve spoke up from two seats back in the opposing row. "Well, only the atomic destruction of the world and the rebuilding of a lot of society on Earth. I can't really suggest that you missed anything there."

"How many interplanetary wars have we been in since we hit Yollin space?" Michael turned to the big black ex-special forces man who had been with Bethany Anne since before Michael had been found the first time.

"Well, there were the Yollins," Darryl answered, "the Karillians or Yarees, and the Leath, plus a lot of smaller events."

"The Yaree *were* the Leath," Scott corrected.

"I tend to think of it as Yaree world and Leath world," Darryl clarified.

"You'd have to think of the Yollins as a two-parter too,"

John supplied. "The first one was King Yoll, and Bethany Anne had to straighten out the holdovers who didn't appreciate her version of the emancipation proclamation against their caste system."

"That went on for a while," Gabrielle agreed.

Tabitha spoke up from the back, where she was sitting next to Peter. "I'd add the Federation as another."

Michael looked over his shoulder and spoke a touch louder. "The Federation?"

"It's been more of a war of words, politics, and counter-moves among the systems," Tabitha clarified. "She got her dad involved in more ways than one, and has had to stay in the background, only showing herself to scare some of the other polities."

"So," John brought it back around to this present operation, "I understand we have a lead on who has been attacking us. We're gonna do…what?"

"Kill them," Michael answered.

Planet Soboth (Previously Territory 7732), Undisclosed location, Open Out-ring, Non-Federation

Az looked at his private tablet for the fifth time. He'd had one text to tell him missiles had been fired.

And one more that had stopped mid-send. *"Target is res…"*

"Res" what?

With no specific information he had to assume the worst, however unlikely that was. No one took out over a thousand missiles and a hundred and twelve ships except the large governments with their massive fleets. No one, not on some backward little forgotten company planet, was going to overcome the number of ships he had pulled together.

Stretching his favors, he had called in everyone. One last hurrah to take over the planet.

Now no word was coming back through the transponder systems they used for talking between systems. Even if the messages had been caught up in queues at one of the stations, he should have received one by now.

Az needed to consider if he wanted to show up at the conglomerate's headquarters and act like the CEO he was or stay hidden. If he went there his location would shield him from a major attack, since no one would attack Adolphin.

He nodded once and leaning forward, he stabbed a button. "Uleq?"

"Sir?" The Torcellan's voice came back immediately.

"I'm going to head out to Adolphin. I need to do a flag visit, remind them that the big guy comes in and works in the big office."

"You want us to stay here or travel with you?"

Az hesitated. "What do *you* want to do?" he asked, seeing Uleq shrugging his shoulders in his mind's eye. The Torcellan was a soft spineless sponge. Az rolled his eyes before Uleq got back to him.

"Stay here, I guess. I've got projects that could take me out-system in the direction opposite Adolphin. Much as I love the weather and the food, I would hate to travel all that way just to come back."

"Okay. I'll be back in about a month," Az continued.

"You, Imon, and I can follow up on special projects through the usual communications channels." Which meant hidden messages. "Let me know if there are any general projects I need to review while on Adolphin."

"I will," he confirmed. "Take care."

Az nodded and stabbed the button again. Some days there was just so much of his partner he could take before he wanted to walk into his office down the hall and unscrew his head from his shoulders.

Az stood up from his desk, grabbing his tablets and the case he carried them in. The secret tablet went into a hidden pouch that was shielded from typical spaceport security. Not usually a problem, since once he got to the next major world he would rent a personal craft to take him to Adolphin.

On the company's dime, of course.

He locked his office and headed for his suite, but then he got a bad feeling and turned to head directly to the transportation level.

There was no time like the present to leave.

22

High Tortuga, Hidden Space Fleet Base, Nursery

Bethany Anne was resting with her eyes closed when her breathing turned erratic. Her eyes beneath the lids jerked back and forth and her sleep was punctured by fractured dreams.

She was back on Earth.

Her hands subconsciously grasped the covers, squeezing them as scenes of destruction insinuated themselves and voices, screams, and death played out on the video screen of her mind.

Michael was dead.

Her back arched and her head tilted at an impossible angle into the pillow as a silent scream erupted from her soul.

BETHANY ANNE! TOM's voice ripped through her consciousness.

Her eyes flew open. She was lying on her back in her bed, sheets torn up around her. She breathed a sigh of relief, spying the two advanced hybrid Pod-cribs her children rested comfortably in next to her.

But there *was no Michael.*

Her eyes flashed red and her chest heaved uncontrollably as she fought to hold herself together.

This is bullshit!

Bethany Anne rolled out of bed. ***ADAM, prepare my armor and tell the Guardians I want thirty of their best.***

>>Okay. Are we going somewhere? <<

Yes, she replied, walking into her shower to get the stink of the nightmares washed off. ***We are going to protect the father of my children...***

—

Bethany Anne locked on the latest armor Jean had made for her.

It was jet-black and sexy as hell. This new set wasn't composed of connected links, but instead damn-close-to-impregnable plate. It ruined her mobility, but so long as she was inside it there wasn't much on the planet that could kill her.

She hoped.

She deliberated for a moment. She wasn't sure if she should take the children or leave them here in the safety of the base, but she listened to her instincts and allowed herself to *feel* the truth.

"You guys are coming with me," she whispered, keeping her voice soothing as she grabbed her helmet and walked out of her armor closet to the two Pod-cribs.

Both infants were sleeping. She ran a hand across the permaglass that allowed her to see them. "You are *our* children. I'd wish you an easy life, but that isn't in my power to provide. Hell, it's not in anyone's power; life doesn't work that way. But I promise you love, an abundance of aunts and uncles who won't ever let you out of their sight, and tough workouts."

She smiled. "And a father to enjoy it all with, *so help me God.*"

Three minutes later, five men in armored suits were allowed into her suite to help Bethany Anne bring the little Pod-cribs with them to the *G'laxix Sphaea,* a hundred-foot-long ship which had cloaking abilities.

And a captain she could trust with her children's lives.

High Tortuga, *G'laxix Sphaea,* Ships Bay 001

Bethany Anne confirmed the Pods were locked in properly before she made her way to the bridge. Inside there were four people; two Bethany Anne didn't recognize, but she did know Captain Kael-ven T'chmon, and…

"Kiel!" She grinned.

Kael-ven shook his head. "The captain of the ship gets no respect…URGH!" He coughed as Bethany Anne's other arm squeezed him. "Watch that hug there or this could be a short trip."

"You large liar." Bethany Anne patted Kael-ven on his hard exoskeleton. "Thanks for working with me on this."

"Of course," Kael-ven nodded to something he was reading on his screen before sending the instructions to take them out, cloaking the ship with a swipe and a tap. "I'd have been offended if you hadn't asked."

"Well, you didn't ask *me,*" Kiel grumped, "but I will

accept your surprise and elation at my presence as your apology."

Bethany Anne hugged the old Yollin mercenary and Marine officer. "Oh, shut up. I was freaking out that Michael was dying and I wasn't there to save him, so I get a pass."

The front bridge screens showed the outside of the ship. The craggy walls swung by as they zigzagged through a canyon before breaking toward the sky, streaking upward toward their rendezvous with the battleship.

Kael-ven turned his upper body in his chair; his four legs were wrapped around the base. "I imagine you have placed an operational gag order on anyone involved in this little effort?"

"Of course," Bethany Anne agreed, sitting down a moment. "Can you bring up video of the children?" A moment later, one of the screens at the front switched to show the two Pod-cribs and the four Guardians, two on each side of the babies. "Ok, excellent. And by 'of course,'" she clarified, "I mean I had people do it."

A voice came over the speakers. "And by people, she means an AI," ADAM explained. "Hello, Kael-ven, Kiel."

Kiel dipped his head. "Hello, Your Omniscience."

ADAM sniffed. "I'm not sure I can live up to that title, but I rather like it."

Bethany Anne pointed to the location on her skull where ADAM's chip was embedded. "If his ego gets so large that I start having headaches, I will find you and kick your ass."

"ADAM working on his ego will be good for you both," Kiel continued. "I've had to assist Kael-ven with his ego issues as planetary potentate, so I am extremely qualified to help ADAM through any issues as well."

"I can assure you," ADAM replied, "that I have no issues with ego. Ego becomes a problem when people either ascribe to themselves capabilities they do not have, or when those who *do* possess such abilities are compelled to have their self-worth recognized by those around them. Either way it is self-delusion."

Kiel grunted. "Hmmph. Seems to me like you are *already* going down the path of self-delusion. I'll watch you very closely."

Kael-ven interrupted the argument between his friend and the AI. "I've got the Battleship *C. Hewgley* on track to allow us to dock and snuggle up, then we Gate in twenty minutes. I hate to be all captain-y and demanding, my Queen," he jerked a thumb backward, "but get your armored ass to the back and lock in."

Bethany Anne stood and patted Kiel on the shoulder. "Wow, grumpy pilot!" She looked around. "Where's Snow?"

"My precious white dog didn't want to get out of bed to go on this trip. She told me to tell you hello, and that Ashur and Bellatrix called last night and they are fine." He jerked his thumb again. "Now go. I've got a job to do, so catching up on our pets is for later."

Bethany Anne's mumbled cursing followed her down the hall.

Planet Soboth (Previously Territory 7732), Undisclosed location, Open Out-ring, Non-Federation

"Dammit!" Uleq cursed under his breath. The income

for the core world's water purification services went down half a percent each year. As he walked down the hallway toward his office he heard a palm slam against a desk in Imon's office.

Uleq stuck his head into the Shrillexian's office. "What happened?"

Imon aimed his glare at the intruder for a moment, then waved a hand. "Come in and close the door." He leaned back in his chair, waiting for Uleq to sit down in front of his desk.

"It seems," Imon ground out the words, his voice tense, "that a group of my fellows on Goptek Major has been taken out."

Uleq put his tablet down on the desk in front of him. "Shrillexians?" Imon nodded. "How is that even... Who could do it?"

"Well, plenty I can think of, but none of them were on-planet at the time. The bigger issue is that they got away. The city police shut down the port, but a total of five ships left between the time of the murder and when the space-port was shut down. I have," he waved a hand at his tablet, "refined the data and the information suggests an Ixtali took them out. Probably the same Ixtali who was asking questions of those who moved the warehouse materials from Goptek Minor to Major."

"On Az's request," Uleq pointed out.

Imon's eyes flicked to Uleq and stayed there for a moment, then he shrugged. "True."

Uleq leaned back. "So, is it possible that one Ixtali could take out your team?"

"Highly unlikely, so that means there was a team

already in place and this Ixtali pulled them into an ambush." He grimaced. "Which means security on this operation has been breached."

"They couldn't have made them?"

Imon shrugged, "Unlikely. The Ixtalis are known for their intelligence and spycraft, not their fighting abilities. An Ixtali would certainly not be able to slit one's neck," he pointed at each side of his neck, "stab another in the neck, and shoot the third as he ran." He shook his head. "No Shrillexian would run from a fair fight, and by definition a Shrillexian against an Ixtali is fair."

Imon tapped his hand against his desk. "No, the obvious answer is that it was an ambush. They tried to kill all three with knives to keep it quiet, but Str'ek caught on and tried to flee. He was shot down in cold blood."

Uleq was careful not to show his amusement at Imon's turn of phrase. Still, he snickered internally at Imon's complaint about his thug being 'killed in cold blood' when the purpose of the male's being there was to kill someone on Imon's orders.

He wasn't in good spirits.

Uleq grabbed his tablet and stood up. "Well, I'm going to go get us a drink."

Imon looked up. "We don't drink except on the last workday of the week."

Uleq shrugged. "Let's drink to the fallen, then. At the moment, I believe I could learn to drink for some reason every day."

Imon nodded. "It is getting that way." He waved Uleq off. "Go get it, I'll drink with you."

Planet Adolphin

It had taken Az a week to travel from the out-ring to Adolphin. As his ship sliced through the atmosphere, its clean lines and unique ceramic siding offered everyone the opportunity to admire the multi-billion-credit personal yacht of business moguls and royalty speeding past.

Ignoring those who were beneath them.

Conglomerates often had a central location for their main office, but not many ever expected to see the highest of the high who worked there. It was a common occurrence to find reporters from news agencies around the systems camping outside to try to get a word with the elite and powerful if they should appear unexpectedly.

A single comment might be worth millions in the right hands as the powerful organizations manipulated markets.

However, the big fish, so to speak, did have to show up from time to time, and Az planned to use this to his advantage.

Adolphin was a well-defended world. No one would bring world-busting ships here and start attacking; it wouldn't be prudent.

Any mercenary group large enough to battle their way in knew damn well that it would be political suicide. Smaller pirate or mercenary groups would lack the resources necessary to fight their way through the protective military space-based weapons platforms layered over Adolphin.

Adolphin was neutral ground, too many systems' large business entities had representation and assets here.

A mercenary company who harmed assets on Adolphin would find themselves ejected from all major star systems in three weeks flat. It would be little better than an oversized pirate association after that.

No, Az had decided he would hide in plain sight and allow the world to protect him. He was fully capable of handling his personal protection, and that was another reason Adolphin worked for him.

What you did on your personal (or corporate) property was your business on this world. So long as you didn't harm others, you could build up a personal army and the local authorities wouldn't blink.

So long as you didn't use those assets to attack anyone.

Protection only.

Of course, KGB had a corporate shuttle bay large enough to allow Az's ship to land.

He took six from his protection detail and another six from operations he'd ordered to come with him as he left the ship and headed into the corporate shuttle operations center while vetted support personnel went to work on the ship.

Standing straight, the Leath CEO smiled and waved at those lucky enough to be outside as he strolled in, ensuring that the many news drones caught sight of him as he and his entourage swept past on their way inside.

One of the more aggressive rumor-mongering news organizations flew their drone over the boundary into corporate space, but the drone got less than two feet inside their space before it dropped out of the sky. A small anti-drone launcher had fired three missiles and downed it without so much as a warning to the news organization to stay out of their airspace.

Az spent little time inside the building, just spoke with

a few workers and signed tablets for two others excited to meet him. Then he and his group disappeared into the vast underground mag-lift travel system.

And were gone.

Planet Adolphin

The Leath-built ship sliced through the atmosphere on the path provided by system traffic.

Unlike Goptek, Adolphin had been settled hundreds of years before and had quickly become a place where many conglomerates based their main offices.

It was a world with arching skyways and beautiful parks. Addix enjoyed watching the thousands of ships which crisscrossed the sky. Due to the prevalence of money the world had a decentralized port structure, with many private ports.

"Lady?" Addix called as they headed slightly away from the middle of the city.

"Yes?" the ship's EI replied.

"Isn't the KGB headquarters downtown?"

"Yes, but for us to secure a landing location which is trusted by the city yet not so strict that our credentials will be checked too closely we had to go out of town some little way. The farther we go from the city center, the less we have to worry about the diligence of the private port in its interactions with the city."

Addix thought about this. On the one hand it meant she would have to walk farther or find private transportation, but on the other there would be less scrutiny.

"Very good," Addix replied. "But next time you go

outside my operation parameters please inform me in advance."

"Understood."

Addix weighed her options and decided to choose knives. She could argue the case for knives, but Jean Dukes?

Not so much.

Besides, she was here strictly on reconnaissance, with zero expectation of getting herself in the middle of a gun battle. At least, she hoped that would be the case.

Addix's mandibles tapped together as she thought. Adolphin had decentralized access; there wasn't one single place where ships that could navigate space and atmosphere were required to land for immigration and customs.

Lady, the ship's EI, had given the planet's authorities their bona fides. These credentials were good until she landed, and all she could do was hope the shit didn't hit the fan if their efforts to identify her came up positive.

As long as nothing she did tripped their systems and she didn't provide anyone with a reason to investigate her further—like wearing very unique weapons which could be traced back to the Etheric Empress—she would be at no additional risk of exposure.

Addix sighed. "Knives and wits. Let's hope I have more than enough of the one and not too few of the other."

—

Three days later, Addix was stymied. She had been to KGB headquarters on three different occasions in three different guises and had the same outcome all three times.

The CEO was not here, he was not accepting requests

for interviews, and no, they did *not* know when he might show up.

Addix was walking along a route of thought, one of many that criss-crossed the city, when a shadow passed overhead. Addix looked up and gawked. It was a Messeir Breat personal yacht—beautiful, and rare even on *this* world.

Almost blindingly white, there were brown squares which formed a stylized "MB" along the craft's side as it cut through the air in the direction she had just come from.

"Damn, I want one of those," she grumped as she continued walking. Easily half the people around her had stopped to pay attention to the yacht and talk about it, which was an indication that good design translated across species.

It didn't matter that the most recent yachts didn't have the speed, the gating ability or the sheer *power* of *The Lady Princess,* the one that flew overhead was drop-dead sexy. As Stephen would say, it was like providing a human male with a female who was all body and no brains.

She didn't speak, just squealed.

Ixtali sexual desires were driven by pheromones more than physical attributes, but the Messeir Breat that had just flown over helped Addix understand Stephen's comment in a way that had previously eluded her.

Addix continued down the alley, annoyed she had no way to figure out where the CEO was. She had called for the team to prepare and come here, but now the best they would be able to do would be a hit-and-run operation to acquire intelligence. She had Lady working on insinuating herself into the data lines throughout the city.

But so was everyone else.

Perhaps an AI could break into their systems, but she doubted the EI could get past their firewalls.

Addix sighed. No, this was going to require something other than digital theft.

Adolphin, Aboard *The Lady Princess*

"Lady," Addix called, pulling off her robe. She rarely wore it anymore when she was alone since it was vastly impractical.

"Yes?"

She sat down on her specialized chair on the bridge and leaned back. "Lock us up and request permission to leave in twelve hours. I've got nothing to go on at the moment, and I'd rather meet the team in space. I'll give them the schematics of the building and you can provide access to your digital efforts to date. Perhaps ArchAngel will provide insight."

Addix knew Lady was an EI rather than an AI, but she would bet credits that she had just sniffed because Addix had suggested an AI might be able to hack the KGB's computer network where she couldn't.

"Well," Lady began, "what if I told you I know exactly when CEO Az Th'loo will arrive on Adolphin?"

Addix straightened. "Don't play with me. Do you?"

"Yes."

"Well, when?"

"He is here now," the EI replied.

The forward projection screen came to life and displayed drone footage, probably from a news drone, of the beautiful ship she had seen just an hour before. The text underneath announced in bold that **CEO Az Th'loo had returned to Adolphin after a one-year absence**, and the reporter waxed enthusiastically about his surprise visit to the conglomerate's corporate offices.

"Sonofabitch," she whispered. "That asshole just flew right over me." Her mandibles tapped together in shock. "It's better to be lucky than good sometimes."

"I will assume," Lady told her, "you just said that *you* are lucky and *I* am good?"

Addix chuckled. "Of course, Lady, of course." She considered her options. "Keep our spot here, but inform the owner we are going to go sightseeing for two or three days."

"The *ArchAngel II* will be in-system tonight."

"Okay, one or two days," she amended. "If we are secured, take us out."

"What do you want me to do with my data discovery efforts?"

Addix mulled that request. "Did you put anything in that will give us away?"

"No, my programs are modeled after the best data acquisition spiders. Only if they acquire information as designated by the filters will they call back for the advanced data exploit support."

"And how close to yours are the best data acquisition spiders?"

"There are none better."

"That you have encountered."

"Well." There went that sniff again. How had Addix

ended up with a touchy EI? "That is true. I have not yet encountered any superior hacking algorithms."

She felt a slight wobble so she glanced at the readouts to confirm they were headed out. "So, if they *are* better than the ones you programmed," Addix continued, refusing to drop the argument, "you might possibly never know you don't have the best, right?"

This time Lady didn't answer right away.

Addix leaned back in her chair, "I'm going to take a nap. Why don't you get back to me with your answer when I wake up?"

23

Planet Adolphin, CEO's Personal Residence

Az's personal transport slid into the bay, barely touching down before four of his security personnel got out and headed for the entry. The first confirmed the security hadn't been tampered with, then issued the security code for the day.

It changed every planetary day.

The doors unlocked and they went in, sweeping the house's main, upper, and basement levels before providing the "all clear" so Az could leave the shuttle. This was their typical order of business when he first arrived.

Az swept through the inside service area and into the kitchen from the main bay. Normally he would enter and exit through the front door and never see these parts of the residence.

They were for the workers, not for him.

However, security wanted to keep him out of sight right now, since the news drones had been alerted to his presence and were hovering some distance away. They were close enough for their long-range optics to get a clear shot.

"Damn, those newsies are annoying," Az grumped to his lead security operative.

"Sorry, but it's the price you pay to be at the top, sir," he replied as he headed out to secure the back of the house.

"I know. That's why I stay away so much." Az waved him off and headed upstairs to his personal suite. When he turned the corner at the top of the stairs, he nodded to the two guards stationed outside his double-wide suite doors. "I'm just going to take a nap, then make a quick trip to the office."

The short nap ended up being a full night's sleep and the team left before early rush hour in the morning.

Az had been more tired than he had thought.

His executive shuttle's darkened windows allowed him to see out, but no one outside could see in so he took in his surroundings for a few minutes as the local star curved across the horizon. The buildings' white spires shone brightly as the city below them woke up.

Az pulled up his tablet to check his schedule for the day. Anytime he was in the city he had three days of boring and tedious meetings to attend before anything else could be scheduled—yet another reason for staying out of the corporate office.

He was dressed in an impeccably tailored Geuuitve suit, which had been modified for his Leath build. It accentuated his square jaw.

He was, he thought, a very striking figure when dressed for the high-level business atmosphere of Adolphin. He couldn't wear military garb anymore for obvious reasons, but his business attire announced his power.

As the shuttle set down he went through his secondary mailbox, but there was nothing he needed to know from his partners.

Good. He didn't want to deal with either Uleq or Imon at the moment.

It took the better part of half a stan to reach his office suite. When she greeted him, his personal assistant acted like he was there every day.

"First meeting, mid-morning. This will allow you to review any presentation notes necessary. For every meeting there is a second tab where I've summarized the content—the information you might need and any secondary conclusions from others. On the third tab are the political entities that will be affected by the decisions discussed in that meeting."

Az thanked her and accepted the tablet, pocketing his own. With a press of his finger, he pulled up his message queue as he closed his office's door behind himself.

Imon had sent a message that had been routed through a tertiary email location, arriving since he had stepped into the building.

"Goptek Major Operation partially successful. Unfortunately, three cases of food poisoning affecting our people. No consumers known to be affected."

Az read it again.

Three of Imon's people had been killed, and he didn't have a body or know who had done it?

Az reached up and rubbed a tusk and his eyes narrowed. Who could be onto their operation? More importantly, *how* had someone gotten onto their operation?

The only logical answer was that it was those he was trying to eradicate. Apparently they didn't think that staying on Devon until Az was successful was a viable solution. Further, they had resources that could find the connection with the foodstuffs, get information on Goptek Major, and kill the team stationed there to take out anyone sniffing around.

And get back off-planet.

That could and would explain how his allies who had attacked the planet had been wiped out; if they knew in advance they could have set up an ambush. A little impractical to suggest that all the ships had been destroyed, but plausible. Hell, as an ex-military man he could think of three ways to make it happen.

Mines were solutions one and two. Massive ships slugging it out would be a third, but the most unlikely.

No, it had probably been an ambush.

And they had tracked the missing missiles to Goptek Major. Az looked at the plan for that operation and noted that Uleq had provided proper instructions, but then his eyes narrowed.

Uleq had tagged all of them as having come from him. *That back-stabbing Torcellan.*

Az tapped a button on his tablet and his secretary answered, "Sir?"

"Cancel all meetings. Not feeling well, I don't think I've come out of this last trip healthy. Tell everyone I apologize and I'll get back with them as soon as I'm better."

"But sir…"

He cut her off. His stomach was queasy, but it wasn't due to travel.

Az pulled out his personal tablet and connected to a private message queue. After typing **We no longer need Torin's help** he slipped the tablet back into his pocket and opened his door. Putting up a hand to stop his secretary's immediate comments he left, taking the back stairs to the fastest path out of the building.

It didn't take a half-stan to leave the place.

When Az exited the building his personal shuttle was waiting with the doors open and two of his security guards standing by. He slipped inside and they followed, closing the doors.

"Not the main house," he told them. "Take me to my chalet."

If there was going to be a fight, he wanted to be surrounded by enough land to make sure it wouldn't spill over and hit the neighbors.

In deep space far from the Planet Adolphin

The Lady Princess was dark, barely releasing any energy when the alarms went off.

Addix bolted awake from her nap.

"Sorry!" The alarms shut off. "The proximity alarms were still set. I didn't expect *ArchAngel* to arrive so close to us."

Addix looked at the screen in front of the captain's chair. Her nap had gone on for longer than she had expected.

The *ArchAngel II* was too far away to see with the naked

eye, but close enough that on the screen she appeared to be practically sitting on top of them.

"Take us in." Addix yawned. "I'll get dressed and meet our new team members. Make sure we communicate with ArchAngel for any supplies we might need. Stock us up."

"Understood, Addix."

Fifteen minutes later their ship was swallowed by one of the ship's bays on the *ArchAngel II*.

—

"So." Addix pointed to the different seats in the conference room on *The Lady Princess*. "We can sit and chat, or you can get some sleep in the suites over there." She looked around. "You will probably need to get out of your armor if you want to sleep. There are two areas in the back of the ship for supplies. Plenty of room there to change, since I'm not trading at the moment."

Michael had spoken with Addix from time to time but had never worked with the insect-looking alien. Bethany Anne had spoken highly of the spymaster and that was enough for him. "Who is our target?" he asked.

Akio stayed standing as did Eve, but John, Eric, Scott, Darryl, Tabitha, and Gabrielle found places to sit.

Addix, her black robe covering her body, pointed to a wall behind Michael. He turned to see an image.

"He is ugly," Michael stated flatly. "Looks like a standing warthog."

John chuckled, shaking his head. "You are going to have to understand that we work with dozens of different species here in space, Michael. You can't just randomly toss out comments about their looks."

Michael stared blankly at John, who put up his hands.

"Right. Sensitivity awareness and training can start *next* decade." He looked at Gabrielle. "You might make a note of that for BA."

She smirked.

Michael returned his attention to Addix.

She pointed to the video. "This is the CEO of Kertheck G'loxx and B'rkleth, otherwise known as KGB. This conglomerate spans dozens of worlds and multiple systems. It was under his authority, implemented by the vice-president, that the materials were moved from Goptek Minor to Goptek Major, leaving the missiles without any security. They had been marked as foodstuffs in the inventory system, so no one paid them much attention. The pirates arrived, on-loaded the missiles, and took off. It wasn't until the news broke about the event that anyone started looking, and that was how I found out about it."

"From the news?" Michael asked.

"Yes. One of our contacts sent us the information."

Michael just nodded his understanding.

She continued, "When I arrived on Goptek Major I entertained two employees of KGB who told me that the system hadn't been updated appropriately. And when I left those contacts, I was attacked in an alley."

"You went into an alley and they attacked you, or you lead them into an alley and attacked *them*?" Michael asked.

"The latter," she clarified. Apparently he was accustomed to being the hunter, not the prey. Like recognized like, it seemed.

"What were they?"

"Three Shrillexians. A hit team," she answered. "We had

lost two assets—one down, one dead. Bethany Anne wanted me to personally work this angle."

Michael was watching the screen, etching the face in front of him into his brain. "She made a good choice."

Addix looked at John Grimes, who had opened his mouth to say something. He glanced at Michael and shut it.

Addix wondered why he was being so quiet.

"Where is he now?" Michael asked.

Addix was about to answer when Lady interrupted, "He has left the corporate headquarters in the business quarter and flown out. Destination is expected to be his chalet."

Addix' eyes narrowed. "Why would he rush to his chalet? I would have expected him to have a month of meetings."

"The guilty flee when no one is looking, but in this case I suspect he is onto *us* being onto *him*," Akio answered.

Addix's mandibles tapped in frustration. "Lady, did your data acquisition efforts alert him?"

"Unlikely," the EI answered. "Until I reconnect with the system I can't verify that, however."

"Assume they did, or we did, or someone did," Michael stated. "Why would he choose to go to a chalet? Is this similar to a chalet in Europe—a beautiful home up in the mountains away from everyone else?"

"His is, yes." Pictures of a modern-looking domicile appeared on the wall. The images had been pulled from magazine pages.

"Someone got their house in last year's *House Beautiful,*" Gabrielle commented. "And it *is* beautiful."

"Too stark, too much rock," Eve argued. "Needs more rounded corners."

John eyed the huge building. "Don't worry, we are going to help him remodel."

Tabitha looked from Eve to Akio and raised an eyebrow.

Akio shrugged. He wasn't sure if their little EI in an android body had ascended to AI yet—and now wasn't the time to have that discussion—but one of the ways to tell was that the EI started offering opinions that weren't based on facts.

Like whether this house was pretty.

"Okay." Michael's eyes narrowed. "Go back two images. He has the high ground. Going up the side of that mountain is asking for someone to drop explosives on your head. Why wouldn't we just blow it off the mountain?"

"Adolphin has a weird set of laws. It boils down to this: if you use missiles or armaments similar to missiles they will hunt you down. If however you keep all weapons, including rounds fired, destruction, and so forth on the property, then whatever happens is considered a personal issue."

"What about a typical robbery?" Scott asked.

Addix shrugged, "If you kill them on your property there are no questions asked, but if someone comes looking for a body you have to prove the killing was warranted. Most immediately call for the police to investigate. If you fail to speak about deaths or other infractions on your property, the cops assume you have something to hide and try to prove you guilty."

"That's..." Scott thought about it a moment. "Rather proficient."

"Yes, so to summarize: bring the attention of the police

to the situation as soon as possible so forensics can confirm what happened or you are guilty unless proven innocent."

"I assume they have enough coverage over the planet to figure out missiles, but what about vapor?"

"Don't do it, Michael," John Grimes interrupted. Michael turned his attention to John, whose face was stone-cold serious. "Don't even *think* of taking off the armor. Not only would Bethany Anne kill us—and by 'us' I mean you three times over and the rest of us just the once very, very slowly, but the capabilities of defensive armaments on this world are a lot better than anything that was ever available back on Earth. If they don't have shields that would fry you in your Myst state, there is a good chance they can tell something is there. You solidify and you die."

Michael thought about it for a moment. "I can attack while still mostly Myst."

"Who knows what can harm you as Myst?" John shook his head. "Don't chance it. We haven't had enough opportunities to figure out what can hurt you in that state."

Michael frowned. "We should have tested this."

Akio told his friend, "They have technology here that makes what we faced in the Hadron Collider look like tinker toys."

"And if you think for one minute," Darryl commented, "that any of us would purposely and with intent try to shoot, kill, stab, or poke you in any way, shape, or form just so we could confirm if you could be hurt in Myst form while Bethany Anne was pregnant?" He shook his head. "You are out of your *Gott Verdammt* mind."

The side of Michael's mouth curved up. "Good point."

He turned back to the video wall. "What about air defenses?"

Lady interjected, "I've been able to tap into satellite images. I can't give us the highest resolution, but it is clear enough that there are three anti-ship emplacements on the property."

"Puck them?" Akio suggested.

Addix thought about that solution. "Use the one-pound pucks? They should work, and if we carry them on our bodies the law would be on our side. Are you thinking of an airborne insertion?"

"Yes," Akio supplied. He walked to the wall, tapping a finger on the aerial shot. "We need more data, but if the law says all damage must stay on their land then we must abide by that."

"Why are we doing that again?" Gabrielle asked. "We hit, we leave…who cares?"

"To minimize blowback on High Tortuga," Addix answered simply. "This is a very advanced world, and we don't want them creating a special file to figure out who carried out the raid. So long as we are successful and abide by the rules it will be an open and shut case—no blowback on High Tortuga whatsoever."

"It *is* a rather interesting legal model," Michael agreed. "Plus, I want to confirm," he touched the side of his head, "that this is the person who has attacked my family. If so, I'll kill him…slowly."

Gabrielle nodded, satisfied that her question had been answered. She knew that even if she had found a loophole…

Michael was going to do this face to face anyway.

24

Planet Adolphin - Personal Chalet

Az reached into his coat pocket and pulled out his tablet. It would take hours for the round-trip confirmation that Imon had finished the job to reach him.

That little Torcellan had been too unwilling to get his hands dirty by killing. The only positive aspect of his weak-spine was that it allowed Az to not worry so much about a physical backstabbing. He should get confirmation from Imon within a half day, maybe a day tops depending on what Uleq was doing.

They arrived at the drop-off on top of the chalet. He had ordered a team of Leath mercenaries to meet him there, having negotiated with the company's commander for them to be supplied for three weeks.

He checked the time. They should arrive in about a stan. *Good.*

His executive shuttle would now move to a secondary parking area.

"Engage the anti-air defense and make sure the mercenaries have the right security signs before allowing them to enter," Az commanded his security team lead, who tapped his earpiece to pass on the commands.

He reached the doorway to the stairs that led into the chalet and disappeared.

Adolphin System, ArchAngel II,

Admiral Thomas was reviewing the after-action report of the attack on High Tortuga. He liked the results, but there were always ways to make it better.

A red light flashed on his video screen and he looked up at ArchAngel's face.

"Hello, Admiral."

"What can I do for you, ArchAngel?"

A second face appeared on the screen. "I'm sorry, that wasn't me."

Both faces smirked at the Admiral. His eyes narrowed and he glanced from one to the other. He closed his eyes for a moment, breathing in deeply and then exhaling before opening his eyes and smiling at the first image of Bethany Anne. "Tell me you didn't just arrive in the system, Bethany Anne?"

"Of course not," she supplied, and Admiral Thomas started to smile. "I got here three minutes ago. I've just been catching up with updates while you worked on the AAR."

His smile vanished. ArchAngel would have immediately notified him if any other ship had arrived unexpectedly—unless Bethany Anne was aboard. How that woman had gotten even the AIs to swear fealty to her was beyond his understanding. "Perhaps next time," he grumbled, "Arch-Angel would be so kind as to let me know immediately that another asset has entered the theatre of operations?"

"But I'm not." She winked. "You have set the radius of the theatre of operations as being from your location to the planet. We are outside that radius."

"By how much?" he asked.

"Well, the *Hewgley* is at least fifteen miles from you."

"And you?"

She smiled brightly. "If I put on a space suit I could knock on your door. Permission to land the *G'laxix Sphaea*?"

"Depends." He smiled sweetly at her. "Were you looking for someone?"

"Well, of course." Her eyes narrowed. "Is that jackass gone already?"

"I have no idea which jackass you are referring to. Do you mean—"

"Michael," she interrupted. "Michael is the jackass I'm talking about at this moment. The father of our children. The man who needs—"

Admiral Thomas put up a hand and she quit talking. "Already left to go on-planet. I would have thought you'd have asked that already."

"I thought it would take a while to get set up," she admitted.

"Didn't have to. Addix was waiting here for us. Michael was anxious to go, so it was a quick in to pick them up and a fast goodbye."

"Dammit," Bethany Anne grumped, "Addix needs to be a

little less effective when it doesn't work for my plans." She turned her head. "Kael-ven! Head to the planet." She turned back to the Admiral. "Maybe I'll stop by for dinner later."

"Before you go, where are the children?"

This time the second face of Bethany Anne, the avatar of the *ArchAngel,* answered. "They are staying on the Battleship *C. Hewgley,* Admiral. I will guard them with my life."

Admiral Thomas sighed. "Of course you will, Arch-Angel. We all will."

Ship *The Lady Princess*, Two Hours Out from Adolphin

Lady's voice came out of the speakers. "We have an incoming message from Bethany Anne."

"Put it up on the wall," Michael replied.

Michael had expected to see a tired Bethany Anne with a small smile on her face as she held one or the other of their children in her arms, but the woman who stared at him was angry. He turned around, but when he saw no one behind him he turned back to her. "What happened?"

"You *died,*" she replied.

"Not lately." His deadpan delivery did nothing for her. "Okay, so that didn't go as planned. May I ask what we are talking about and where you are?"

"I had a bad dream where you died and I woke up fearing that our children would have no father for the rest of their lives. I don't remember much about my mom, Michael."

"Okay," he replied, and sighed; empathy wasn't his

strongest superpower. In fact, as a superpower it ranked right up there with his ability to leap tall buildings in a single bound.

Which was to say it sucked horribly, but he knew he needed to try. That much he understood, even with John and Eric off to the side waving frantically and pantomiming who-knew-what shit?

"Am I to understand," Michael continued, "that you had a bad dream? And in this dream I died very painfully, and you woke up fearing that our children would become fatherless?" He made a face. "And due to this fear, you packed up our children, departed a somewhat secure planet, Gated here, left them, and are intending to go with me into a military operation?"

"Yes." She grimaced. "And don't describe it like I'm an emotional wreck just waiting to careen out of control and obliterate any semblance of objectivity as I smash into the rocks of melodramatic tempestuousness."

"I wouldn't think of it," Michael lied.

John, Darryl, and Scott smiled and gave him thumbs-ups. Eric was grimacing and rubbing his arm where Gabrielle had just punched him. Eric gave him a wink from the eye opposite Gabrielle.

"And our children?" he asked. Truth be told, he didn't mind Bethany Anne coming here, but she had promised to watch over their children. Was this how their relationship was going to be?

"A battleship, forty Guardians, and a superdreadnought are protecting them. They are in their little Pod-cribs and I held them for an hour each on our way here. I figure we get in, kill some people, and get out. By the time they wake up again we can each hold one."

"And have you named them yet?" Michael asked.

"Not without you, Michael." She glanced up. "I see we will be arriving thirty minutes after you will, so slow down. Let's coordinate our attack efforts, ruin someone's life—or many lives—and then get back to the ship, shall we?"

He could only nod.

Great. Neither one of them was the stay-at-home type.

It was a good thing there were no Child Protective Agencies around. He would hate to have to kill someone who was trying to take his children because it was their job.

Planet Adolphin, Upper Atmosphere

It took three hours for the team to connect, land in a deserted area, and transfer to the *G'laxix Sphaea.* When that was done they headed toward the chalet and *The Lady Princess* lifted back into space.

If they needed her she would be ready and waiting, but if they didn't everyone would ride back on the *G'laxix Sphaea*.

Bethany Anne walked off the ship and greeted Michael with a kiss, then eyed Addix as she approached. "Leave it," she told her spymistress.

Addix looked down at herself, mandibles tapping in confusion. "What?"

"The robe," Bethany Anne clarified, waving the hand that wasn't holding onto Michael toward Addix's outfit. "It doesn't help your ability to fight. You are dropping on the chalet with us, yes?"

"I am," Addix confirmed. She was the spymistress for High Tortuga and this was the equivalent of going dungeon-diving for a possible treasure-trove of information. She wasn't going to allow any of these intelligence neophytes to screw up her treasure box.

Michael's right eyebrow lifted.

Dammit! Mind reading. She should leave her professional snootiness to swim in her mind some other time. Bethany Anne didn't read the minds of her friends. Michael was apparently not on board in that department.

Michael smiled as Bethany Anne spoke. "Then leave your robe. No one here is going to judge how you look."

Had she read John's mind about Michael? Was this her version of sensitivity training for him? She glanced at Michael's eyes; his mirth was evident. She reached over her shoulder and lifted the robe off over her head. She could have ripped it, unbuckled it, or just taken it off normally, but for some reason she felt like it was a rebirth.

Addix tossed the robe past the two of them as Scott came up beside her and put an arm on her shoulder.

"Feels good, doesn't it?" he asked.

—

They all got back on the *G'laxix Sphaea.* Twenty minutes later they were looking at spy drone footage.

"Where the hell did they get Leath executive-level armor?" Scott bitched. "Not as good as Jean's, but fucking good enough."

"How many are his personal bodyguards?" Michael asked. "Probably none?"

Eve came in just then and moved over to the ops room's video screens without a single sound. She pointed to one of the armored figures. They were all larger than a normal human, and only John and Darryl in their group were tall enough to stand amongst them. "These Leath are—"

"Large," Michael interrupted, "and ugly."

"We have Leath friends." Bethany Anne sighed.

"So we have large ugly friends?" Michael quipped. "Why are you giving me the evil eye? Is this similar to how you never tell a friend their new baby is ugly?" His eyes darted around the room. "Except my children, who are very cute."

The chuckles around the room helped reduce the tension and Eve drew their attention back to the problem at hand, saying, "These are mercenaries-for-hire who work for higher-level company executives, not governments. Normally they control the tactics and take care of things without input, but since our man is ex-military they are probably working together."

"What's the chance they have a dome?"

She pointed to three spots on the screen. "Anti-aircraft shields here, here, and here.... If you can shoot up, you can shoot down. Not many have the ability to curve the protection fields."

Michael spoke. "First time a puck hits we lose the advantage of stealth."

John chuckled. "And that is different from Bethany Anne's normal method *how*?"

"You aren't supporting me here, John," she grumped. "Granted, shock-and-awe *is* my preferred style."

Michael shrugged. "I'm told this armor beats parachutes. We jump, we drop pucks, disable the anti-aircraft, land, and find the target."

"How thick is the roof?" Akio asked. "We could puck our own hole in the roof for quick entry."

"We have enough," Tabitha pointed around the room, "for three insertions."

"Michael and I go in from the top." Bethany Anne pointed. "Gabrielle, John, and Eric, west side. Scott and Darryl, east. Eve and Tabitha north, and Addix and Akio go in from the south side."

"Great!" Scott clapped, "Everyone meets in the middle!"

Five minutes later Kael-ven's voice came over the system. "This is your captain speaking. I'm opening the back ramp in thirty seconds. Anyone wishing to fall, hoping the armor's antigravity kicks in before you pancake on the ground, please jump out. Anyone not crazy, please stay on board."

Kiel stayed with Kael-ven. "I'm on second-string, so I'll keep an eye on the rear in case it goes to shit," he told Bethany Anne. "Kael-ven and I will be here to help you guys get back aboard, and we'll lay a shit-ton of fire down if you need it."

In the back, everyone locked their helmets on.

—

Bethany Anne jumped first, her body head down as she plunged through the atmosphere toward her target. Markers on her facemask pinpointed the locations of the three anti-aircraft emplacements, the main house, a new one for the exit from the roof to below, and three…no, five tangos.

"ADAM?"

"Yes."

"Make sure you watch everyone's suit. I don't want the newbies forgetting they need to control their descent and, as Kael-ven put it, 'pancake into the ground.' Give them a reminder right now that you will be taking control if they don't."

"Tabitha, Akio, and Addix have confirmed that they will allow me to control their descent."

"Not Michael?"

"No."

"Figures." She sighed. "Watch him anyway."

Three seconds later the pucks dislodged from her armor and streaked down ahead of her. "SHIT!" She saw a missile erupt from one of the anti-air emplacements just before the pucks slammed into them and bodies flew everywhere, two of them in flames.

The missile was slicing toward them when it exploded and two voices exclaimed jubilantly over Bethany Anne's comm.

"That was mine, Akio," Michael stated calmly.

"I think not, Michael-san," Akio replied. "It should be obvious from the trajectory that I made the shot."

"Are you two arguing as we fall?" Gabrielle asked. "Seriously?"

They all heard both Michael and Akio chuckle. "This is how the game is played. Now, because of your interference we have to credit half a missile-kill to each of us," Akio replied.

John chuckled gruffly. "Game on!"

A moment later Bethany Anne released two more one-pound pucks. The antigrav Etheric drivers sped them up and the two unstoppable kinetic rounds slammed into the roof of the building, the pucks hitting within a fraction of a second of each other.

All eleven of the armored figures turned feet-first in mid-descent and used the last five hundred feet to slow down enough that the landing wouldn't shatter their knees and hips.

Two figures rushed ahead of where Gabrielle had landed on the west side. *"BOYS!"* she yelled.

On the roof, Michael was bitching.

"How did those not make a hole in the roof?" he asked as he and Bethany Anne confirmed the mercs in the emplacements were out of commission. Michael was moving around the corner of the roof to the door when a gauntleted hand smashed into his helmet, sending him over the edge of the building.

"Michael!" Bethany Anne raced to the corner as a seven-foot-tall Leath walked out from behind the wall that had hidden him.

Bethany Anne was the smaller of the two, but she drove her shoulder into the armored mercenary and knocked him off the edge after Michael.

"GOTT VERDAMMT!" Michael's voice, filled with surprise and anger, rolled through her helmet and Bethany Anne jumped off the two-story building, reducing her weight as she neared the ground.

She found Michael underneath the armored Leath, who had apparently flattened him. Michael's arms snaked up to grab the helmeted figure's head and he twisted. The mercenary had been flailing but stopped when something snapped and his helmet was suddenly twisted two-thirds of the way around.

Bethany Anne chuckled as she grabbed the Leath's arm and yanked the dead suit of armor—and dead mercenary—off him.

"I was just about to figure out a way back up," Michael bitched as he stood up, "when it began raining Leath."

"We get up by commanding the antigrav to reduce our weight to fifty-percent normal and jumping," she explained and crouched, then jumped, her body soaring back up and over the lip of the roof.

Michael commanded aloud, "Set weight to fifty percent."

"Set," his HUD replied.

Michael judged the amount of strength necessary and pushed off the ground.

Bethany Anne was expecting to see Michael fly up over the edge of the roof, but when she heard a loud *CRUNCH* she walked to the edge and looked down.

Michael was on his back.

"What are you *doing*? We don't have time to be fucking around, Michael!"

"You said fifty percent," he bitched, standing up. "That was heavier than I thought it would be, so I didn't jump as hard as I needed to." He bent at the legs and exerted himself, and this time he landed next to her.

"I said fifty-percent of *normal*." She followed Michael, who was already kicking in the stairway door. The two of them headed down the stairs.

By that point Akio had already counted out three take-downs and John two over the comm.

The two of them went from room to room. "Clear!" one would call, then alternated the lead when they went on to the next.

Bethany Anne was going down more stairs with Michael behind her and bitching about a complete lack of opportunity when Akio's voice came over the system.

"Four."

—

Az went to the basement, locked the metal door, and sat back. He now had four feet of the same metal battleships used between him and whoever was out there.

He'd just had a one-word reply from Imon. **Done**.

At least that was one project finished.

Az's mercenary team was going to be wiped out. Perhaps they would be able to kill a few of the attackers, perhaps they wouldn't. However, he had requested that two chalet-leveling missiles be fired at his location.

He would survive inside this bunker. Those outside?

Not so much.

25

On the G'laxix Sphaea

"We have two incoming missiles, angle two-two-three," Kiel informed Kael-ven from the weapons console. "Instructions?"

Kael-ven looked at the screen. "Thirty seconds to arrival. What do you suggest?"

"Intercepting them. You could place the ship in between, using the shields to protect us against the damage."

Kael-ven snorted. "This is why you aren't Navy. How about we shoot them down?"

"Sure. Not as much risk, but whatever the captain wants," Kiel grumped. "Four turrets aimed at the missiles. Ready to fire at the captain's command."

Kael-ven engaged the comm channel to those below. "Suggest finding shelter. It's going to be raining missile parts in a moment."

Kiel kept his finger poised for a few more seconds, but

the turrets began firing before he pressed the control. "What?" He lifted his hand before turning to his friend. "I didn't fire them!"

Kael-ven chuckled. "Did you really think I would trust a Marine to fire Navy weapons when my friends' lives were on the line?"

"Well, who did?"

Kael-ven shook his head. "I left it to the EI."

Planet Adolphin, Az's Chalet, Bunker

Az heard the banging on the door to his bunker room and smiled. There were seven more…six more…five more… His eyes opened large when the outside video showed destruction on a far smaller scale.

His missiles had been destroyed.

Planet Adolphin, Az's Chalet, Outside Bunker

Bethany Anne, shaking out her right fist, pointed with her left to the metal door that had stopped her from entering the next room. "That's a hard door."

"Are you done?" Michael asked. The indentations in the door were impressive but didn't seem to have done anything to it structurally. John and Eric showed up behind them on the steps that led to the bunker.

"What, you have a better idea?" Bethany Anne huffed. Her eyes grew wide when Michael, who had been standing there with his helmet off smiled and disappeared, his empty armor crumpling to the floor now that his body was no longer holding it up.

"MICHAEL!" she screamed, her eyes flaring red in anger as she turned toward the door.

And disappeared.

John and Eric stared at Michael's empty armor.

"Well...*fuck,*" John murmured.

—

Az was watching the four armored figures in front of the bunker's door in confusion when the audio feed cut out. He was reaching over to turn it back on when the human male disappeared and the human female pulled her helmet off, screaming.

Then he heard voices.

Az jumped up from the security station. The bunker had a bed, a small kitchenette, and plenty of electronics to both tell him what was going on outside it, and it could also connect him with external contacts.

He had placed another order for missiles and some more mercenaries just two minutes previously.

YOU are the one behind the attacks... Interesting, a military mind using pirates to do your dirty work and help you get to the top.

Az's head darted around as he tried to pinpoint the source of the voice.

The one who attacked Devon... Attacked my family... Attacked others for your greed.

Az sneered. "I take what I want. It's the law of the jungle."

The mental voice laughed. *Then it is a shame that the jungle has come for* you!

"Bring it." Az sneered just as a human woman with her hair floating, her face and hands crackling with energy, and her red eyes blazing appeared in front of him.

He stared as her hair turned white and her face black. "WHERE. IS. *HE?*"

"Bitch, I don't … ARGHH!" Az's armored body sans helmet slammed into the electronics suite. Sparks flew as he fell over the console to land awkwardly on the floor. He went for his gun, but she grabbed his hand between a vice-like forefinger and thumb, twisting his arm around and breaking his wrist.

He screamed in pain as she asked him in a gravelly voice, "I said…"

"I DON'T KNOW!" Az yelled, reaching for a knife with his left hand.

She broke his arm and kicked out his legs and his back slammed to the floor. A red ball of energy appeared in her hand as she straddled the massive Leath, then she pushed the sizzling ball into his left hand. She held it down with her right knee as the knife and his flesh melted. Smoke and the smell of burnt flesh wafted through the bunker.

"I'm pretty fucking impatient," she hissed.

Michael's voice spoke from beside her. "You *always* are."

Bethany Anne's gleaming red eyes jerked to Michael, but before she could say anything he pointed to the Leath. "He is the guilty party, and *payback?*"

Baba Yaga turned back to the Leath beneath her. "YOU just tried to kill my *CHILDREN!*"

Az looked at her with fear in his eyes. He now knew who this woman was.

Death had come for him, *and she was a bitch.*

His screams went on for a while. Michael held him

down and Baba Yaga took her time burning through the armor over his chest, gravity directing the melting metal to his ribs and his heart.

"You scared me." She eyed Michael as she stood up.

Michael smirked. It wasn't the first time he had accomplished that feat, and it probably wouldn't be the last. However, the way her hair was floating around her was doing things to him. "I'm hot for you right now, so can we save the bitch session for later?"

Bethany Anne stared at him, her face slowly changing back to white and her hair back to black. She stepped off the body.

"Did you just play me?" She tilted her head, narrowing her eyes at him.

"No," Michael replied. "I was working to confirm he was the guilty party when you showed up.

"Was he?" she asked. "The guilty party?"

"The main one, yes." He glanced at the body. "But there are two more—or were. One, a Shrillexian, killed the other, a white-haired albino human."

"Torcellan," Bethany Anne corrected.

"Right, that," Michael agreed. He looked at the destroyed electronics. There were some that were still working. "I wonder what opens the door?"

"What about sex?"

Michael waved a hand under his nose. "Not the right smell for that."

"Okay." She shrugged. "Frankly, I don't know how we'd manage it with this armor on anyway." Bethany Anne went to the door and pushed a button.

It did nothing.

She hit a second button and a series of clicks and clunks came from the door mechanism. A moment later the door opened to reveal their people.

"Oh, geez!" Scott covered his nose. "What the hell did you guys do in here?"

Addix stepped around Bethany Anne.

There was gnashing of mandibles. *"WHAT DID YOU DO TO HIS COMMUNICATIONS CONSOLE!"* she shrieked.

Planet Soboth (Previously Territory 7732), Undisclosed location, Open Out-ring, Non-Federation

Uleq, wearing a gas mask, walked through the silence. He stepped over an arm that was lying outside a cubicle as he made his way back into Imon's office.

Imon was dead, slumped over his desk with a glass still in his hands.

Uleq shook his head and tossed a tablet on Imon's desk. "Poor choice of who to follow. There is always a new generation ready to take over when the old can't understand that times have changed. You should never have accepted a drink after work with me. Eventually there might be poison in it."

He turned and stepped out, closing the door behind him. Passing through quiet halls with more than a few dead bodies, Uleq made his way out to the spaceport. There was another Torcellan waiting for him.

Nodding, Uleq boarded the small spacecraft and the other Torcellan came up the ramp behind him. As it closed behind them, they took off their masks.

Soon, the ship was in space, heading in the opposite direction from Adolphin.

Back in the base the tablet on Imon's desk glowed, a simple word fading in and out…

"DONE."

High Tortuga, Hidden Space Fleet Base, Queen's Nursery

Bethany Anne smiled down at the baby boy, his hand grasping the smallest part of her finger and squeezing it in his sleep.

"Ow, Gabriel!" she hissed. The pain lessened. "Strong little bugger."

Bethany Anne?

Yes, TOM?

I'd like to tell you something.

Hmmm? she murmured. ***Isn't Alexis the cutest little girl?***

Yes.

Bethany Anne sighed and stepped out of the room, closing the door softly behind her as she padded to her bedroom. Michael was already up, having gone outside to work on how to cook dinosaur meat—or whatever the hell it was that he planned on hunting with William.

They had purchased some meat in a small village outside the forest to practice grilling, but Bethany Anne wanted nothing to do with it.

For now, they had twelve long-distance scout ships looking for clues to where the Kurtherians might be. As soon as they had the information, she and her team would ship out and track the fuckers down.

Until then, she planned on working on High Tortuga

and the MPPS governmental system—and raising a couple of children.

And developing her magic.

"What is it, TOM?" she asked, remembering that he had started the conversation.

You might want to sit down.

Oh goody, she responded. ***One of* those *conversations.***

Bethany Anne skipped the bedroom, heading instead for the living room and a Coke. This seemed like a Coke talk.

She opened it and took a swallow and then sat down. "Go for it," she told him.

A half-second later Coke spewed out of her mouth and her eyes opened wide in surprise.

"YOU'RE A FUCKING *PRIEST?*" she yelled. "I thought you were a pilot!"

Well, in my culture they are the same thing. So, lost in translation?

It's been a hundred and seventy years, give or take, she thundered. ***Why has this not come up before? I'd think you could have given me a little clarification when the two words were so obviously different!***

Bethany Anne went to the snacks area, grabbed two rags out of a drawer, and tried to clean up the Coke mess.

Fortunately her synthetics cleaned easily.

TOM sighed. **The best answer I can give you is, you scared me.**

Not this bullshit about learning too quickly again?

Yes, in a nutshell. Perhaps a tiny, less complicated nutshell.

Why the hell? Bethany Anne heard a small cry and

stopped, her head turning toward the bedroom where the children were sleeping.

The crying stopped.

Okay, so why the hell, she continued, taking the rags to the sink to wash them out, ***are you just telling me this now?***

I think that for you to have a chance of succeeding if we encounter other Kurtherians—at least those more adept with the Etheric—you need to be guided by my knowledge. The challenge will be for you to stay here in the present.

Why will it be a struggle?

All of us who know, struggle. Every day is an acknowledgment that we know how to ascend; we see the peace, the love, the delight in that, and yet we choose to stay here. Until Michael came back and Gabriel and Alexis arrived I didn't know if you had what it took to say no to ascending, so I didn't teach you in case... Well, in case you chose to take the less painful route.

Bethany Anne thought about his comments for a moment. He was here to train protectors to defend against and defeat the Seven. She was, for all practical purposes, his avatar. ***So you could ascend at any time, TOM?***

Yes.

And you have to fight it every day?

No.

Why not?

Because I have *you.*

All the anger she was feeling fell away from her heart and Bethany Anne slowly sat down on the carpet, raised her hands to her eyes, and cried.

Fully a minute later ADAM spoke to TOM. >>**Is this**

good? << He was trying to discern the meaning behind her crying.

I don't know, but it was the truth.

>>So should I tell her now? <<

TOM snorted. **No fucking way.**

FINIS

AUTHOR NOTES - MICHAEL ANDERLE

MAY 9, 2018

The Author hit the record button. "This is Michael Anderle, the Author who has been blessed by receiving permission to chronicle the experiences of Bethany Anne Reynolds, now Bethany Anne Nacht, from the time she was pulled into the UnknownWorld to a time in the far future."

He continued, "Unfortunately there are too many stories that revolve around Bethany Anne for a single—or many—authors to chronicle."

He glanced up. The woman in front of him had her legs crossed and was wearing black high-heeled shoes with red soles.

"That's not true." Bethany Anne held the Coke, complete with straw, away from her mouth. "There are *certainly* enough authors—but would my story really be interesting enough?"

"Well, okay," the Author agreed. "Unfortunately,

Bethany Anne has too many stories for a practical number of authors to pull together her stories."

She interrupted, "I don't know if I'd agree it was *impractical*. Perhaps you just need help."

Exasperated, the Author asked, "Like who?"

She took a sip of her Coke through her straw while she contemplated. "Well, ADAM and the EIs he can tap could do it, and quickly."

The Author countered, "Do you believe they would be able to take the input and provide the correct emotional resonance?"

"Um…" Bethany Anne chewed on that for a moment. "Not sure. I guess they could read a few thousand—or ten thousand—stories known for their emotional substance and make a pretty good pass at it."

The Author opened his mouth, then shut it. "Okay, that would be a fair test. It would certainly get more of your stories out. Now, what filters would you place on the story?"

"Filters?"

"Yes." Michael reached up and scratched his forehead. "Do you, for example, want every part of every day? Would you like to include, for example, trips to the restroom?"

"Ughh, no." She shook her head. "However, that is easy to filter out. In fact, they could probably go through the first twenty-one books and categorize each of the scenes. Then they would extrapolate if my stories had some sort of congruence and place them in an ordered list. From there…what?"

Michael raised an eyebrow. "So what happens if we need to tell this in chronological order?"

"You mean if we needed to skip stuff?" She thought for a moment. "A little tougher."

"Sure," he agreed, "but I was thinking how one chooses to carve out only certain scenes to wrap them up into a cohesive story for the readers?"

>>I can work with fans,<< ADAM interjected.

I think that is his point, Bethany Anne sent. ***He is suggesting that you*** **will** ***need to work with humans.***

>>Well, of course I will. Eventually they will be reading the stories, right?<<

How are you going to choose the most relevant ones?

>>I can create grading scales based on emotional content, issues between characters, and opportunities for miscommunication.<<

Why miscommunication?

>>Amusement value. It seems many humans find it funny when there is miscommunication.<<

Bethany Anne thought back to a few times where miscommunication had been a part of her life and made a face of disgust. "I think there would have to be at least an editor in the mix. Someone who could realistically choose which pieces of the stories were worth telling and those I might not want shared."

The Author nodded. He took a sip of his own Coke, but his was in a bottle. "So, will you think about it?"

"About what?" she asked, confused by the question.

"About having ADAM provide more snippets of your life so we can give the fans more of your past, not just your future."

Bethany Anne's smile was wry. "Smart, Mr. Author Man. That was damned smart."

He shrugged, eyeing the empty bottle; the elixir of life he had just finished. He looked at her and winked. "Well, I have to have something to keep selling to support my Mexican Coke habit."

Bethany Anne snorted. "Now *that* might be one of the few habits I *can* support." She tapped her fingers on her leg. "Let me think about it."

"All I can do is ask," he replied, looking pitifully at her glass. She glanced down at her drink.

"Hell no!" She turned aside, protecting the drink with her body as she pointed to the kitchen. "Go get your own."

THANK YOU so much for reading this first book in the SECOND series of Bethany Anne's adventures!

Just a smidgen over two years and six months ago I released my first book, *Death Becomes Her*, and now I'm releasing book twenty-two about this incredible woman.

She (and her stories) have changed not only *my* life, but the lives of my family and many OTHER authors, editors, artists, and audio talent as we pull together in doing what we love to do so much.

Tell stories!

That is the one constant all of us share: the love of stories.

I can't speak for my collaborators, but I can tell you that I personally *love* creating these new stories. Placing emotions and characters together with events that make us feel amazing as we read them (sometimes the only respite from life) and wish, just once or twice, that I could spend time with *them*.

My friends in the stories.

Two and a half years ago—with a lot of anxiety—I put my little story out there for people to read. And it turned out pretty well, even if it *was* a bit crazy.

Now I'm going to do something *else* that may be a bit crazy and hope like hell I'm not the *only* sumbitch who thinks this idea might be fun.

LMBPN (my publishing/entertainment company) is going to work on creating a cool fucking experience for fans based in Vegas.

Why?

Because I want to have an opportunity to party with friends—those friends I've found on Facebook, Amazon, Goodreads, and other places.

I've met some of you at restaurants, military bases, and conventions.

I have encouraged a lot of fans, and now many of my fans are now *authors.*

It started with just four and now the great-grandchild of that effort is continuing with the **FANS Write for the FANS** projects—but that isn't the end of my desire.

No…it isn't at all. I have a dream, and that dream (perhaps hallucination) would be to party like it's 1999 in Vegas with a thousand of the most awesome people in the world.

Readers.

People just like me, no matter what color, gender, age, ethnicity, political affiliation, or ANY of that shit that bugs the world.

People who love books, love audio books, love the worlds, the games, the stories, the characters, and the joy reading brings into our lives. We can support each other just by being ourselves.

I don't want it to be a normal convention—which is to say I recognize that there are fun parts of conventions and just freaking *weird* parts.

I want an LMBPN convention to be entertaining for some, educational for others, relationship-building for all and a place to party year in, year out with each other knowing that if you want something different…

It's VEGAS baby!

You can always find something in that city.

We have started this by attaching a fan event to the end of the 20BooksTo50k author convention in Vegas in November 2018, which has six hundred or more authors coming from around the world. Some of these authors have yet to hit the button, and others have fifty books or more.

You can't be near a 20BooksTo50k convention without stumbling over authors.

Honest! Many of them go from the sessions to the restrooms and you stumble over them. They are often thinking about some 'Ah-HA!' moment from a few minutes ago, or some new concept for a story because they were chatting with another author and they run into shit.

Or you... Whichever one happens first. (Editor's note: It's true, and watch your toes!)

This year 20Books Vegas runs from Tuesday to Thursday, November 6-8th, 2018.

We are hoping we can get just *two hundred* of you crazy motherfuckers who love *The Kurtherian Gambit, Oriceran, Protected by the Damned,* and *Mr. Brownstone* to come join us and party.

Many authors involved with LMBPN (and many

others) will be in Vegas during that week, having a hell of a time.

Would you consider joining us?

Then, I want everyone to look at next year, 2019 to see what we can do together.

I'm willing to put the money down to grab the dates for the weekend following the 20Booksto50k Convention (early November) to put on an **EVENT** in 2019 to cherish what brings us together.

For 2019 I don't just want to put tables together, but hold an event that merges and blurs the lines between authors, fans, and readers both text and audio.

Eventually including more "stuff." However, that's for the future. For now, what we have are stories…

And a strong-assed desire to party with our friends.

If we can get enough people to say "I'm in," LMBPN will put down money to make this a hell of a party…

A party to *blow the doors off.* Where new authors get the chance to share their work, find new fans, and make ever-lasting relationships to grow their fan base.

For fans to reach out and help new talent become something that they never could without *YOU* in the mix.

Where we celebrate everyone who is a part of the massively entertaining activity called "reading" whether we write, edit, do covers, help with beta reading, arc teams, or JIT.

So…what do you say?

Does anyone think this might be fun?

Anyone willing to join us in 2018 to kick this off at the

micro level, helping us figure things out and get our feet wet so that maybe in a few years…

Oh…*in a few years….*

We will take over the Las Vegas Convention Center—the largest in the *WORLD*.

Because if *that* isn't a "H#LY SH!T" goal, *what is?*

Ad Aeternitatem,

MICHAEL TODD ANDERLE

EDITOR NOTES - LYNNE STIEGLER

WRITTEN MAY 2, 2018

First, thank you for reading this far! We appreciate your willingness to venture into the jungle at the end of the book. So why are we here?

A long time ago, in a galaxy far, far away…wait, wrong universe. In this universe, a woman got a bad case of bronchitis and could do nothing but lie there and read. She had a book on her Kindle by some guy named Anderle, *Death Becomes Her,* and she finished it really fast. Then she read the next one in the series, and the next, and…

Forty-eight hours and sixteen books later, she messaged that Anderle guy on Facebook and told him it was a great series (he is one *hell* of a storyteller) but he needed a good editor. (She didn't tell him at that point that she used to edit for Baen). Conversations ensued, he sent her a book to edit, and the rest is history.

Fast forward to present day: I never knew I'd spend *any* of my time trying to figure out the best way to punctuate "wrinkled-ass llama-sniffing fudge-shoveler." Or should it be "wrinkle-assed?" Ah, well...that's a frequent problem, especially with TKG. And Pandora often makes me blush (and cackle) while I edit.

But seriously... For the last year, I've been proud and privileged to be that Anderle guy's editor. But not only his! To date I have edited over a hundred books for more than twenty authors in the Kurtherian Gambit universe as well as Oriceran (an Anderle/Carr creation, check it out if you haven't already). Now I'm lucky enough to work with *Protected by the Damned* and *The Unbelievable Mr. Brownstone.*

Who'da thunk? Because it *was* luck. Michael and the LMBPN family are some of the most talented, warmest, and most caring and giving people I've ever met in my life. I'm honored to be part of the team.

Many of the authors who publish through LMBPN are new to the game (and indie publishing is a whole new oeuvre anyway), but that Anderle guy has set it up so they can get advice and assistance from word one to post-publication. (Being an author is freakin' scary, as some of you know. You put your heart and soul out there for everyone to see...and pick at. (Note: I wound up letting my husband, who has been an author for decades, edit these editor notes. Hard on the ego. He says the author has final say, but when the editor is authoring and the author is editing, how does that work, exactly?)

Not only that, the Anderle guy goes out of his way to help people, although that doesn't get nearly as much publicity as Bethany Anne's new baby. Because of his willingness to work with new authors, some of his people have regained a family house, gotten off welfare, and been able to quit their day jobs. He's given an elderly woman a new lease on life (and vastly improved her vocabulary of expletives). The list goes on and on.

While I'm at it, I'd like to give a shout-out to Stephen Campbell, LMBPN's production manager, who doesn't get mentioned in *Author Notes* nearly often enough. He's the backbone of LMBPN, making sure everything is on track and wrestling the alligators at the 'Zon. It's due to him that our works get published at all, and I for one appreciate him. Well, I know Michael (and everyone else) does too, and I will speak for him just this once.

Anyway, enough drabble. Hope you loved the book. I did—kept having to stop just reading and go back to editing. Check us out on Facebook if you haven't already at https://www.facebook.com/TheKurtherianGambitBooks/. And if you want to play in this universe (and soon Oriceran, which will have its own anthology in about three months), head over to https://www.facebook.com/groups/TKGFansWrite/ and submit your story for consideration for publication in the next anthology. Submission just closed for this one a few days ago, but that gives you enough time to develop a story for the next one.

And hey…I'll be your editor! (*Grins evilly*)

Ad Aeternitatem,

Lynne Stiegler

BOOKS BY MICHAEL ANDERLE

For a complete list of books by Michael Anderle, please visit:

www.lmbpn.com/ma-books/

All LMBPN Audiobooks are Available at Audible.com and iTunes

To see all LMBPN audiobooks, including those written by Michael Anderle please visit:

www.lmbpn.com/audible

CONNECT WITH MICHAEL ANDERLE

Michael Anderle Social

Website:

http://kurtherianbooks.com/

Email List:

http://kurtherianbooks.com/email-list/

Facebook Here:

https://www.facebook.com/OriceranUniverse/

https://www.facebook.com/TheKurtherianGambitBooks/

Made in the USA
Monee, IL
31 July 2020

37306746R00198